BEHOLDING

bee

Also by Kimberly Newton Fusco

The Wonder of Charlie Anne
Tending to Grace

BEHOLDING

bee

Kimberly Newton Fusco

Alfred A. Knopf
new york

THIS IS A BORZOI BOOK PUBLISHED BY ALFRED A. KNOPF

Visit us on the Web! randomhouse.com/kids

Educators and librarians, for a variety of teaching tools, visit us at
RHTeachersLibrarians.com

Library of Congress Cataloging-in-Publication Data
Fusco, Kimberly Newton.
Beholding Bee / Kimberly Newton Fusco. — 1st ed.
p. cm.
Summary: In 1942, when life turns sour at the carnival that has always been her home, eleven-year-old Bee takes her dog, Peabody, and piglet, Cordelia, and sets out to find a real home, aided by two women only Bee and her pets can see.
ISBN 978-0-375-86836-8 (trade) — ISBN 978-0-375-96836-5 (lib. bdg.) —
ISBN 978-0-375-89886-0 (ebook)
[1. Disfigured persons—Fiction. 2. Self-esteem—Fiction. 3. Runaways—Fiction. 4. Carnivals—Fiction. 5. Orphans—Fiction. 6. Identity—Fiction.] I. Title.
PZ7.F96666Beh 2013
[Fic]—dc23
2012005091

The text of this book is set in 12-point Goudy.

Printed in the United States of America

February 2013

10 9 8 7 6 5 4 3

First Edition

*For the memory of
my beloved great-grandmother,
Dorcas Brewster Newton*

June 1942

Part I

1

The way I got the diamond on my face happened like this.

I was sleeping in the back of our hauling truck one night after Pauline shut down our hot dog cart and Ellis closed the merry-go-round and the Ferris wheel, and then, after every one of the stars had blinked out for the night so no one could see, that is when an angel came and kissed me on the cheek.

That is the way Pauline sees it.

Other folks say different things, like "What a shame, what a shame." I hear them when I am chopping onions and Pauline is frying hot dogs. "Now there's a heavy load for a little slip of a thing to carry." They make it sound like I am lugging coal.

I hear one lady tell her girl I must have done something horrid to be stained all over my face like that. Or maybe my mama is the one who did something awful, or maybe my daddy, and I am the one being punished.

"Stay away, stay away," the big girls say. But they come up to our hot dog cart for a closer look. And they poke each other and whisper, as if I am not standing right in front of them, "Careful or you'll catch it," like I have the flu. And the boys ask did I get burned all over my face, or am I marked by the Evil Eye, and they holler at each other: "Run or you'll get it on you."

But Pauline holds me and whispers they are not right. Otherwise, why would I have a beautiful jewel on my cheek the color of a rose at dusk and they do not?

I do so like Pauline's way of looking at things.

2

When you have a diamond shining on your face, you have rules about things.

First, I keep it hidden. There is a hose outside every place where we hook up, because we need water to run our traveling show. Pauline and I keep a bucket and a sponge in the back of our hauling truck. Water from a hose is cold as cherry Popsicles but if you let the bucket sit in the sun all day it heats up and at night Pauline pours out her apple shampoo and we take turns washing our hair.

Pauline has a big towel and she wraps my hair and then combs it out and I don't yell out much because she is mostly gentle. Then she braids my hair and when it dries she lets it loose and it falls all soft in twists and curls and hides the diamond on my cheek. Because when you have a jewel on your face, some days you might not want to show everyone who feels like looking.

Second, I make sure I am always close to Pauline so when somebody comes up asking for hot dogs, I can turn my cheek toward her, where it is safe. I am always out of harm's way when I am near Pauline. I spoon onions and sauerkraut on hot dogs and wrap everything in squares of wax paper, all the time keeping my cheek turned to her.

Third, I make Pauline buy lemons so I can squeeze the juice on my cheek before I go to bed. The lemon juice stings as it slides over my diamond, and sometimes I scrub a little. I have not noticed it working yet, but Pauline says keep trying because you never know how things will turn out. Life is just full of surprises.

3

Hot dogs are Pauline's job. We park our cart right between the merry-go-round making its *dee-dee-da-dee* racket and the Ferris wheel playing "The Farmer in the Dell" so many times you start wondering if maybe the rat should eat the cat, just once. You really do.

Ellis runs our traveling show and says hot dogs make a lot of money when folks know they are there. So he wants us right where folks can see us and he makes Pauline and me paint the cart with red and white stripes every spring and hang balloons all over it until it is as bright as the sun on your face.

This is especially important since President Roosevelt declared war last December and young men are getting shipped overseas. This has got Ellis barking at everyone all the time. Business is dried up. Pauline fries up a whole crate less of hot dogs now, but children and mamas and grandmas and grandpas still buy a few, and they smother them with the onions I chop every day until my eyes hurt so much I am sure they are bleeding, and the tears are dripping down, rolling right over my diamond.

Those are my jobs. Chopping onions and lining up the bottles of mustard and ketchup and scooping one tiny spoon of sugar into everyone's coffee because this spring sugar rationing started. Folks are greedy like pigs. They always want more. When you can't have something, you want it awful bad.

My other job is making sure there is enough celery salt, because somebody who likes celery salt gets in an awful tizzy if you do not have any left. They poke their finger at you and say what is the matter with you, girl, there is no celery salt, and I might get so bothered I could forget to keep my hair pulled tight across my cheek to hide my diamond.

We also serve honey buns. They are big and fat and we buy them from bakeries in long cardboard boxes. They are made with honey and corn syrup, not sugar, of course, and they sit like a flat tire in your belly, but I love them. I eat them by the bucketload and Pauline wonders why I am still small as a chickadee. My job is to keep the honey buns beneath a little screen. They look nice under there and flies do not get at them. We do get a lot of pests around here.

My other job is to find me and Pauline a home. I told Pauline I would take over this job because she is not so good at it. She keeps forgetting what she is supposed to be doing. "Pauline, look at that one with all the flower boxes," I point out when we pull into Trenton, or into Springfield, "Pauline, we would be so happy here. Look at that swing on that front porch," but she is always writing poems in one of her little notebooks and not paying attention. "Oh, Bee, it's not so easy to leave."

I don't know why. It would be easy as pie, one foot in front of the other. So I keep watching in each town we roll into, the whole caravan of us. I am always sitting up in the cab of the hauling truck between Bobby, who runs the Little Pig Race, and Pauline. I look out the window for our new home. I will know it when I see it.

4

The warning light inside me goes on and off, on and off, as soon as I hear the creeping around outside and the whispering. I am in the john doing my business. The hairs on my arms stick up. I hold my breath.

"I think she went in here," says a low girl's voice.

"You're not sure?"

"I saw her coming this way but I didn't see where she went. You were the one who was supposed to be watching."

"No, you were. I gave you one job and it was to watch her while I was getting a strawberry pop. And you messed it up, you little dummy."

I hitch up my overalls and pull my legs up and wrap my arms around myself, making myself as small as I can without falling in.

"Kick it."

"Me? I don't want to kick it. You kick it."

"Oh, forget it, you baby," and then there is a loud thump against the door. "What you doing so long in there? Some of us have to go, you know."

I hold my breath. I wonder how long the lock will hold. I think it is the two girls with the shined-up saddle shoes who were watching me chop onions. I kept turning my cheek to Pauline, but they hopped from one end of the hot dog cart to the other, poking each other and giggling and asking me are there any onions on the hot dogs because they don't like onions and are there any pickles left and is there any new mustard because this one is all gone. I know what they were up to. They wanted to have themselves a look.

"Buy something or scat," Pauline told them, waving her hot dog fork in angry circles.

There is more kicking and I whisper a little prayer the lock will hold. There are hushed voices and then somebody kicks on the door again.

"When you coming out?"

I don't answer. I pull my legs up tighter. I hold my breath deep inside my chest. I wait.

"We know it's you in there. Some of us want a turn, you know."

"Maybe she's trying to scrub it off. Do you think she got burned?"

"No. Mama tells me when you have one of those you are born with it. Mamas want to cry when that happens."

Do not, do not, do not. I pull my legs even closer to my chest.

"Will I get one?"

"No, I said you are *BORN WITH IT*. Why are you such a retard? If you don't have one by now, you're not going to get one."

"Good, because I would just want to die if I looked like that."

I reach up and touch the diamond on my cheek. I trace my finger along the place where my face ends and the mark begins. The girls are kicking again. They are kicking hard. The door buckles.

I pull my legs tighter and hide my face in my knees. My tears are sliding over my diamond.

"Hey, what's going on in here?" It is Pauline. Her voice is low and hard, mixed with the kind of dare you feel when you want to give somebody a taste of their own medicine.

"Forget it."

"She's too ugly for us anyway."

Am not, am not, am not.

"Get out of here, now. Bee? Bee, are you in there?" Pauline knocks on the door. "Don't listen to them, Bee. Bee?"

I reach for the lock and unhook it. Slowly I open the door. And then I am up and I am in Pauline's arms. I let her hold me and I feel her breath on me and her heart beating. I smell the apple shampoo in her hair and I feel the aching in my heart. I know you should not judge a book by its cover, but most folks do. I am trembling and then the tears are rolling all over my diamond and I am wondering what to do about all that is wrong with me.

"Don't listen to them, Bee." Pauline runs her fingers through my curls. I wrap myself tighter around her and bury my face in her neck.

I won't, I won't, I won't.

It is a whisper only I can hear.

5

Pauline slides her arm around me and we head back to the hot dog cart. She asked Bobby to watch things while she went looking for me. Already folks are piled up.

Bobby wears thick glasses and needs to slick his hair down all the time. He notices my tears and pulls a piece of ruby licorice from his shirt pocket and hands it to me. It is a little oily from the bandanna sitting beside it that he uses to wipe up everything.

Pauline says Bobby does not talk much because he has been on the road so long he has seen everything a person could see. Now he has nothing more to say. I do wonder what he saw.

The licorice smells like pigs. Everything about Bobby smells like pigs. Pauline does not like pigs or the smell of pigs or men with the smell of pigs on them.

But I do. I think baby pigs smell very nice and their snouts tickle your neck when they are nuzzling you. I like pigs and I like Bobby very much. And I know Bobby is sweet on Pauline the way I am sweet on honey buns.

"Thanks," Pauline tells Bobby, tying her apron and scrunching her nose.

When lunch slows and we are caught up Pauline tells me I can have a break. I hurry over by Bobby because I also like licorice very much.

Bobby is in charge of four piglets: LaVerne, Big Ben,

Vivian, and Cordelia. He trains them to run around a path he sets up in each place we stop. They run for the finish line as fast as horses at the track because they are awful intent on getting the corn Bobby hides at the end.

Folks like to watch this very much. They make bets on which piglet will win the race. Usually it is LaVerne because she is such a greedy little pig, but sometimes it is Big Ben.

It is never Cordelia. She is the runt of the litter and she doesn't run as fast as the others and one of her ears droops. Also, she is more interested in looking at a dragonfly hovering on the fence post, or maybe a bumblebee. I tell her she is a dreamer with her head in the clouds. Folks who do not know this about her will say bad things, like what a slowpoke and even worse things that hurt her feelings awful bad. She needs a lot of snuggling after that to get back to feeling good about things. It turns out I am very good at this.

6

I watch Bobby get the piglets lined up and in their starting boxes and then he holds up his fingers, one, two, three, and he pulls the lever and the fronts of the boxes flop down and the piglets fly out. This time Cordelia starts out in front because she is chasing a dragonfly and folks are clapping and screaming and then LaVerne pushes right past and wins a gold paper crown. Folks laugh and clap when they see a pig wearing a crown and they buy more tickets.

A little girl keeps turning around and staring at me when she should be clapping and cheering for Cordelia. Lord knows it might help Cordelia believe in herself a little more.

"Does it hurt?" she wants to know, and then her mama is pulling her away.

I am not inclined to answer things like that. I can see in her eyes, though, how this little girl does not mean anything bad by it. When you spend as much time watching folks looking at my diamond as I do, you can tell what's inside of them without looking too deep. It's like knowing what's in a bologna sandwich without lifting the bread.

Pauline tells me I have a sixth sense, like a gift you get when one of your other senses is missing. "Like when you can't see, your hearing is really good, Bee, or when your hearing is gone, your heart is big." We are lying on our mattresses in the back of our hauling truck. She is writing in her little notebook.

The shine from the moon is peeking into the truck. "Or when you can see somebody other folks can't?" I whisper.

Pauline knows I am talking about the old lady in the orange flappy hat. She has been showing up since my mama and papa's funeral. Now that I am older and getting teased, she comes more often. She is sure to appear on the days that truly are very, very bad, the days when a boy says, "What's the matter, did you get burned all over your face?" or when a mama tells her girls to stay away from me. Those are the days she comes.

Pauline does not like me talking about the lady in the orange flappy hat. I think it's because Pauline can't see her, and I do wonder why that is. "Stop talking fairy tales," she tells me, rolling over.

I want to tell her I know life is not a fairy tale and bad wolves like Ellis do not always hide in the woods. Sometimes they are standing right in front of you.

7

We are all on pins and needles wondering about what is happening in Germany and Japan. When there's a war on, you feel like you are waiting for something bad to fall on your head. You know when you go to sleep that when you wake up the whole world could be upside down. Like when Pauline and I were frying Spam and potatoes for supper at our campground in Florida, waiting for spring, and we heard on the radio about all our sailors lost at Pearl Harbor. Folks everywhere were crying at the sadness of it all, even me.

Then came the gasoline rationing on the East Coast and we couldn't get hardly any sugar. Ellis lost half of the men who worked for him, the ones who ran off and signed on with the army. No one thinks Fat Man Sam will go, on account of his size, and Ellis is too old, but I am worried about Bobby. Pauline says sometimes the army changes its mind about soldiers wearing glasses when the war heats up.

I pull off my apron and hurry over to Cordelia when Pauline starts talking like this. I do like Bobby very much.

To get to the piglets, I have to squish through a lot of mud. It has been raining since we got into Buffalo and if there's one thing even worse for a traveling show than a war, it is rain. Ellis shuts off the music when it's been drizzling because it's not worth spending the money to open, so it is very peaceful and the only sound is my work boots smacking the ground.

Cissy runs the Guess How Much You Weigh booth and looks up from the checker game she is playing with Pete the Alligator Man. He keeps a live baby alligator in a cage and wrestles with it in a tin tub of water. The things folks will pay good money for is beyond me. Fat Man Sam sits on his chair, unable to get up from eating so many hot dogs. "Bee," he calls to me as I hurry by.

I stop, knowing what he will ask me.

"Can you get me another hot dog?"

I shake my head. I am in an awful hurry.

"Beeeeee."

"I can't now. I have to go see the piglets. I will in a few minutes."

There is always a job to do at a traveling show.

8

Ellis thinks he is the hero of my life. He thinks how since he kept me on, he is deserving of some sort of award.

He is not.

"Watch her," he told Pauline. She was sixteen and was already working for him when my mama and papa died in the truck crash in Florida one winter. I was four. Pauline told me Ellis wanted to drop me off at an orphan house and leave me there but I held on to Pauline so tight he gave up trying to break us apart. He said I might grow up to be of use to him, looking like I did, and he told Pauline she could come off the merry-go-round and take over my mama's job running the hot dog cart and watching me.

Pauline says I would not let go of her hand for six months after that. Ellis told her if anybody nosed around asking what a little girl with a mark on her face was doing without a mama or a daddy, he would drop me off somewhere, because the last thing he needed was trouble. "You can sleep in the back of the truck," he said, and that is how we do it now.

When we are traveling from one town to another, we carry tents in the back of our truck. Bobby drives and Pauline spends the time with her face in her notebook, wrinkling her nose and wishing she did not have to sit near a man who smells like pigs. I'm thinking of telling her maybe she is the one who could use some glasses.

When we pull into a town, we unload and then Pauline

and I get our bedroom back. We could close up the back doors to keep out mosquitoes and wolves, but then the inside of our truck would get hot as a fire pit. Sometimes you have to make a choice in life. So we leave the doors open and I string up a purple curtain because when you are sleeping in the back of a hauling truck you do not want anybody coming in and bothering you.

9

Pauline shakes like a leaf when Ellis tells her do this or do that. Sometimes I ask her why she does whatever he says and she says we are lucky to have a job.

"Well?" says Ellis. He is watching Pauline. She is standing there looking at the money in her hand, and then she looks at me. He wants her to go to Woolworth's and buy paint. He tells me I can't go. He pulls a piece of Beech-Nut chewing gum from his shirt pocket, unwraps it, and pops it in his mouth. He flicks the foil on the ground and it lands at Pauline's feet. She bends over, picks it up, and puts it in her apron.

Pauline pulls me to her and whispers, "Get all those onions chopped and then start the hot dogs. Don't worry. I'll be right back. And don't let the hot dogs burn." She looks over at Ellis and then she hurries to the truck, starts it, and drives off.

Ellis stays in the shadow of the hot dog cart watching me. He likes shade. He is very pale. His cowboy hat hides his face so you can't see his eyes, but I know there are snakes under there.

I try to act like I do not know he is looking at me, but I cannot help reaching up and checking to be sure my hair hides the diamond on my cheek. I used to think that when I got bigger the mark would get smaller. But stains on your face do not work like that. They get bigger when you get bigger. My diamond stretches from my eyebrow to under my cheek. It is a map of all my heartache.

Pauline says everyone has troubles. Some folks have troubles on the outside for everyone to see, and some have troubles on the inside where they hide and fester. "But everyone has something, Bee. So you are not alone."

I think it must be way easier to have troubles on the inside where no one can see. I tell her this. She says there are some things I might not understand because I am only eleven. I tell her I understand things pretty good.

I try and think about the onions I am chopping and if I can make them small enough to disappear. I try and make myself disappear. I am a candle blown out, a whisper at night, an old lady in an orange flappy hat. I try and make myself nobody at all.

The tears from all the onions are rolling right down over my diamond and I do not want to wipe them off because that would draw attention. I do not need to be a flag waving, not with Ellis standing there.

He spits his gum out and grinds it in the dirt and right away pulls another piece from his pocket and folds it up and stuffs it into his mouth. Then he walks right up next to me. I smell the sweet Beech-Nut. He reaches for my hair and pulls it up and looks at my face. I stiffen, unable to move, boulders in my shoes. There is an awful waiting.

"If that thing were a real diamond, you'd be worth a fortune," he whispers.

I yank my hair out of his hands. Real tears mix with onion tears and I do not look up until he walks away.

10

At night when all the rides are closed and all the folks are gone home, Bobby and Eldora, Fat Man Sam and Cissy and Pete the Alligator Man and everyone else who still works for Ellis go out on the town and talk about the war and about the rationing and if there's going to be enough gasoline to get us to the next city.

We get extra gas because we are in the entertainment business, but it is still bad and Ellis is saying he wants to set up a stay-put show somewhere.

They talk about all these things when they go out, but Pauline and I stay and play the ha-ha game. Even with our purple curtain open it is too hot to be in our tin can without windows so we go outside and lie in the grass and kick off our work boots and look up at the stars. Pauline tells me stories about when I was little, like how I saw some fancy saddle shoes at Woolworth's and I boohooed over them for an awful long time, but there wasn't any money for them, so she painted a white stripe right across my work boots, and after that I was so happy I wore them to bed, dirt and all.

"I did not." I am red in the face because I do remember those boots.

"Did, too. I wrote it down." She holds up a little notebook, not the one she writes her poems in but a different one, one with a shiny gold cover. This is the one she uses to write down things I've been doing since Ellis put us together, called *The Story of Bee*. She reads the whole tale, how I wailed and wailed. She reaches over and tickles me. I try not to be the first to laugh, but sooner or later one of us starts to giggle, and that is why we call it the ha-ha game.

When I ask her why she writes things about me in her little notebook, here's what she says: "Because no one did for me, Bee. And now since I don't have anyone to remind me about things, I don't remember hardly anything about when I was little."

I look up at the stars. I try and feel inside what she is feeling, about not remembering what it was like to be eleven. I stretch out on the grass and breathe deeply and snuggle up next to her. The Big Dipper overhead is pointing to the North Star, just like always. "Do you think we could find a real home, Pauline?"

I think maybe she is sleeping. She doesn't answer for a long while. But then she says, "It might be hard, Bee."

"But could we do that, could we get ourselves loved like that so somebody would want to keep us?"

"I don't know, Sweet Pea Bee."

I can hear the tired-from-standing-on-your-feet-all-day sound in her voice. I tell her how I would like to go live in a real house where I would not have to worry about folks bothering about my diamond all the time and does she think she might like to live there, too, and she says, "Sure, Bee, whatever you want," just as she is fading off.

I like that about her.

I like how when she is tired she mostly goes along with my ideas.

11

Pauline knows Woolworth's the way some folks know stars. She can spot one light-years away.

She likes picking out things a lot better than she likes frying hot dogs, so she finds plenty of reasons to take Ellis's truck and get us to one, no matter what town we are in.

Pauline takes me by the arm and leads me through the door. She lets me look at *Superman* and *Captain America* and *The Spirit* comic books and then we go over by the doll-houses with the little wooden ranges and refrigerators and the rugs and the wallpaper painted right on the walls. I think about how I would like to live in a house like this one, with a kitchen. I would like a real birthday cake, one that somebody who loved me made for me, not a quick-hurry-up slice at a diner somewhere.

Pauline hurries me past the Rita Hayworth paper dolls and the music elephants and the toy Plymouth automobiles and the Popeye crayons. She rushes me through the sweater and underwear aisles (sometimes scooping up things for me because I am growing so) to the books. Pauline is the one who taught me to read and now I have books on the stars and the planets and on bird identification and all about sea-shells, trees, wildflowers, and the weather. I can tell an oak tree from a hickory by the shape of its leaves and I know a storm is on the way just by the smell of the air. It is good to know about a lot of things, Pauline says.

Woolworth's offers a lot of protection for somebody like me because folks are generally running around like chickens with their heads cut off looking for toothpaste and laundry soap and shampoo. I have to be careful at the cash register of not looking somebody in the eye, because if you're going to have trouble at a Woolworth's, that's where it will happen. Folks stare when they are standing in line with nothing to do and they get irritated from the waiting. And then you have a feeding frenzy with folks looking and whispering and Pauline has to rush me out the door.

12

One night, Pauline is breathing softly and I am almost asleep inside our hauling truck when, as quick as a snap of my fingers, I am awake.

I listen. The outdoors rings with the call of peepers, but nothing else. Inside, the truck is quiet. I'm not sure what startled me.

I nestle back in my mattress and pull the sheet to my chin. A full moon shines against our purple curtain, sending a stream of light into the back of our hauling truck. I look around and all is as it should be. Pauline has flung her arm up over her head and one of her feet hangs off the mattress. She wears socks to bed, even in the heat of summer.

Pauline's mattress is pushed against one side of the truck, mine is against the other. Deeper inside the truck is where we keep our crates full of clothes and our books and checkers and my comics. My eyes cannot cut through the dark back there, but nothing seems out of place. My heart rattles, though, and I am very hot.

I pull the sheet off and try and think about something else. I think about how Cordelia likes her back scratched and how she wiggles her tail all the time and how she can find an apple you are hiding in your shirt in an instant. Baby pigs are very smart that way.

The purple curtain moves, and I pick up one of my work boots very quietly and get ready to throw it. And then, just inside the curtain, I see the lady in the orange flappy hat. She is leaning against her cane, watching me.

I open my eyes wide. I look over at Pauline. She is snoring softly.

The old lady smiles warmly. She points toward Pauline and holds her finger to her lips. Then she hobbles closer. My heart flips in my chest and sweat forms on the back of my neck.

"You really are cute as a bug's ear, aren't you?" she whispers.

Pauline stops snoring and rolls back toward me. "Bee?"

I look at her quickly. She sits up, rubbing her eyes. When I look back the lady in the orange hat is gone.

"Did you see her?" I whisper.

"Who?"

"The lady in the flappy hat."

"Oh, Bee," says Pauline, flipping over and pulling her pillow over her head. "There's nobody here. Now go to sleep." Her voice is muffled, but I can hear the mad.

I look around the hauling truck again, searching as best I can in all the dark corners.

I have seen the lady in the flappy hat many times before, but three things are different this time: she never came in the truck before, she never came on a day when nothing has gone terribly wrong, and she never spoke to me.

I try and keep remembering what her voice sounds like in case Pauline wants to know. As I fall asleep, I wonder what the heck a bug's ear is, anyway.

13

One day when we are outside of Pittsfield, and hardly anyone is coming to the show because all the men are gone to the war and who wants to ride a Tilt-A-Whirl when you can't bring your sweetheart, that's when the temperature climbs past 95. The air is wet with sweat.

No matter how hard you try you cannot get cool when you work at a traveling show. We set up in the middle of a field where the grass feels like dry toast under your feet and I stay as long as I can under the little striped tarp over our hot dog cart. My cheek attracts the sun like butter on a plate. I dunk a cloth in the dishwater and hold it to the back of my neck and then soft against my diamond. In a few minutes the cloth is hot and I have to dunk it and start all over again.

The grill is sizzling and there are flies trying to get at the honey stuck to my fingers. "Please, Pauline, please," I say about a hundred thousand times.

"Bee, I said we'll see." Pauline gets all cranky when the heat gets past ninety. She blows her hair out of her eyes in a loud wet sputter. I sigh. I do not want to make her mad. I want to ask her please again, but if I do, she will tell me I have gone and done it, I have made her mad and she is putting me on quiet time.

"You cannot put me on quiet time anymore. I am eleven."

"Just be quiet, Bee."

Pauline does not like flies all over the food and I bet

I could count a dozen trying to get at our honey buns. I count flies while I wait for Pauline to not be mad at me.

I sigh, over and over, louder and louder. It is too hot for folks to even eat, so the hot dogs get dried out. There was a matted little dog sniffing around this morning when I got up to do my business in the john. He was nosing around the pig bucket, where we put hot dogs nobody wants and the honey buns we cannot keep for another day. Already the piglets are getting very fat. I stuff a few hot dogs into the pocket of my overalls in case I see him again.

We close up at nine in most places. Sunday nights we close at six. It is Sunday night. Pauline throws the last of the hot dogs into the bucket. I scrub the cutting board. You never can get all the onion juice out of the wood. I wash the knives and lock them in the trunk and push it to the back of the cart.

Ellis shuts off the music and all the lights. Fat Man Sam and Bobby and Eldora make plans for where they will go out on the town. I am glad Pauline does not go with them. "Dump out the dishwater," she tells me, and she heads for our hauling truck. "Oh, and Bee?" Pauline turns, a big smile across her face. "Are you a little hot?"

If you ever saw a Little Pig Race in a traveling show like ours, and you saw how fast those baby pigs fly around the track, then you have an idea how fast I rush to our truck, climb the stepladder Bobby made for us, and whip the purple curtain open. Even with my legs all wobbly from standing on them all day, I can fling off my apron, unhitch my overalls, and jump into my swimsuit. I wrap myself in my towel and put my work boots back on. Finally, I think, *finally, finally, finally.*

No matter where we go, there is always an old swimming hole somewhere to swim in. You just have to ask one of the girls with the dirty ears or one of the boys who sneak smokes behind the trucks because chances are kids like that know where to find an old swimming hole. I just make sure to let Pauline ask for directions.

I jump out of the truck. "It's up the road," Pauline says a minute later when she steps out. Her hair is down around her waist. Boys look at me for one reason, but they look at Pauline for another. She is pretty as a buttercup, I tell her. I do not tell her too often because I do not want her to get any ideas about boys and leaving me.

"Did you get the flashlight?"

"Yes," I say, turning it on to test it.

"Don't waste the batteries, Bee."

She tells me this every time. I roll my eyes. If she saw me doing this she would tell me girls who roll their eyes can just sit by themselves in the hot truck. This is why I do not let her see.

There are no lights at swimming holes and sometimes we stay so long the stars come out. That makes them very safe if you do not want folks looking at you when you are busy splashing like a trout.

"They said it was up past the filling station."

"I didn't hear you asking anybody."

"It was a surprise, Bee."

I look for a narrow path. Cars and trucks slow and drivers look at Pauline. Sometimes boys hoot at her. I pull my hair over my diamond and keep my eyes on my feet.

"It's not far," Pauline says soon as I find the path and

30

rush straight up a hill. Swimming holes are usually like that. First you climb and then when you get to the top and look down over, it steals your breath away.

"Tree frogs around Pittsfield are louder than anywhere, don't you think, Pauline?" I am skipping very fast, so happy to be off the road and closer to the swimming hole.

"Shush," she says from behind.

We walk after that as quiet as old tree stumps. We get up a steep part and the path swings a little to the left and then we are at the top looking down at a dark hidden pond covered with shadows. Everything smells heavy with wet leaves and damp mud at a swimming hole. I breathe deeply. It all smells very good.

A frog bellows on one side and another answers near us. The pond is about the size of four of our hauling trucks pushed together. Around and around we look, checking every tree and every rock. You cannot be too careful. "Stay here," she says.

Pauline climbs down the bank and wades into the water to test it, one toe at a time. I am frustrated the way I am when somebody cannot decide what to put on a hot dog and I have to stand and wait for about two thousand years. Pauline says I could learn a thing about patience. I tell her I already know plenty.

Already my towel is on a rock and I am jumping up and down. If I am hot and steamy the water will feel even better on my skin.

"How is it?" I can hardly bear the waiting. A fish jumps and ripples rush out to Pauline and touch her before she is waist-deep.

"It is really fine," she says, diving in. Then she swims on

her back to the middle of the pond. Every so often one of her work boots rises above the surface. We wear them because of all the mud at the bottom and because of snapping turtles. Pauline laughs out loud. "Well, don't just stand there, Bee."

Pauline is a wader, but I myself am a jumper. My smile pushes across my cheeks. Ready set go, I rush off the rock, fly through the air, and slip feet-first into the inky depths.

The water yanks the breath out of me and when I find it again, I lie back, my hair swimming behind me, and I look up at the moon, just rising. I flip over and dive down, deep, deep, to where the biggest trout hide, and I am laughing so hard inside myself that I wonder if the fish can hear me.

When I rise to the surface, Pauline swims over and tells me I can climb onto her back. We paddle around pretending we are different animals: frogs, horses, dogs, mountain lions. I am too happy to worry about the diamond on my cheek when we go swimming. That is why I like this so much. I jump off Pauline and paddle from one end of the pond to the other, back and forth, over and over. I breathe deeply and dive to the bottom again and again.

When it is getting late, Pauline has to tell me about a hundred times to get out of the water.

"Bee?"

I dive down so I do not have to hear her telling me to get out.

"Bee?" she is saying when I come up for air, but that is all I hear, because I dive right back down again.

"Bee?" Pauline is saying when I come up, and this time there is mad around her voice.

"What?"

"I said a million times already that it is time to go."

"Oh, I didn't hear you." I smile at the water. And then I dive down once more because I have to thank the trout and the sunfish and the rocks and the mud and the turtles and everything else below the surface of the water. It has been a very wonderful night.

I wrap my towel around and around and sit on the rock and listen to the tree frogs. An owl hoots "who cooks for you, who cooks for you" in the distance.

"What kind?" asks Pauline as she sits down beside me.

"Barred," I say, screeching "who cooks for you" back to the woods. It is good to know about many things.

Then we check for leeches. Other than snapping turtles, leeches are the only downside I can think of to a swimming hole. Leeches like to suck on your legs and your arms and sometimes your back. They are hard to get off because they change shape from short and stubby to long and thin, quick as a wink, like an accordion. That's why it is good not to swim alone. I know some folks get all worked up about leeches, about how they suck at the skin between your toes. I want to tell them, worse things could happen than a leech stuck to your belly.

14

The heat soars and we head to Vermont—Barre and Montpelier and then Burlington. We find swimming holes everywhere we go.

One morning a new man is standing next to Ellis before we even open. His eyes are flying over Pauline. Pauline takes one look and grabs my shoulder and pulls me toward the hot dog cart. She starts the grill and throws hot dogs on. I peel an onion.

Before I get the first one chopped, there is Ellis bringing the new man over. He is tall and dark and looks like Cary Grant in a cowboy hat. I pull my hair tight.

They walk up to the cart and watch us for a minute. Ellis keeps his hat pulled low. I feel like a sausage getting looked over. I am pulling my hair so tight over my diamond my head hurts. This is not an easy thing to do when you are chopping onions. It means you chop with one hand. It also means you are slow. Ellis notices things like this, so I hold my hair down with my chin and chop faster.

"This is Arthur," he tells Pauline. "He needs to learn the ropes. I want you to show him around."

The new man tips his cowboy hat at Pauline. She smiles and Ellis points to me. "You can run things."

I stop chopping. "But I can't do all this by myself—not all the onions and all the hot dogs and all the sauerkraut and all the popcorn and pink lemonade, not without Pauline."

Ellis raises the brim of his hat and I imagine the snakes under there. I think they are black as oil. "Did you hear me? I said get to work. Or does that thing on your face affect your hearing, too?" He looks at Pauline. "You know, I think it's about time she stood in the look-see booth and started earning her keep."

Pauline shudders from the terrible things Ellis says. Already the trembling in my legs has begun. Pauline puts down her spatula and steps closer to me.

"Bee's too little to have folks gawking like that." I feel Pauline shiver through her apron. "She wouldn't earn you any money if she cried all the time she was standing in your look-see booth."

Ellis chews on this for a moment and then grins at Pauline. "Okay, but I won't wait forever." He reaches out to touch my diamond, drooling over when I am grown, but I turn away and wrap myself like a vine all around Pauline and bury my face in her apple blossom hair.

"I didn't say you could show Arthur around tomorrow," he growls. "I want you to show him around *NOW*." He points at me. "And stop holding your hair like that. Folks like to look. For such a little girl, you sure can draw a crowd." This time he laughs. Pauline sucks in her breath.

Arthur sweeps his eyes over my face and stops at my diamond. An overstuffed lady with two girls in pink headbands walks up wanting something to eat. I step toward Pauline, but already Ellis is pulling off her apron and throwing it on the counter. Then he is leading her away.

All day I have to fry hot dogs while Pauline shows Arthur around. I burn my fingers over and over because I am not paying attention to hot dogs. I am holding my hair over my cheek and watching what Pauline is doing.

She stops at each game—the Hoop-La and the Penny Pitch and the Museum of Mystery, where Eldora does her divining. Then Pauline shows Arthur the merry-go-round. I see them meeting up with Silas Meany the Man Without a Stomach who sucks his breath in so far it looks like he was born without a belly and Theodore the Cripple whose leg is twisted and thin as a pencil from polio and Fat Man Sam who tells everybody he is twice the size he was when he finished school. He can't squish himself into the Ferris wheel seats anymore. I see Pauline showing Arthur all about how Ellis wants everyone to keep their eyes on the ground at all times because wallets go flying and he wants them scooped up before anybody notices they are gone. I watch Pauline explaining how to start and stop all the rides and how to hook the safety belts on. Arthur is nodding and asking her questions. I notice she is smiling a lot.

For a moment I think maybe I see the lady in the orange flappy hat limping toward me. But the sun is beating hard and I rub at my eyes and when I look back, there is nothing there but a boy who is dragging a little girl up to the hot dog cart.

He points at me. I know what they are up to. I pull my hair over my face like a curtain and turn away. I give them nothing to look at.

15

At noon I have an awful crick in my neck and my fingers are sticky from selling so many honey buns.

I do everything with one hand so I can keep my hair tight over my cheek. Finally I smear some of the honey from a honey bun on my face and press my hair in it. When it dries I feel like spikes of glass are stuck on my skin.

At about three, I look over and see Pauline pull the ponytail out of her hair so her curls fly down her shoulders, and Arthur is watching the whole thing.

When I turn off the grill at nine, Pauline comes over and tells me Arthur wants to take her to the all-night diner and do I think that would be all right?

"Oh good, I'm starving." I rip off my apron.

"No, Bee. You sweep up, then go to bed. We have to get up early because Ellis wants to open by ten. The radio says we're going to get rain for the rest of the weekend."

"But I do not want to be alone. I can't fall asleep without you."

"Oh, Bee. Yes, you can."

"No, I can't. You know I can't."

Pauline turns to Arthur, standing right beside her. "Wait a minute, okay?" She puts her arm around my shoulders and walks me about five steps so Arthur cannot hear. She bends down and whispers in my ear, "Bee, I haven't ever had a boyfriend. Not here working for Ellis. I really want to go. I won't be late. You'll be okay. All right?"

She waits for me to answer.

I don't. I stare at my work boots. I look at the Beech-Nut foils and the dirty popcorn all over the ground. By the time I look up, Pauline is already walking away.

When I finish sweeping around the hot dog cart and go into the hauling truck, I sit on my mattress for a long time. I think long and hard on why Pauline did not want me to go with her. I hear Fat Man Sam and Eldora and everyone climb into Ellis's truck and go out. They are singing "Boogie Woogie Bugle Boy" and they will be yelling it when they get back and Eldora will make Fat Man Sam put his bedroll outside.

I am afraid to fall asleep until Pauline comes back. I listen to the Ferris wheel creaking as it rocks in the wind and to dogs barking in the distance. Finally, around midnight, I hear Pauline outside the truck giggling. Arthur says, "Good night, Lady Light." I roll my eyes in the dark.

Pauline climbs the ladder and then comes over by me. I pretend I am asleep, and I sigh a lot so she knows I am very unhappy.

"Bee?"

I make a few soft snores.

"Bee, don't be mad. I haven't had a boyfriend before."

I want to tell her how she does not need a boyfriend, how all she needs is me, how all we need is a place to live far away from Ellis and now Arthur. But if I say anything, she will know I am awake.

Pretty soon Pauline climbs onto her own mattress and rolls over and then she is sleeping for real and it is very hot and I am awake for a long, long time. Finally, when I can't make myself fall asleep, I take my bedroll outside and lie down under the stars. I try and play the ha-ha game by myself, but it does not work. I look up at the Big Dipper and think about things for a long time. I tell it how Pauline and I need a home right away.

Then I wait for the old lady in the orange flappy hat.

16

The next morning I am being licked on my face. I think for sure I am being kissed by an angel. I am not.

"Stop that," I say, wiping goo off my diamond, getting up off the wet ground, and looking in the soft eyes of the little matted dog. He tilts his head and watches me. His fur is caked with mud.

"I don't have any more hot dogs. I left them all for you last night. Did you eat them all?"

He tilts his head to the other side. One of his ears sticks straight up. The other bends like it is doing a front flip.

"Well, whose fault is that, anyway?" I fold up my bedroll. I look him in the face.

"Woof!"

"Shush up," I say, standing. "You'll wake everybody up."

But the dog does not shush. He flops on the ground and rolls over, wiggling his paws in the air, wagging the place where a tail ought to be, if only he had one. He wiggles all over like he is happy to see me. I know it is because of the hot dogs.

"I do not have any more. I gave them to you. Remember?"

He rolls all the way over and back up on his feet and when he is doing this he is kicking up dirt all over me and in my hair.

"Stop that!" I say, trying to get the dirt out of my eyes and off my face, and when I do he runs around me in a circle and then comes right back to sit down.

"Ellis is going to hear you. He doesn't let any dogs in our traveling show. You do not want to be in hot water with Ellis, believe me."

The little dog rolls over, wiggles his paws in the air, jumps up, wags his stump of a tail, and while he is doing all this he kicks up even more dirt in my face.

"Get out of here. I do not have any more hot dogs. I am sorry I gave you any in the first place. Now get."

The little dog sits and tips his head to one side, and then the other. He keeps trying to wag his tail, but since he doesn't have one, he wiggles most of his body instead.

You can't help but giggle. No one is up yet, not even Pauline. The dog lies down and watches me. I scrunch my nose. "You sure do smell awful." This only makes him wag his tail harder.

"Don't you know this is no place for a dog?" He sits up and watches me. I look at his belly. It is very thin.

"Roll over."

He gets down on his belly, and then rolls over like he knows all about behaving. He sits up and then we both just look at each other. He tilts his head again like he is trying to figure me out. I pull my hair across my cheek. He notices a stick a few feet away. He looks at it and then back at me, at the stick and then back at me. I know he is trying to decide.

Then he leaps for the stick. He is so small and the stick is so big he cannot get his mouth around it. He goes at it over and over, wrestling with it, until finally he sinks his teeth in and drags it over to me. He sits right in front of me, his head tilted again like he doesn't understand why I am not throwing the stick.

"It's all wet. I'm not touching that."

The dog raises his flopped ear. Now they are muddy flags sticking straight up. He wags his stumpy tail. His whole body is wiggling faster, faster, faster. "Woof!" he says, like I am slow or something, like I do not know what he wants and he has to explain the whole thing very carefully to me.

"Oh, all right, but just once." I throw the stick out past our hauling truck and wipe my hands on my overalls. The little dog jumps after it and I head for the hot dog cart.

A minute later, there he is, dragging the stick and dropping it at my feet.

17

That's when the warning light inside me goes on and off, on and off, and the hairs on my arms rise.

I look all around me. The carnival grounds are quiet. Everyone is sleeping from their late night out. I haven't even seen anybody make their way to the john.

I take many deep breaths. The merry-go-round is empty and there is no one by the Penny Pitch or the Hoop-La. All is quiet out by the Little Pig Race. Bobby keeps the four piglets locked up tight in their shed overnight with plenty of fresh straw because, just like everyone else, pigs like a nice clean bed at night. "The idea that pigs like to be dirty is hogwash," Bobby says. The trucks where everybody sleeps are still. The little dog and I are alone.

I drop a hot dog on a plate and put it on the ground. The little dog eats it in one gobble. I give him another hot dog and then another.

I pull the bucket I use to wash my hair over to the hose and fill it with water. The little dog is watching me very carefully. He comes over to the water and gives it a sniff. I know it is very cold, but I can't do anything about that now. I reach over and pat him on the head and then I scratch between his ears. Already my fingers are covered with mud. I pick him up and he licks my cheek.

I lower him into the water and very slowly I rub his fur with apple shampoo. "Don't tell Pauline," I whisper. I lather first his back and then the top of his head and then down around his belly, where I can feel his thin stomach and his slim ribs. I scratch around his ears and all down his bony chest and his legs. He closes his eyes. If he were a cat, he would purr.

There are many stickle burrs stuck in his fur, and when I pull at them he whines, so I let them be. I swish him all over and pour more and more of Pauline's shampoo over him, squeezing the last of the suds out of the bottle. I look hard at his stump of a tail. "What happened to you?" I whisper, and then I wash his funny ears. Finally I lift him out and wrap him in my towel. He shivers, and when I put him down he shakes puddles all over me.

"Stop that," I say, wiping the water off my face, but I can hardly believe what I see. "Well, look at you," I say, all admiring, because the little matted dog is now the color of sweet butterscotch.

And then he growls. At the same time, my warning light goes on and off, on and off.

18

They have no shirts under their overalls and no shoes. How they got up to us so fast without me knowing, I do not know, and I have to cuss at myself. I scoop the little dog into my arms and pull my hair over my cheek.

"She's the one," the rounder one is saying.

"Show it to us." The taller boy steps closer.

I step back against the hot dog cart.

"You get burned or something? You one of the retards they hire for folks to look at?"

The little dog whines. I feel the metal counter pushing into my backside. I shake my head. I am not that girl.

"Well, we mean to have ourselves a look. Isn't that right?" He looks back at the rounder boy, who is nodding.

The tall boy laughs. He takes another step closer. I would back up if there was anywhere to go. The little dog yips a few times, then whines, then backs into my armpit.

"Maybe you got the Evil Eye on you. Show it to us." His spit flies. He reaches for my hair. I push his hand away.

The rounder boy grins wide. He has watermelon cheeks. "Seems she don't want you touching her."

The little dog pulls himself out of my armpit and barks and then backs up like a turtle into my armpit again. It is awful hard to keep him still while I am trying to keep the side of my face hidden. I am sorry the honey is worn off my cheek.

The taller boy licks his lips. He is so close I smell orange pop on his breath. He reaches for my hair again.

That is too much. The little dog howls and then barks, sounding much bigger than he is. I have to struggle to keep him in my arms and I let go of my hair and it bounces away and suddenly my diamond is shining for everyone to see.

"Wow," says the round boy, "will you look at that." He takes a step back.

What they aren't expecting is Bobby right behind them. "We're closed," Bobby growls. He is not wearing a shirt, just his overalls and work boots.

"We weren't doing nothing," the round boy says, backing up more, and then the taller one is saying, "We don't want no trouble," and then they are turning and running away. The tall one outruns the rounder boy and the little dog is trying to leap out of my arms so he can chase them out of our traveling show.

Bobby puts his hand on my shoulder and looks into my eyes. I try and hold back the tears.

Bobby nods at the dog. The dog wags his stumpy tail. The edges of Bobby's mouth lift.

"I'll keep my eye out for those boys. You keep that dog away from Ellis." Then he turns and walks away.

19

The little dog and I both need a hot dog after that. It is nearly time for everyone to start waking up, so I get the grill started.

"Do you have a name?" The little dog looks at me, tilts his head, and then a worm floating in a little puddle catches his eye. He goes over for a closer look.

I think of all the boy names I know besides Arthur or Ellis or Fat Man Sam or Pete the Alligator Man.

"Roy? Is that your name?"

The dog sniffs at the worm.

"Hal, Jim?"

The dog pokes at the worm with his paw.

"Dexter? Theodore? Dean?"

The dog sticks his mouth in the puddle and grabs the worm with his teeth. He shakes it in the air and drops it at my feet.

"That is really disgusting." I go over and flip hot dogs. "All right. If you're not going to help, I'll call you Nobody. How would you like that? Here, Nobody, here, Nobody!"

The dog looks at me. He tilts his head again and sticks up both of his ears. Then he goes back to the worm.

"Oh, forget it." I take the hot dogs off the grill. The little dog forgets all about the worm and hurries over to me. He wags his stumpy tail.

I put a hot dog on a plate and put it on the ground. He

gulps it down and looks up at the Peabody Frankfurter box. "Woof!"

I look at him and back at the box. He wags his stumpy tail so fast he gets himself off balance. He looks at the box and whines.

"Peabody? Is that the name you want?" I cannot tell if he likes the name or if he wants another hot dog. But it is good enough for me. And that is how I give my dog a name.

20

That night Pauline goes off with Arthur and Fat Man Sam and all the others. She has been mad about Peabody all day. She thinks we will be in hot water when Ellis gets back from Poughkeepsie, where he is thinking of setting up a stay-put show.

I do not even ask her to take me with her. Instead, I bring Peabody into our truck. I turn on the big flashlight and show him my mattress, hard as our grill. I puff up my bedroll. I show him how we keep our clothes in old apple crates and how we keep the purple curtain closed. Already mosquitoes are getting in and I fix the curtain so there isn't any space between the cloth and the sides of the truck.

I fluff up my pillow. I lie on my belly and watch Peabody. I tap the mattress and show him where he can lie down, right beside me. I tell him all about my life, how I came to be with the traveling show and with Ellis and with Pauline.

"Pauline has been very good except now she is with Arthur." Peabody tilts his head so he looks as if he is interested in what I am saying. "Ellis does not like dogs and he will get rid of you if he finds you."

It turns out it doesn't take long to love a dog. I pull Peabody close and smell the sweet warm smell of him. After a while, he licks my face. I ask him where did he come from and tell him I do not know what Pauline will do when she sees him in the truck with me, so I will think of something.

A trash can knocks over outside. I turn off the flashlight. "Traveling shows attract a lot of skunks," I whisper. Peabody is all interested in what is outside. He sits up and whines.

"Shush." I scratch him behind the ears. He keeps watching the purple curtain with both of his ears raised up.

"Do you know about the ha-ha game?" I try to get his attention on other things. He tilts his head. "Well, it's when you tell stories about when you were little. The ones that make you laugh. We do not tell the ones that make us sad." I think about Pauline for a minute and then make myself stop because it is not a good idea to think about things that make you tearful when you are all contented. It tends to cloud things up.

I pull Peabody closer. It is so hot. "Do you like swimming holes?" Peabody wags his stumpy tail. I tell him all about how Pauline and I go swimming. "I don't go swimming without Pauline, though."

I rub his ear. "Sometimes when I am alone I go out and watch the stars. Do you like the stars?" Peabody tilts his head. "It's a good star night tonight. There's no moon." Peabody wags his stumpy tail and that is a good enough answer for me.

It is very dark. I wave my flashlight and Peabody and I go slow to make sure there are no skunks. I pull my bedroll out past the Little Pig Race. We have to stop so I can let Cordelia and the others out of their shed so I can scratch them for a while. Peabody sniffs at them and I lift Cordelia over the fence and bring her onto the bedroll with me and Peabody. She snuggles up against us so I will rub her backside. Pigs are awful loving when you give them half a chance.

"That's the Big Dipper." Peabody's fur is soft on my cheek. Cordelia is nuzzling around my belly. "And that is the North Star. It is a very important star if you are trying to find your way home."

A crow caws. Peabody lifts his head and looks up. Another crow caws. I shiver. Peabody jumps up, looking through the dark. It is awful late for crows to be cawing. I scan the shadows with my flashlight. Peabody whines. Another crow caws. I think maybe I should shut Cordelia and the others in the shed.

"You wait here." I pat Peabody's back so he knows he should stay put. My legs are wobbly from standing on them all day. "I need to lock you up in case," I say, lifting Cordelia into her pen.

Before I can say Jack Sprat those boys from before are coming up on us. Peabody raises the fur on his back and growls.

"Well, look what we found!" The tall boy and the round boy with watermelon cheeks stand grinning, as close to us as dug graves. They wait in the shadows of Cordelia's pen, their ball caps pulled low. Another boy stands a little off to the side. He is smaller, thinner. Like the others, he has no shoes.

"What do we have here?" says the taller boy. "Is it the ugly girl?"

The round boy laughs. Peabody barks.

"And her ugly dog, too?"

I pick up Peabody. His fur is standing on end. I hold him close. I look for Cordelia, hoping the boys don't notice her. I don't know what they'd do to a baby pig. I try and pull my hair tight, but it is hard to do when I am holding a dog. I look back at our hauling truck, wondering how quick my legs could get us there.

The tall boy steps closer and kicks the pigpen. Cordelia and the others scramble. Peabody whimpers.

"Knock it off." I try and make my voice a boulder in my chest. I hold my dog tight.

The boy laughs. "What's the matter, ugly girl? You don't like us?" He grins. He looks at his friends. "She don't like us."

The round boy laughs. The little boy backs up. "I—I—I think we should leave her alone. My mama says we should stay away from her."

"Naaaah," the tall boy says. "Why would we want to do that? She's just a girl. An ugly old girl. We're just getting started."

Peabody growls. I pull him tighter.

"I know what happened to you." The tall boy reaches for my diamond. Peabody growls again. I step back. My legs are Jell-O. He laughs. Then in a low voice, he says, "Grab her!"

My legs quiver as I hold Peabody and leap away and dash toward our truck. Pauline is all I can think of as I run. I want Pauline. I want her to give these boys a taste of their own medicine. And then I want her to hold me so tight I can smell the apple shampoo in her hair.

"Catch her!" the tall boy yells. Bare feet slap the dirt behind me. I try and push myself faster but I am on shaking legs. The footsteps behind me get closer. There is no voice in my chest. My legs wobble and then I am pushed from behind and I fall, hitting the ground with my arms around Peabody and the weight of the tall boy on top of me.

"Don't be a baby," he whispers in my ear.

"Flip her over, flip her over!" the round boy screams.

"Careful or you'll catch it," whimpers the little one. "Don't touch her mark."

I hold tight to Peabody. He is trying to wiggle out of my arms. I hold on tighter.

The boy pulls me over and wipes my hair off my face. He touches my cheek, running his dirty fingers all over the edge where my diamond begins. Peabody howls and wiggles out of my grasp.

I shudder. I hold my breath, and then when the boy runs his fingers close enough, I grab his hand and send my teeth deep into the thin skin between his thumb and his finger. He screams that terrible high-pitched screech cats make at night. When I let go of him, he is already crying. He sucks at his hand.

"She's marked you!" the youngest boy shrieks. Tears rush down his face.

Peabody barks and howls. He leaps between me and the boys. That's when there is another sound, this time a bear growling.

Bobby grabs the tallest boy and flings him off me like a bag of potatoes. Then he picks up the little one and hurls him past the first.

The round boy runs over and drags the little one to his feet and then the tall one is running up the hill and away from our traveling show and the other two are chasing after.

Bobby helps me up and as soon as I am off the ground, I throw myself on him, sobbing, and you can tell he does not know much about children or what you are supposed to do when one is crying, because his arms are stiff as barn boards as they wrap around me.

"You run slower than Cordelia," he says after a while, patting my head in a way that feels more like a thumping, but I don't really care because it is Bobby.

"You're going to have to run faster than that if you're going to look after that little dog."

It is more words than I have ever heard him put together, and for some reason it makes me cry awful hard.

21

The next morning before the sun is hardly up, Peabody and I are out by the Little Pig Race, with Bobby holding up his watch. "If I can teach pigs to run, I can teach a girl." I am not sure if I should take offense or not.

Training girls is different, though, because Bobby does not use corn. He uses his pocket watch, and the memory of those boys.

"Tie those tight," he says, pointing at my work boots. I wind the laces around and around the top of each boot to keep them from dragging. I can't do anything about the holes in the soles.

"See those woods and that hill and that pine tree at the top?"

I put my hand up to block the sun, just rising. There is a field that heads straight into woods that climb steeply. I will have to climb over at least one stone wall before I reach the trees. My legs still shake from last night. Bobby looks to see if I am paying attention. "Running in the woods will build stamina. And it will make you fast. Now, the trick is to remember those boys with every step you take. Slow down if you have to, but do not stop. You will find your second wind."

He's talking way more than I have ever heard him before. I look at the pine tree at the top. It is straight up. Peabody is grinning, he is so excited about what is going to happen.

"Ready?"

I want to shake my head, but I remember the boys. Bobby holds up his arm.

"Get set, go!" He drops his arm and I run out past him, my Jell-O legs trying to hold me up. Peabody is right beside me jumping and yipping and barking, he is so happy to be flying so fast over the parched grass.

My legs are sore from last night but they carry me out, out, out through the long grass toward the woods.

I spook a dozen mourning doves and they flap into the air. Peabody darts out after them, his stumpy tail waving in front of me. Already my legs are telling me to quit.

As soon as I enter the woods and start climbing, I am running through cement. My lungs are two sloshing buckets of water. When I reach the stone wall I inch myself up and over and then flop onto my side, I am so out of breath. Peabody lies down beside me and whines. I watch a beetle and a butterfly, and feel just like Cordelia.

I lie there a long time so my heart can get back to beating regular, and because my head feels awful dizzy. Peabody whines louder. I look up at the oak trees, so high overhead. "Oh, all right," I say finally, pulling myself up because Bobby has his pocket watch and I am remembering the tall boy and how fast he can run.

It hardly takes a few steps uphill and the blood is pounding in my head again. I trip on a log hidden in old leaves. Peabody is already far ahead. He sits down and watches me run up the steep hill, my legs high-stepping boulders and logs like I am running through very deep snow. It is very hard to run in the woods and very hard to run uphill. I wonder what Bobby is thinking.

Finally, I reach the pine tree at the top and flop onto the ground, my chest heaving.

"That's it," I wheeze, "I am not a runner."

After Peabody starts whining again like maybe it is time to get going, I pull myself to my feet and hobble back downhill to Bobby. Peabody yips all around my feet, like he is a sheepdog and I am an old ewe. I climb over the stone wall and then I limp all the way back to the Little Pig Race.

Bobby has stretched a string between the fence and an old fold-up chair and he wants me to run through, but I wilt on the ground before I get there.

"That's twenty-two minutes," he says, shaking his head, looking at me sprawled in the dirt, and tucking the watch back into his overalls. "We'll try again tomorrow."

He walks off toward the pigs. Peabody runs off after him.

It takes a few minutes for my head to stop pounding and my pulse to quit racing. I pull off my work boots and peel down my socks. My feet are red and puffy and soft and slow and very sore. I am ashamed of them the way I am ashamed of my face.

22

A band of silver circles Pauline's finger. It glitters in the sun. She waves it in front of me.

"Look, Bee." She moves it slowly past my eyes, waving her hand so the light bounces off.

I know it is from Arthur. I do not mention I can see plain as day it is foil from a stick of gum. I bet even Peabody can tell. Nobody who's serious about things gives a girl a gum-foil ring. Bobby would give her the real thing. Of that I am sure.

I take a hot dog off the grill and throw it to Peabody.

"You can't do that," says Pauline. "Ellis will kill us."

"He's not here, remember?" I pull three onions from the box and cut off their papery skins. While I am doing this I find reasons to give Pauline many disapproving looks. She is too busy frying up hot dogs to notice. Arthur comes by on his way to the john and tips his cowboy hat at Pauline. She giggles. I roll my eyes.

"Isn't it a beautiful day, Bee?" she asks after he is past. "I just love days like this, with the sun all shining and everything so happy."

I look at Peabody. He is lying beside me inside the hot dog cart. I fold my arms across my chest. "I didn't notice."

She looks at me a minute, then sighs and turns back to the grill.

"I haven't had a boyfriend ever, Bee. Can't you just be happy for me?"

Before I even have a chance to unfold my arms, Arthur is right beside us asking Pauline if she could help him with the merry-go-round. She looks at me and I keep my arms crossed and won't take my eyes off the onions.

"Oh, Bee," she says.

I look at Peabody. He is watching Pauline. Already she is untying her apron. I do not know what has gotten into her.

23

Arthur is a tidal wave washing over us, pulling Pauline out to sea and leaving me and Peabody all alone on the shore.

"I have to help Arthur again tomorrow," Pauline is saying that night as she rushes around her side of our hauling truck, slipping a new dress over her head. "Ellis wants to put him in charge of the stay-put show he wants to set up in Poughkeepsie, so I have to teach him everything that goes on here."

I curl up on my bedroll with Peabody against me. "But what about Bobby?" I whisper. "He likes you very much."

"The pig man? He doesn't like me like that, Bee."

I look at her. "How can you not know he likes you so much?"

"I like Arthur, Bee."

"But he's rotten. It's like he's bewitched you, Pauline, and what about me? I know you would never go out all the time and leave me if you were thinking right. Why aren't you thinking right?"

Pauline stops putting on her dress-up shoes from Woolworth's and comes over and tries to squeeze me, but I turn away. When she loosens her hold, I rush out of the truck and Peabody follows right behind.

24

The next morning I am tucked tight in my bedroll when someone bangs on our hauling truck. Pauline jumps up. Peabody growls. I cover my face.

"Bee?"

It is Bobby.

"What's he doing here?" whispers Pauline, pulling the covers close to her chin.

"He's been teaching me to run."

"Run? Why?"

"If you were here more, you'd know that, Pauline." My legs are still wobbly from yesterday, but I get up and climb into my overalls. Peabody pushes his nose out the curtain.

"You think I'm doing this for my health?" Bobby asks when I get the curtain open. He is leaning against the truck with his pocket watch and his ready, set, go and his rules about starting slow and ending fast.

"I'm not running anymore."

"Why not?"

I look back at Pauline, who is turned to us, listening.

"Because I hate it."

Bobby spits off to the side. "How's quitting going to keep those boys from stealing your dog? Or worse?"

Peabody tilts his head and looks at me.

"I'm terrible at it."

"Well, I have some things I need to show you. Running

in the woods, jumping over stone walls and logs, running uphill and down, all this will make you fast. You'll get better, I promise. You're not a quitter, are you?"

Maybe I am. "I have to get ready to open the hot dog cart."

"You've got time. Come on. Besides, we'll be setting up outside of Nashua tomorrow and who knows if there will be a good place to run?"

I cross my arms in front of me and glare at him. Peabody whines.

Bobby crosses his arms, too. "Probably best if you remember those boys every time you feel like quitting."

I look at him with his thick-rimmed glasses and his coal-dark hair shooting up in a hundred directions and I know that if Pauline gave him half a chance, things might go better for us.

25

Morning after morning, before anybody is up, me and Peabody are out past the Little Pig Race and Bobby has his pocket watch in the air.

It turns out there are plenty of woods outside of Nashua.

"You have to start out slow," Bobby tells me for the hundredth time. "Then pick up speed as you go. That's what went wrong. If you use up all your heart at the start, you'll never find your second wind."

He checks my laces. They are tied twice. "If you get tired, slow down before you fall down. Got it? And go straight uphill, climb rocks, jump over trees. Understand?"

I nod.

"At the top of the hill, turn around and fly down as fast as you can. And keep your arms at a forty-five-degree angle. Like this." He bends my arms at the elbow. "Raise them and push back with each step so it's like you're pulling back a lever. Try it. And don't stoop like that."

He tells me so many things I can't keep them in my head. Peabody wags his stumpy tail. Cordelia and LaVerne nose around the edge of their pen waiting to see somebody else race for a change.

"Ready?" says Bobby.

I nod.

"Set, go!"

And we are off.

I start off fast like a rabbit and then go slow like a turtle, straight into the woods, then fast like a rabbit and slow like a turtle.

"No, no, no!" Bobby is yelling, following me until I reach the woods.

I slow down until I am a turtle and I keep that pace until I am over a stone wall, have jumped a pile of logs, and have climbed a sheet of ledge. I try and come up with all the words I know for *turtle* and *tortoise: sluggish, slow, determined.* I plod forward until I reach the top of the hill and then head down again.

When I get out of the woods, I see Cordelia sticking her snout through the fence and the sight of her sets me on fire and I am a rabbit all the way back until I fall at Bobby's feet.

"Not fast enough," Bobby says when I am rolling in the dirt, choking as I try to suck air into my lungs. "Twice a day. We'll do this morning and night."

26

My muscles are aching. My shins feel like there is a knife slitting them, top to bottom. My face is burned from the sun and the sweat pours down my chest and the back of my neck.

"Eighteen minutes," he says the next morning in Portland. "You're still running like a girl."

"I *am* a girl." I glare at him.

He spits out across Peabody's head toward me. It nearly hits me. I think maybe I am mad as a wet hen. I suck up spit and shoot it back. It lands in a soft wet drip on the top of my work boot.

He grins. "That all you got?"

My face is hot from already being mad at him and now even hotter from seeing the spit on my boot.

"There's an art to spitting. Most girls don't know how. Do you want to learn?"

"No, I do not want you to teach me to spit."

I clomp off with the spit on my boot. I don't wipe it off until I get to the truck.

27

"Okay, here's how you do it." Bobby sucks up spit in his mouth. I am out watching him feed the piglets the next morning and I am not so mad anymore. He scratches each of them behind the ears and talks all sweet to them and calls them Sweet Pea and Darling Dear and Honey Pie. When I am not so mad I think how they are lucky to have him.

"You have to get a lot of spit worked up in your mouth. Whoosh your mouth like this until you get a lot." He swishes his mouth around. "Then gather the spit on the edge of your tongue and pucker your lips. Then blow as hard as you can."

Bobby sends a wad of spit off toward the stone wall. He turns back to me. "Spitting is a good thing to know how to do. You never know when it will come in handy."

I look at Peabody. I think about the tall boy and the round boy with the watermelon cheeks, and how much I would like to send a mouthful of spit straight at them. I swish my mouth trying to come up with enough saliva. I work at it for quite a while and then move the spit to the end of my tongue. This is not as easy as it looks. Finally, I open my mouth and blow as hard as I can. A very small gob of spit lands on Peabody's head.

Peabody rushes over and hides behind the pig shed. Bobby grins and shakes his head. "What a girl." Then he goes over and picks up Peabody and wipes the spit off his head with his bandanna. "Make sure you're up fifteen minutes earlier tomorrow morning. I want to get you running faster."

I fume. Bobby goes by the pig shed. Peabody won't look me in the eye. I tell him how I didn't mean for it to happen and that I am sorry. He needs a lot of snuggling after that to get back to feeling good about things. Just like Cordelia.

28

Ellis comes back all fired up about setting up a show in Poughkeepsie. He makes us all go over by Eldora's Museum of Mystery and sit in the waiting-for-your-fortune chairs and hear what he has to say: "There's a big factory making Army tanks down there. Lots and lots of folks are working, folks who will have money to burn at night. You get my drift?"

Fat Man Sam and Pete the Alligator Man nod. "Yessiree," says Silas Meany the Man Without a Stomach. I hold my hair over my face and hear Peabody start whining in the back of our hauling truck.

Pauline winces. I hold my breath.

"This war ain't gonna end soon, so what we'll do is set up another show, a stay-put show in Poughkeepsie," Ellis says. "Some of you will come with me and some will finish out the year with this show and then go south for the winter." He looks over to the trucks. "What is that noise?"

I grab Pauline's arm. She looks at me and shakes her head very slowly.

Then Bobby steps up. "One of the pigs has been feeling poorly and has been making an awful racket."

"Well, do something about it. Can't have no sick pigs around here. I thought you said you knew how to take care of pigs."

"Yes, sir," says Bobby, and then Ellis gets started telling

about a new booth he wants to set up in Poughkeepsie, something he heard about from a show out in Chicago.

"It's called an African Dip. You put a colored boy in a cage and people pay good money to throw balls at a lever. If they hit it right, the boy drops in the water. Pulls in bucketloads of money, too."

Ellis laughs. I shudder. I can only imagine what he would do to my little dog.

I tell Pauline as soon as we get away from Ellis that I think we better find a home for ourselves pretty quick. "Me too, Sweet Pea Bee." And then she goes off to help Arthur with the Tilt-A-Whirl.

That night Pauline is feeling bad about leaving me all day. She wants to know if I want to play the ha-ha game. I sigh a few times to let her know I am not sure if she is worth my time. Then when I am afraid she might think about changing her mind, I tell her I will give her one more chance.

We drag our bedrolls out onto the grass. Peabody snuggles up beside me. Pauline looks up at the sky. I am looking at my work boots.

Pauline is so quiet I think she has fallen asleep. I snuggle up next to her. She slides her arm around me.

"Bee, I have something important to tell you."

I am wide awake.

"Are you listening?"

I nod my head in the dark.

Peabody looks up.

"Ellis says I have to go join up with his show in Poughkeepsie."

"No, Pauline. I want to go to Florida."

Pauline sighs. I don't like it when she sighs.

She is quiet for a minute and then says, "Ellis told me I can't bring you, Bee. He wants you to run the hot dog cart here. I told him I couldn't leave you, I couldn't go anywhere without you, that we've been together since you were four. He told me I had to do what he said or he would put you in an orphan home tomorrow."

Even in the dark, I know there are tears winding their way down Pauline's face. I don't have any words in me. All I can do is reach over and grab hold of her and let her pull me to her and my tears start flowing and Peabody whines in my ear.

Pauline holds me. "I am so sorry, Bee." She says it over and over and over and we hold each other for a long time under the stars. When Pauline falls asleep, I stay awake and wait for the lady in the orange flappy hat.

29

It all happens so fast. Bobby is working on the pigpen, fixing where a family was leaning too hard and broke the boards. Every so often he looks over at Pauline.

She doesn't notice him. She is loading her things in Arthur's truck for the trip to Poughkeepsie. She carries out the bedroll, then the mattress, then the apple crates of clothes, and finally the shoe box with all her little notebooks filled with her poems. She keeps looking over at me and I know her face is red from all the crying about leaving me.

With each load, my tears roll faster. Bobby keeps clearing his throat and he lifts Cordelia out of the pen and brings her over and puts her in my arms just as the first *ting, ting, tings* of August hail start falling, a thin pattering of ice all over us. I brush the bits from between Cordelia's ears and run my fingers through the tracks they leave behind.

"Can't you do anything?" I sob as Bobby just stands there watching Pauline packing her things. "I know you like her."

Bobby gets all red in the face. He takes Cordelia from my arms because Pauline is walking toward us. He doesn't look Pauline in the eye.

But I do. "Don't go, don't go, don't go," I sob. I hold on to her neck and get myself tangled in her hair.

Pauline sobs. Her whole body shakes. "Bee, I'll be back before the winter comes. Ellis promised. We'll go to Florida together." I know Ellis's promises are good as pie crusts. They are always crumbling. "I didn't know it would turn out like this, Bee. Honest, I didn't." She cries more and more.

While I am all tangled up in Pauline's hair, Arthur comes over to see what is taking so long.

"Let her be," Bobby tells him.

But Arthur doesn't listen. "Ellis wants us to meet him in Poughkeepsie tonight," he says, pulling Pauline's arm and leading her away. I sink to the ground and the bits of hail are not *ting, ting, ting*ing, they are pelt, pelt, pelting. When I look up, Arthur is helping Pauline into the truck and she is turning and twisting to try and keep her eyes on me and then he is slamming the truck door and taking her away.

Peabody licks the streams of water off my cheek. I throw myself into the grass. He lies down beside me so I can bury my face in his fur and sob.

In a moment, Bobby pulls me off the soaking ground and leads me and Peabody to Eldora's Museum of Mystery, where there are fat sofas to sit on and peanuts to eat. Just before we go inside, I think maybe I see the thin fading outline of an orange flappy hat.

30

Folks hand over their money by the fistful at Eldora's Museum of Mystery. This is because Eldora tells folks what they want to hear.

Basically, everybody wants to know two things from Eldora: will they get the love of their life, and will they get rich. This makes it very easy for a diviner like Eldora. She tells them yes, yes to all the questions that they are hopeful about, and she throws in just a teeny bit of trouble to make things sound right. She promises the girls will get husbands who look like Cary Grant, and the young men will each get an Ingrid Bergman. She tells everybody they will get a gold mine of money, too. It is hard to believe there is that much gold to go around.

Fat Man Sam says what Eldora does is a sin against God and nature, but Eldora tells him to shush up and he forgets all about sinning and everything else when he wants Eldora to tell his fortune awful bad.

"She gives me the creeps," Pauline used to say, telling me to stay away from Crazy Eldora with the Bright Yellow Hair, as we all call her. But Eldora never gave me any trouble. She's the one who told me about how lemons would make my diamond disappear if I used enough of them.

When Bobby and I walk into the tent, we are dripping from all the rain and the hail. Eldora is laying out her cards on a small fold-up table.

"We came to get dry, and that's it." Bobby drops onto a fat sofa. I sink down beside him and look around for the dish of peanuts. There's a dead butterfly on the wall that Eldora pinned to a piece of cardboard, its wings fanned wide so everyone can have a good look. It is so sad, I turn so I can't see. Peabody jumps on my lap and turns around a few times before lying down. He has his eyes on Eldora.

Bobby leans back and shuts his eyes. "We don't need any of your monkey business."

Eldora jangles her bracelets as she deals her cards. Her yellow hair is tied up in silk scarves and she wears a church choir robe she found outside Manchester. The sleeves are so long they cover the cards and you can't see what is happening under there.

"That's what you think I do in here? Tell folks voodoo and that sort of thing?"

"Something like that." He opens one eye. "Doesn't amount to a hill of beans, as far as I can tell."

I watch Eldora carefully. It is good to get my mind off things. Eldora scoops up the cards and fans them out across the table in a rainbow. Then she scoops them up again and shuffles them, making lots of interesting snapping and popping sounds, and she sets one card on the table, face-down.

"This is the past," Eldora whispers in her slow and heavy divining voice. She turns the card over. It is the queen of hearts. She makes her voice so smoky I cough. "You had an affectionate, caring woman in your past."

Yes. Yes, I did. I scratch Peabody between the ears and try not to feel the ache of Pauline leaving.

"That's enough." Bobby opens his eyes and glares at Eldora. "We just want a place out of the weather."

The fortune-teller acts like she is in a trance and cannot hear anything from this world. She scoops up the queen card and pushes it into the middle of the deck. She puts the deck on the table and fans all the cards out again and pulls them back. Bobby folds his arms over his chest and closes his eyes. She scoops up the deck and splits it into three parts and stacks them together. She flips the bottom card onto the top. I hold my breath. Peabody watches everything she does. One of his ears is sticking up.

She lays the top card on the table.

"This is the present."

I cannot keep my heart from thumping.

She looks at me. "Do you want to know?" Her voice is hoarse. "Some folks don't want to know."

I look at Bobby. He is breathing slowly. I picture Pauline walking off with Arthur.

"You can't get to your right future if you don't take a hard look at your present." Eldora waits for an answer.

I nod quickly.

Eldora flips over a three of spades. She looks at it for a moment and shuts her eyes for a very long time. I look nervously over at Bobby. He is snoring softly. I check how far it is to the door.

"You've had a break in a relationship." Eldora opens her eyes. "Because of a third person, probably a man."

I let my breath out slowly. Well, no kidding. Eldora watched Pauline giggle all silly over Arthur, same as anyone. I shrug.

"This is the future." Eldora takes so long to flip over the last card I just about lose my patience and turn it over myself. When she finally snaps it onto the table, she lets out a tiny moan. She turns to me and stares.

"What? What is it?"

"Child," she says softly. "I had no idea."

I push Peabody onto the floor and jump up and Eldora covers the card with her hand, but not before I see it is the nine of spades.

"Is that bad?" I ask her, even though I do not give a fig about her predictions and fortune-telling. "Is it bad?" I search her eyes for truth. She looks away. I search through my sixth sense that Pauline told me I had so much of to see if I can figure out what it means to get a nine of spades.

Bobby opens his eyes and takes it all in, seeing everything in an instant. "Come on, Bee," he says, jumping up. I lift Peabody into my arms.

"Hold on to that funny-looking dog," Eldora says carefully, just sitting there and not doing anything about my future card that is sitting faceup. "A friend like that is worth more than gold."

I don't need anybody telling me that, I think as I carry Peabody out into the rain. I already know that all by myself.

31

That night, Pauline's side of our hauling truck is a blank piece of paper, empty, picked clean as an old stew bone. She left only one thing, her little notebook, *The Story of Bee*, which is sitting on my pillow. I look at it, pick it up, fan through it, and throw it on her side of the truck.

Peabody snuggles up close to me. I hold him for a very long time, breathing in the warm smell of his fur, my eyes settled on Pauline's empty place. "Why did she do it? Why did she go like that?"

Peabody wiggles closer so there is no space between. He answers with just his eyes; he is sorry about everything. It turns out that dogs are very good to talk to.

32

"I can't."

"You can."

"I can't."

"Yes, you can," Bobby says. "Now, let's see you run to that tree out there."

I shake my head. It is early morning in Rutland. I haven't run since Pauline left us two weeks ago. Who can run with such a big hole in her heart?

"I want to try something different," he says. "You're ready to work on your speed. I also want to watch your form. I have noticed you've been trying to take strides that are too long. You might think that makes you run faster, but it slows you down."

Bobby is wearing an old pair of white shoes I have never seen before. They have red leather stripes on the side and they are worn through to his big toes.

"Like this." He runs a few feet, his legs stretched out as far as they will go. "See, I don't want you to do this." He takes a shorter stride. "See, like this."

"I can't."

"What do you mean you can't?" He yanks his glasses off and wipes the dust off the lenses. His hair pokes out the back of his cap.

"I'm trying to make you a better runner, Bee. I know you

can do it. But all you're telling me is you can't, you can't, you can't. But you can, Bee. You have to want to get better. You have to look for your own finish line and tell yourself you will cross it, even with Pauline gone, and you have to keep trying and trying and you will find the strength deep inside yourself, and when you find it, you will be proud, really, really proud. When you have a goal like that, you will get better, I promise."

I look up at Mr. Talk My Ear Off. Things have certainly changed.

Bobby doesn't say anything. He walks over by the pig-pen, opens the gate, and steps inside. Cordelia is the first to nuzzle all over him. Then Big Ben comes and then LaVerne and Vivian. Even pigs love him. I don't know what's the matter with Pauline.

Bobby holds Cordelia up over the pen so I will come get her. It is awful hard to resist a piglet when she is looking at you like that. I go over and take her, feel the warm tickling as she nuzzles my neck.

"How do you know so much about running?" I ask after a while.

He laughs at the way Cordelia is trying to get up onto my shoulder. "I held the record for the mile at my high school, Bee. They used to call me the Hurricane."

Peabody does not like all the attention I am giving Cordelia and he noses at my leg trying to get me to scratch him between the ears.

"How come I don't ever see you run?"

"I got tripped and busted my knee. I can't run much any-more. That's another reason the Army won't take me." He rubs Peabody's back. "Army doc wouldn't clear me. But I'm tough, same as you, Bee. Now put that pig down and get moving."

"I can't. I'm a terrible runner."

"You can."

"I can't."

He leans against the fence and takes off his glasses again and wipes them off. He crosses his arms against his chest.

"Bee, I have something I need to tell you."

I look over at him quickly.

"I'm going to be leaving here, too."

I sit down before I fall. Cordelia nuzzles in my hair.

"There's a factory in York, Maine, Bee, and they want workers to build bomber engines. It's not that far from here. I saw the signs when we were going through Portland."

I wipe my face on my sleeve.

"Oh, don't cry." He kneels down beside me and wipes my face with the old bandanna he keeps in his pocket. It smells like pigs. I don't want him to stop.

"I've been trying to talk myself out of it, but I have to do something better for myself than running pig races. I've asked Eldora to keep an eye on you and she's promised not to pull any voodoo." He pats my head. It feels like a thumping.

I sob into his shoulder. "But it's my birthday next week. You can't leave before my birthday."

He pulls away and wipes my tears. "Your birthday? I didn't know, Bee."

"You can't leave me. You can't."

He sighs several times. "Oh, Bee. I can't wait another day. I've got everything worked out. If I can't fly a bomber with these eyes, at least I can build bomber engines. And who knows, maybe as the war goes on, they'll loosen up the rules and let men like me serve."

I reach up and put my arms around him. "But I don't want you to go. Everyone is always leaving me. I just want you to stay. I'll run. I promise I will. I'll run every morning and every night, and every afternoon, too. You can call me the Hurricane. Maybe you can make Pauline come back to us."

He squeezes me hard. It is not easy to hug someone with a piglet between you, but I let Bobby squeeze me tight. "I wanted to give you one more lesson before I go. It's getting late now, so we'll try tomorrow morning soon as you get up. But it has to be early because Ellis is coming back and I need to leave before he gets here."

Bobby asks if I will promise not to tell anyone where he is going and then he walks off to pack. He leaves Cordelia in my arms. It is hard to cry when a piglet is looking so sweet on you. But I do anyway.

33

It is so hard to sleep without Pauline. I hide myself deep in my bedroll and try and keep the tall boy and the small boy and the round boy with the watermelon cheeks out of my head.

I roll all around inside my bedroll and Peabody has to get up off my belly each time and circle around and around until he finds a good spot. He sighs to let me know he is tired of doing this.

When I wake up I am surprised I ever fell asleep. The sun is barely up when I sit up and sink my feet into my work boots.

"Ready?" I ask Peabody as I tie tight knots.

You don't have to ask him twice. He jumps off the mattress and scurries down the ladder. He is getting very good at this now.

The traveling show is very quiet this early in the morning and I don't have to worry about Peabody running free. I knock on Bobby's truck. He opens his curtain after a minute and looks out. His hair could use some greasing down.

"Will you show me more about running?" I ask.

Bobby jumps to the ground with his old white running shoes. We hurry to the pigpen. We don't have much time.

"Run from here to the Ferris wheel," he tells me.

"Come on," I tell Peabody, and I am off, putting one foot

in front of the other, trying not to bounce, trying to make my stride the right length and keep my arms at a forty-five-degree angle.

"Slow, slower," I hear behind me.

Gosh, I think. I am running slower than Cordelia. But I haven't lost my breath, and I circle the Ferris wheel and head back.

"Okay, now fast!" I speed up and for a few moments I can fly. Then my lungs fill with water and I feel my blood pumping in my head. I slow down.

Bobby is grinning when I reach him. "Very good. Very, very good." We sit on the grass so I can catch my breath. Peabody goes over and sniffs at Cordelia.

"So who tripped you?" I look over by the shed where Pete the Alligator Man locks up the alligator and beyond to where Silas Meany sits. The sun warms my face and I undo my laces and tie them again.

"One of the guys from the other team. Guess he wanted to win pretty bad. They used to say I could have beat Jesse Owens if I didn't get busted up. That was stretching it a bit." Bobby grins.

"Who's Jesse Owens?"

"You don't know about Jesse Owens? Where've you been, Bee?" Bobby chuckles. "He is the grandson of a slave, who won four gold medals running in the 1936 Olympics in Berlin. That made Hitler powerful mad. Probably started the war, Hitler was so upset."

"If you were hurt, how'd you end up with Ellis?"

"Well, there were no jobs to be had and Ellis comes through town one day and sees me limping around by the barbershop with nothing to do and he offers me a job. Same way he finds everyone."

"He didn't find me that way."

"No, he didn't." Bobby lets Peabody lick his face.

"Did you know my mama and papa?"

Bobby scratches between Peabody's ears. "No, I came on after that. You were already with Pauline."

Thinking about Pauline is like being all balled up in a blanket and you can't breathe. I try and get air into my lungs. I let out a little sob.

"I will find you after the war when I am done building bombers, Bee."

"How? What if I don't work for Ellis anymore?"

Bobby puts Peabody in my lap. "I have an idea. Wait here."

He jumps up and hurries off to his truck. Peabody jumps off my lap and follows Bobby. He knows a good man when he sees one.

When Bobby comes back he is holding the *Billboard* magazine. He opens it to the middle, and hands it to me.

"See this?"

He points to a small boxed advertisement at the bottom of the Carnivals page.

It reads:

> *Anyone knowing whereabouts of*
> *Virgil Mumford*
> *Please phone or wire at our expense*
> *Urbana, Ill., Jul. 27–31, Farmer City, Ill., Aug. 2–8*

"This is what I'll do, Bee. I'll write like someone is looking for me, Robert Benson, and I will put my address and you can write to me there and let me know how to find you. You'll have to mail off for a subscription." He turns to the front and shows me where to send my money. "If you answer the advertisement, we'll be able to find each other. You can write, can't you?"

"Of course I can write," I snap. "Pauline taught me how."

He reaches over and hugs me. I hug him back for a very long time. I am glad he has learned how to hug a girl, and I am very, very glad his arms are not barn boards anymore.

"Come on," he says, looking up. "Running makes everything better. You'll see. It helps put things in place."

34

"What do you mean he left?" Ellis screams while I am trying to calm Cordelia. She keeps trying to hide in my neck. Ellis makes her miss Bobby very much.

"Where did he go?" Ellis steps closer.

I shrug.

"Well, when did he leave?"

"I don't know. He didn't tell me anything."

He stomps over by Bobby's truck to see if maybe he left some clue behind. Then he comes back before I can get Cordelia safely locked in her shed with the others.

"Well, who's gonna run the pig race? I've got nobody extra right now."

I think that maybe Cordelia and LaVerne and Big Ben and Vivian could use some time off, but I don't tell Ellis. He is standing so close to me now I can smell the Beech-Nut. I am wedged against the fence. I fret over Peabody and if he will stay in our hauling truck.

"If I find out you know where that idiot farmhand went, you are done for." He spits his gum on the ground and stomps on it and I have to snuggle an awful long time with Cordelia to get her to stop shaking.

35

Saturday is the best day of the week for traveling shows like ours. If crowds are going to come, they will come on a Saturday. Not as many folks come on Sunday, on account of it being church day, and the rest of the days of the week everybody is working. But Saturday is show day and Ellis goes all out. It is the worst day to have a birthday. Especially if you are alone.

Every balloon is blown and all the American flags are waving and I get the popcorn started and the taffy for the taffy apples melted. Pete the Alligator Man feeds his alligator extra turkey gizzards so there won't be any mishaps in the tin tub. Eldora puts on her choir robe and wraps her bright yellow hair in scarves. She shuffles her cards. Ellis walks around and around and around, checking on if Sam the Fat Man is sitting where folks can see him and if Silas Meany is sucking in his stomach far enough. I tie Peabody with enough rope so he can lie on our bedroll or go over and sniff around Pauline's side of our hauling truck. I hide a few hot dogs so he won't get bored. "Don't make a sound," I warn. "All we need is for Ellis to find you." He whines into his front paws as I close the curtain behind me and climb down the ladder.

The day starts out fine. There are so many folks waiting for rides on the Tilt-A-Whirl and the merry-go-round and the Ferris wheel that Ellis forgets all about being mad at Bobby. I can't keep up with all the hot dogs that folks are wanting and the popcorn keeps running out. And just as I am starting my third batch, that's when the sky opens up and it starts raining bathtubs of water on top of everyone.

It doesn't take long until the grounds are a soupy mess and folks are screaming and running home. If there's one thing about traveling shows, no one wants to come in the rain.

We pretty much all stand around the rest of the day, me and Fat Man Sam and Eldora and Peabody. We are on pins and needles because Ellis is so mad. He lowers the ticket price to a nickel just to get someone in to at least have their fortune read, but even that doesn't do any good and the show is empty. Ellis makes us all stay on the grounds, so I sit in the hot dog cart, thankful for the little canvas roof. I am afraid to go check on Peabody because Ellis keeps checking on me.

By suppertime the rain stops and Ellis yells, "Places, everyone!" and I fire up the grill and pull my hair over my diamond. Fat Man Sam turns the music up as wives, children, sweethearts, and mamas and aging papas start coming through the gates. They wear galoshes on their feet and yellow slickers and rain hats. They lift their feet like they are high-stepping and hurry over for a hot dog. All the lights are on and the merry-go-round is making its *dee-dee-da-dee* racket and the Ferris wheel is playing "The Farmer in the Dell" over and over. Ellis tells Fat Man Sam to stop sitting and go over and open the Little Pig Race.

And then thunder rumbles. A crooked bolt of lightning strikes and then another and there is a crackling and a buzzing and all the lights go out. The folks sitting so high on the Ferris wheel start screaming they are stuck at the top and all the folks lined up to see Pete the Alligator Man and Eldora's Museum of Mystery start running for the entrance and no one can see much except what the stars light up right in front of them so someone knocks into the hot dog cart and all the ketchup and mustard and celery salt go flying. There is another lightning strike and a loud clap of thunder and that's when I hear my dog start barking.

I throw my apron on the ground and run for my hauling truck, bumping into lots of folks who are running for the road, and they push me and carry me away like I am a twig in a fast-moving tide. I fall and get stepped on and someone kicks my face and all across my diamond. I hold my arms over my head and curl into a ball and get kicked over and over and wait while the sea of folks rush past.

I don't know how he did it, but Peabody got himself loose, and now he is licking my face. I think about what would happen if he got kicked, being so little and all, and I pull myself up and totter quite a bit as I try and get my balance. For just a moment I think I might see the lady in the orange flappy hat, and then I scoop my dog into my arms and hurry across the grounds to our hauling truck. I race up the ladder and dive on my mattress. I hold Peabody and wrap us inside my bedroll, afraid of the folks running around like it is the end of the world.

More and more lightning strikes and thunder booms and each time my dog howls. "Stop it, Peabody. Ellis will hear."

We are just dozing off when there is a banging on the outside of our hauling truck.

"You left the hot dog grill on, you little idiot."

Peabody barks before Ellis gets all the words out. I grab Peabody's nose and hold his mouth shut. He shakes until I let go. He barks again.

Ellis climbs up the ladder and flings open the curtain. He whips his flashlight all over the inside of the hauling truck. I try and hide me and Peabody in the bedroll. But Peabody is growling like he is a bear.

Ellis comes right over to my bedroll. "Get up and get that food cart cleaned up now. And let me tell you one thing, missy. You have two minutes to get rid of that dog. If I ever see it again, I will toss it in the next river we come to."

He glares at me and the flashlight makes his eyes yellow. I shake and wait for him to leave. He looks all around the truck, at my bedroll, at Peabody, at the empty place where Pauline used to be.

"Two minutes," he says again. He stomps off and something inside of me cracks and something inside of me snaps and I know right then and there that I need a new plan for my life.

36

It is heartbreaking to say goodbye to a pig, especially one as fine as Cordelia. She nuzzles your neck and looks you in the eye all soft, like she just knows what you are thinking, and she does not like it at all.

I scratch her backside for a long time and rub her neck and itch the places on her head she likes itched so well. I look in her eyes. I do not fib and tell her I will be back soon. I tell her the truth.

"It is not safe here for Peabody. That's why we are leaving." I pick up the stick Bobby kept for back scratching and find all her itchy spots. She likes it especially well. She keeps coming back for more.

"If leaving is a bad idea, I will know it pretty quick and then I will think of another plan." I tell Cordelia this in between kisses on her face.

I cut a piece of rope and tie it to Peabody's collar. We have never run on the road but if we are going to find a home, it's the only way. Already Peabody is squirming and pulling at the rope because if there's one thing about him, he does not like getting tied up.

Cordelia is sticking her head through the slats in the pen, watching. I go over and scratch her one more time and bend down and kiss her on the face. "I will find you when I get settled." I look her in the eye and feel my tears well up.

At the last minute I tucked a dozen hot dogs in my socks

and Pauline's little notebook in the pocket of my overalls. My heart told me it would not let me leave those pages flopped upside down on the floor of the truck, even if I am never going to read a word. A heart is like that. If you listen, it will give you marching orders.

This is also the reason I climb up the boards of the pen and jump inside and wrap my arms one last time around Cordelia and let her crawl into my lap and nibble my ear. Soon they are all piling on top of me: LaVerne, Vivian, and Big Ben, all grunting, all pushing to get to the bits of corn hiding in my pocket. Then I climb out of the pen. I reach back through the fence and give Cordelia one last hug. The only thing that pulls me away is the thought that Ellis will soon be up.

Our traveling show is quiet this early in the morning. Only the crows fighting over specks of popcorn and bits of taffy make any noise. I look past Eldora's Museum of Mystery to the Tilt-A-Whirl and the Ridee-O and the Ferris wheel.

Without Bobby to say get ready, set, go, Peabody and I just look at each other. I turn and see Cordelia's sweet piglet face poking through the fence. I know her tail is wiggling on the other side. My heart throbs. You can only take so many goodbyes in life. So I do the only thing a twelve-year-old girl with love in her heart can do. I go over and lift Cordelia out of the pen and set her on the ground.

"Ready, Peabody?" I whisper.

He wags his stumpy tail. That is my answer.

"Let's go."

Peabody shoots out in front, and my little pig follows. I let them take the lead. It is hard to get excited about running when you cannot see the finish line.

37

I do not have much of a plan except we need a home that will take a girl with a diamond on her face, a funny-looking dog with a stumpy tail, and a little pig.

We run down the main road past all the big houses with the porches out front and the gingerbread trim that looks like frosting dripping down over everything. Once upon a time I told Pauline a house like that was waiting for us. We just had to find the right one.

Now I make myself watch my feet instead of looking at dreams. A house on the main road would not offer enough protection. I keep looking over my shoulder for Ellis. I would not want to be looking for him all the time.

It is a good thing I brought a pocketful of corn because it is the only thing that keeps Cordelia from running after butterflies. Cars and trucks hurry past, and sometimes they beep because it is not every day you see a girl, a dog with hardly any tail at all, and a baby pig all running down Main Street. They slow down and yell at me like I don't know how to keep my dog and my pig out of the road, and I make sure my hair is tight over my face so they don't see my diamond.

It is very hard to hold your hair over your face when you are running. I am so out of breath I tell Peabody it is time to walk. A boy hoots out of the window of his truck. Peabody notices a squirrel running, and he leaps after him, and it turns out that where Peabody goes, Cordelia wants to go, too, and that's how we turn onto a smaller road.

The houses are smaller here and everyone has a victory garden with tomatoes big as melons hanging over their fences. I breathe deeply and try and get myself calmed down. There are many flower gardens along this road and that means many bees and Peabody is very interested in their buzzing. He keeps trying to stop and watch them and I pull at him and tell him to get his head out of the clouds and to stop acting just like Cordelia.

We pass three girls playing hopscotch and I am very careful to hold my hair tight and I have to pull Cordelia when they start saying things like "Oh, what an odd-looking pig," and she gets herself all puffed up and wants to stop and be all friendly because she doesn't know that they are making fun of her. All she hears is the tone of their voices, sugar-sweet, thick as maple syrup.

38

Each house on the next road is all wrong. One has a yard too small for Peabody to play in, one doesn't have a shed in the back for Cordelia, another has a lady snipping her roses who says, "Shoo, shoo," as soon as she sees my little pig.

Just as we turn onto another road I think maybe I see the lady in the orange flappy hat limping ahead, but as we turn a corner she vanishes and I know I am just fooling myself. We start runnning again and I follow Peabody and Cordelia down another road and I am trying to make sure we are following the general direction of the main road, which I reckon is heading south. Pauline is south.

My chest is heavy and my blood pounds in my head and I want to stop and rest. But I hear Bobby telling me whatever you do, even if you are slow as Christmas, do not stop. Keep going. Press on. That is how you find your second wind. I don't know why he spent so much time on me. I never got much better at running, even with all the things he taught me.

We turn onto a smaller road, this one with a farm with a cow and a horse in the field. The sun is high in the sky and I feel my shoulders blister. I am also getting very thirsty. I run so slow I am almost walking. Peabody is all interested in the cow and he stops and so Cordelia stops and she grunts and squeals and the cow looks up wondering what all the noise is about. This house looks pretty wonderful, I think, with a wide porch and roses climbing all over the sides, but then a yellow dog comes shooting out at us, barking his head off, his mouth open and his teeth showing.

"Bad dog!" I yell, pulling Peabody into my arms and trying to block Cordelia. The dog leaps and growls and jumps and tries to get Peabody, and then my little pig runs squealing down the road, which may not be the smartest thing because big yellow dogs are faster than little pigs. I run after them yelling, "Bad dog!" in my deepest Bobby voice.

The dog catches Cordelia and they roll around the road, my little pig squealing like it is the end of the world. Peabody is on them in a flash, barking and trying to get his teeth into the dog's tail. I reach for his collar and pull until I get the dog off Cordelia. He is not taking no for an answer, though, and as soon as I get him off, he snaps at Peabody, over and over, trying to bite at my dog's little stumpy tail.

I reach into my socks for a hot dog and pull out the whole pile. This catches the dog's attention. He forgets Peabody and sniffs at the hot dogs. He gulps them, one after the other, all twelve of them, and as Peabody and I fly down the road looking for Cordelia I think I have never loved hot dogs so much.

39

We find Cordelia under a row of apple trees. She is rooting around all the ripe fruit on the ground, which is rotting and very sweet-smelling.

There is a big split in her ear, the one that usually stands up the right way, and it is bleeding. "Oh, Cordelia." I look around for something to wipe up the blood and finally decide on my sock, but when I look up, Cordelia is lying down munching an apple and Peabody is licking her ear.

I collapse under one of the trees after that, because if there is one thing I love, it is apples. I eat the fattest one I can find and I keep going, one after the other, until my belly is full of apples. Peabody is not much interested in fruit, and I have no more hot dogs to give him, so when he is done licking Cordelia's ear, he snuggles up next to her belly and goes to sleep. Then we all have a little nap, because who wants to run all day anyway?

When I wake up the sun is straight overhead and I have a bellyache from all the apples and the lady in the orange flappy hat is watching me.

Part II

40

I first saw the lady in the flappy hat right after my mama and papa died. We were at the funeral, sitting in a church in Vermont. Pauline was very surprised Ellis let us stop for a funeral. My grandpa was there, too, sitting in the back with his hands crossed over his chest and a scowl on his face. He had loads of money from the gun factory his family owned during the Civil War, Pauline told me. And he had loads of bullets, too, all ready for my papa when he stole my mama away.

"Your grandpa disowned your mama and he never saw you, as far as I know." Pauline said my grandpa had so much money he couldn't spend it all. She tried to introduce us at the funeral, but he turned away.

Stone angels stood all around the church and were solemn and did not smile and I was afraid. I hid my face in my hands and whimpered. Then an old lady in an orange flappy hat limped up the aisle and sat in the seat in front of us. She turned around and waved. Thin wrinkles outlined her face and when she smiled her cheeks plumped out and she looked very much like a very ripe sweet old apple.

I waved back.

"Who you waving at?" Pauline whispered, looking around.

"The lady."

"What lady?"

"In the hat. Can I have a hat like that?"

Pauline looked all over the place and then pulled me closer. "Do you need some water or something? Are you dizzy?"

I checked to be sure. The lady cinched her pink shawl with a big safety pin. She straightened her hat. I waved again.

"She's right here. Can't you see her?"

Pauline looked around again and then got a worried look all over her face. She felt my forehead to see if I had a fever. When I tried to wave again, she pulled my hand down. "No more of that," she warned me.

At the cemetery there were a lot of gravestones and even more statues and shadows everywhere.

I cried again and buried my face in Pauline. After a while, when the preacher was done with his talk, I saw the lady in the orange flappy hat over by a very tall stone angel, and both she and the angel were waving.

This time I didn't tell Pauline.

One night when Pauline was snoring and I was trying to sleep, the wind howled and rocked our truck like it was a toy. I thought how we were going to blow away. I didn't want to go to heaven and be with my mama and papa and I pulled the bedroll up to my chin and listened as the storm shook our hauling truck like it was a box of candy corn. Then there she was, the lady in the orange flappy hat, opening our purple curtain and peeking into the truck, smiling at me and putting her finger to her lips so I wouldn't wake Pauline. In the instant it took to check if Pauline's eyes were closed, the lady vanished.

One day a big black dog showed up when I was off in the

woods doing my business and it started barking and baring its teeth and I pulled up my overalls quick and backed up and the dog moved closer and closer and lunged at me and I screamed. In the second before I screamed again, the lady in the orange flappy hat appeared. The dog took one look at her, whimpered, and raced off. She held my hand and led me back to Pauline.

When I got older and my diamond got bigger and I started getting teased because folks coming to our traveling show wanted a look-see, the lady in the flappy hat started showing up more often. She came on the bad days, the really bad days when I wanted to make myself invisible. She would appear for just a moment to show me the way out of the crowd and back to our hauling truck, and then she would go.

I didn't tell Pauline about most of the times the lady in the flappy hat came because it made Pauline so upset. Then Pauline read about imaginary friends in the *McCall's* she found at Woolworth's and she asked me a few questions, but when I told her the truth she didn't want to hear anymore.

I didn't want to lose Pauline, so I kept the lady in the flappy hat to myself. I didn't like to keep secrets from Pauline but I couldn't find any other way around it.

41

The lady in the orange flappy hat watches us lying under the apple trees, and when I turn away and nudge Peabody to see if he can see her, too, she is gone.

My belly aches something awful and I am very sorry I ate all those apples. I am also very thirsty. Peabody shakes, he is panting so. Cordelia is up on her feet looking for more apples. "Come on," I say, standing up.

My legs wobble from traveling so far. When we get to the end of the road, another road crooks to the right, and we take that one, and then it bends to the left, and just as it turns right again, I stop short.

"Well, will you look at that?" I can hardly breathe.

The three of us stand looking at a house the color of buttercups, with blueberry shutters and a front porch with rocking chairs still rocking. There is gingerbread trim on all the windows that looks like frosting dripping down. All around the house is a fence with sharp white pickets, because when you live in a house that looks like a birthday cake you do not want folks coming in and bothering you. Of that, I am sure.

There are roses all around—big red roses with plenty of thorns to keep even more bad things out—and a gate with a heavy latch. It is a house with a lot of protection.

"Will you look at all those windows and how tall they are?" I point so Peabody and Cordelia will notice. "They are taller than us all put together."

There is a wide porch, perfect for sleeping outside on a hot summer night, and there is a porch swing, just waiting on a girl to come and lean back and rest her hurting feet. "We'll get water here." I reach down and scratch Peabody between the ears. When I look up, the old lady in the orange flappy hat is standing on the porch. Peabody barks.

"Shush," I say, pulling him up next to me and making him sit and be quiet. Cordelia is watching a dragonfly on the fence.

The sun is blinding against all the buttercup paint and I screen my eyes with my hand because now the lady with the flappy hat has brought a friend. This one is taller, with hair the color of a new silver dollar, and they are both standing under a hanging flowerpot full of pink geraniums. The lady in the orange flappy hat lifts her hand again and waves, but this time the tall one pulls it down.

The glare from the sun bounces off the windows. I narrow my eyes so I can see better. The tall woman disappears right in front of me and then all I can make out is the outline of the orange flappy hat. After a moment, it, too, is gone.

42

Generally it is not a good idea to fret too long over things like ladies who disappear, or ladies who appear, for that matter, or you will lose your nerve. I try to remember how the lady in the orange flappy hat always showed up when I was having a very bad day and she helped make things better. Maybe this is one of those days.

I lift Peabody into my arms. His little butterscotch self up next to me is very reassuring. "We are here," I whisper, "and we are some parched and need something to drink."

I lift the latch on the fence and open the gate and carefully climb the front steps. Peabody wants to get down as soon as we get up on the porch, so I let him. He runs over by the front door and sits and wags his stumpy tail. Usually that is a good sign. Cordelia sniffs at the dried geranium blossoms that have fallen on the floor.

I take a deep breath and knock. I rub the scuffs on the sides of my work boots and wipe at the dirt on my overalls. I pull my hair tight over my cheek.

I give Peabody one more look-over. A leaf hangs off his belly from when he was watching the bees. I brush it off, telling him how first impressions are very important. He looks up at me and then back at the door. He could care less about first impressions. He wags his stumpy tail.

I knock again, nice and loud. We stand there and wait,

the three of us looking at the door for a very long time, and then at each other. Peabody whines.

"Stop that. It is bad luck." I knock again, nice and loud, so I sound like I mean business.

A crow caws in the woods and then another caws and then another. Cordelia looks up. I try and take no notice of all the crows and all that I know about crows and crow warnings from being at traveling shows so long and I knock again, louder this time so I can be heard over the very loud commotion in the woods.

Peabody gets bored and wanders over to the swing and sniffs it. He circles round and round and finds a good spot and lies down, listening to the crows. I go over by Peabody and sit on the swing. I am very thirsty. Ellis has noticed for sure that I am missing by now.

As a general rule of thumb, it is a good idea to think about other things when you are bothered. I tell this to Peabody. He is busy watching a honeybee trying to get to the geraniums.

I make myself count up the good things about my life while I am trying not to worry. "First is you, Peabody." I bend down and scratch his ear. It is standing straight up because he is still watching the honeybee.

"Second is you, Cordelia." She goes over and flops down by Peabody. I smile, my heart filling with the sight of the two of them. "Third is my health. I am strong." I stretch out my legs and look at my wobbly thigh muscles and cross my legs again. Peabody is not watching. "All right then, maybe not that. But I am well fed, but not too much, and I do not have temper fits and I have a happy heart when I am not getting teased about my diamond. I am clean and can read very well. Because of that I know all about the stars and about bird identification and about the weather. I know when sunny days are just around the corner."

Peabody turns to me and raises one ear and it flips over. Then he turns back to the flowerpot. There are now two bees buzzing around the geraniums. Peabody gets up and goes over for a closer look.

I breathe in the clean country air blowing all around me. It is better than Pauline's apple shampoo in my hair. I look back at the door. I stand up.

"Come on, Peabody. Let's try again."

43

I turn the knob slowly, and finding the door unlocked I gently push it open, a tiny bit at a time.

"Hello?" I whisper.

It is very bright inside from the sun that jumps through the windows. There is a big hall inside the door with waxed wood floors and a tall staircase that shoots up to a second floor, and a railing just made for sliding down.

The house is much bigger than it looks from outside. I hold my hair tight over my cheek and step inside. Peabody and Cordelia are right beside me. They are looking up the stairs. I breathe in and out, deep as I can, and try to quiet all the worry thoughts tumbling around inside of me.

"Hello?" I say, this time a little louder. "It's me. It's Beatrice Rose Hockenberry. This is Peabody and Cordelia. We are very thirsty."

There is no answer, only the slight scratch of the curtain lace against the screens. Peabody looks up at me like maybe I should not have thrown all my eggs in one basket, like maybe I should have been sure about how things would turn out before I showed up.

I clear my throat. "It's me, Bee, the girl you keep waving at."

Everything is quiet. Everything smells of lemon wax. On one side of the hall is a fancy sitting room with a sofa and many plump chairs and everything has little lace cloths so your head can lean back without getting the chair dirty. I know this from looking at Pauline's *McCall's* magazines. There are bright rugs on all the floors. Already I know where the Christmas tree should go.

On the other side of the hall is a room filled with many books and bookcases, a desk, a sofa, and stuffed chairs for reading. This is a room to be quiet in, a room to think things over. Pauline would like to write poems in this room. I sigh.

I don't see any mirrors, anywhere. This is a good thing because when you have a diamond on your cheek you don't always feel like looking.

Peabody tips his head. He lifts one ear. He looks down the hall toward the kitchen. Then I hear hushed voices, soft murmurs, and a mumble or two.

Peabody whines. I look at him, my finger on my lips. He whines again and I pick him up.

Then: "Oh, shush, Mrs. Swift."

"You shush up, Mrs. Potter. You shush up now."

I look at Peabody. Cordelia grunts softly. "Hello?" I whisper, not sure if I should turn around and run out the door or get a glass of water first. My throat tightens. I tiptoe toward the water.

Cordelia's little hooves click on the waxed floor. The hall leads to a kitchen with a white stove peeking through the doorway. The stove sits on legs and has many red-painted knobs and a big steel teakettle on top.

"Now there's a stove for cake baking," I whisper. Peabody keeps his eye on a large white sink and water faucet. I notice two hard-boiled eggs on a round table set with a pink-and-white-checked cloth. The eggs sit on a china plate beside a teacup and saucer, a little bowl of sugar, and a creamer. The counters are covered with canning jars and cookie boxes and tall tins of tea biscuits. The back door is open and the smell of roses is everywhere.

I am very still. I feel Peabody's heart flipping. I feel my heart flipping. Finally I clear my throat. "It's me, Bee."

At first all is quiet, but then there are murmurs, and then distinct voices.

"She's only a girl. And a wee one at that."

"She can't be the one."

"Of course she's the one."

"We're not expecting a DOG, Mrs. Potter. And certainly not a PIG."

"Oh, horse feathers! We've been expecting this girl for years."

"We cannot have a dog. You know that would be a very bad idea. And a pig? Good gracious!"

Then more muffled voices coming from the walls, or maybe from under the floors, or from inside the tall cupboard in the corner of the room. It is very hard to tell.

"Did you hear that?" I ask Peabody. He is looking at the sink.

"We are very thirsty," I whisper, looking around the room again, and then I tiptoe over to the faucet and turn it on and watch a heavy dribble the color of butternut squash tumble out.

44

Generally, when you find yourself in a bad situation it is a good idea not to make it worse. Looking at a cup as half empty and going around and around and around your troubles in your head are not the best ways to handle things. It is usually far better to skip right over them and think about sunnier days ahead.

Sometimes this does not work. Sometimes you let the bad thoughts get the better of you. This is what Peabody is doing right now looking at the rusty water.

"Stop whining like that, Peabody. It is bad luck."

Peabody looks up at me like he does not want to think about blue skies ahead. I know what he is getting at. I let the water run for several minutes, hoping for a clear stream, all the while looking behind me and listening for the voices. The water turns muddy.

Before Peabody can say boo, my eyes fill. Thirst will do that to a person. I pull my dog closer to my heart and tell my pig to follow me and I back out of the kitchen and down the hall and out the door.

The sun is pouring through the maple trees, all over me and across Peabody's butterscotch self. I can hardly see anything, on account of the sun and my tears. We get out as far as the first apple tree on the thin ribbon road and sink beneath it.

More than anything, I want Pauline. I want her to come

and get us. I want to hear her say how I shouldn't worry because bright days are right around the corner. I want her to play the ha-ha game with me and tell me how beautiful I am and how I should not worry about crooked roads ahead. They have a way of straightening out when you keep putting one foot in front of the other.

When the thought of Pauline makes me so sad I don't know if I can stand up again, I wonder how many miles stretch between me and Bobby. My tears are falling onto Peabody's sun-covered backside and he is whining in my arm because if there is one thing I am learning, it is that Peabody does not like a girl in tears.

45

"Hello, Beatrice." The voice is a soft whisper, and Peabody jumps up. I turn around, and there, right there, leaning on her cane in the thin ribbon road, is the lady in the orange flappy hat.

"You're not giving up on us so soon, are you?" Her flappy hat is tipped to the side. Her pink wool shawl is cinched tight with a large silver safety pin. You would think she would be hot. Peabody watches her intently, the way he watched the bees on the geraniums. Cordelia is more interested in the apples on the ground. I pull my hair across my cheek. The lady in the flappy hat looks into my eyes again and smiles. It is kind and generous.

"You are in awful need of a home, isn't that right?"

All I can do is stare at the soft wrinkles on her cheeks and around her eyes, which are blue as sky. I look down at my worn-out work boots with the holes in the bottom and remember how I wanted to make a good impression. Peabody barks. I pick him up and push him under my arm, but he backs out and turns around and watches the old woman in the flappy hat.

"I'm sorry Mrs. Swift and I frightened you. We're a little unused to dogs. And it's been years since we had a pig in the house." She laughs softly.

I look at Peabody. His head is tilted and he has one butterscotch ear raised.

"I am Mrs. Potter. Do you like pickled eggs?"

Peabody raises his other ear.

"Pickled beets? Pickled herring? And tea biscuits and strawberry jam?"

I nod. I like anything, as long as it is not hot dogs and onions and sauerkraut.

"Good," she says, "because Mrs. Swift is very busy getting things on the table."

"And water?" I ask. "We are very thirsty."

"The kitchen pipes are rusty. But the well is fresh." She reaches down and scratches Cordelia between the ears. "We have a nice place out back for your little pig. Come see."

Peabody and Cordelia fly off toward the backyard and I pick up the rear. A shed sits behind the house with a little garden fence all around. I open the gate and show Cordelia and Peabody how to get inside the fence. By the time I am in, Cordelia is already rooting under some old cornstalks. I open the door to the shed and peek inside. It is bright with a little window and a pile of old straw on the floor. I breathe in the sweet straw smell and kick some around the floor so my little pig will have a nice bed and before I am even done, Peabody flops in the middle and watches me.

"It is perfect!" I tell this to Cordelia, who is now sniffing around some old squash vines while a red squirrel runs across the fence. The lady in the flappy hat leans against her cane.

I look at Peabody. I think about all the years I have been seeing the lady in the flappy hat when I needed somebody, and now she is right here, up close, smelling like roses. Normally, it is not a good idea to let folks see tears puddle up your eyes. But I am so worn out, I cannot help it now.

The old lady in the flappy hat puts her arm around me. It is light as air.

46

It takes us several minutes to get back to the kitchen because Mrs. Potter hobbles so, especially going up the steps. When we finally get there, Peabody's tongue is dragging on the ground, he is so thirsty.

The woman with hair the color of a new silver dollar is standing at the sink, trying to open a canning jar.

"Who in the world put this on so tight?" she says, looking up. Her eyes are bright, clear, and violet. They move from Mrs. Potter to me and finally to Peabody. "We weren't expecting a dog."

"Now, Mrs. Swift," says Mrs. Potter, limping over to help with the canning jar.

"Oh, don't Mrs. Swift me. A dog is a problem, and you know it. And a pig. What will we ever do with a pig?"

"We'll do fine," says Mrs. Potter, twisting the ring and then, with a knife, popping the lid. "The pig is out in the shed, happy as a clam." She sniffs at the inside of the jar, crinkles her nose, and sets the jar down. "It smells a little old."

There's a pitcher of water on the table and I hurry to it and fill the saucer and put it on the floor for Peabody. He slurps it up in a second and I refill it and fill the teacup for myself. I fill both over and over again.

"Straight from the well. Delicious, isn't it?" Mrs. Potter comes over and sits down.

"We don't feed dogs out of our grandmother's saucers!" Mrs. Swift says, frowning, when she turns around. She hurries over and picks it up off the floor and wipes it on her apron. "Bad dog; bad, bad dog."

Peabody takes one look at her and hurries under the table.

Mrs. Potter pulls a pot from under the sink and sets it on the floor. I fill it with water. Then she slices the eggs and puts a few pieces on a napkin and sets them on the floor. She pulls out a chair for me.

The eggs are a little gray and the yellow centers are a funny shade of blue. Old vinegar soars up my nose. She puts some slices in front of me and I touch the white part. It is quite firm. My stomach rumbles. How long since we've eaten anything but apples? Already I feel them running through me.

Mrs. Swift opens another jar. "What do you think?" Mrs. Potter limps over and sniffs the jar. She shakes her head.

"Well, there's always these." Mrs. Swift brings over a tin of tea biscuits. She pries the rusted top off and pulls a flat biscuit from inside and snaps it to see if it still crunches. It does not. She puts one biscuit on the table and one on the floor for Peabody. He sniffs it and then looks back to Mrs. Swift for something else.

"You'll eat what's put before you," Mrs. Swift tells him, her hands on her hips, her voice stern. That's all Peabody needs to hear. He gobbles the biscuit in one bite.

I nibble on a biscuit. Mrs. Potter laughs. Her face really is an apple, old and soft and folding in on itself. "Is there any cake?" I ask finally. "I really do like cake."

Mrs. Potter and Mrs. Swift look at each other. "Well, we

haven't figured out how to use this stove," says Mrs. Swift. "Maybe you could show us how?"

The stove looks at least one hundred years old. I glance at Peabody.

"If we could find the fireplace, we could use that," says Mrs. Potter. "I know it's behind that wall. Why they ever closed it up, I do not know."

Peabody whines, waiting for another stale biscuit. He is worried about how things are going. I try to think about blue skies ahead.

47

"She almost blew up the kitchen yesterday trying to get things ready," says Mrs. Potter, grinning.

I go over to the stove. It is just like the stove we used at the traveling show, except bigger. There are knobs to turn and a box of matches on top. I light a match and turn the knob and in an instant a yellow flame flickers. "Well, will you look at that," Mrs. Potter says, watching. I put the kettle on to boil.

"You said that yesterday you were getting things ready. What were you getting ready for?"

"Oh, we were getting ready for you, Beatrice," says Mrs. Potter, offering me another tea biscuit.

I watch the two of them. I wonder if they will disappear again. "But how did you know I was coming?"

Mrs. Potter looks at Mrs. Swift and very slowly Mrs. Swift shakes her head at Mrs. Potter.

"Another biscuit?" Mrs. Swift holds a biscuit for Peabody and when the water boils, she pours tea into my cup. There is no milk in the creamer and the sugar is hard as tar, from before the rationing, and when I sip at the tea, it tastes very much like water with a little color added to it.

"I'm afraid it may be a little stale," says Mrs. Swift, watching Peabody gobble down another biscuit. He could care less about tea.

I take another sip. Mrs. Potter tries to scrape some sugar

off the bottom of the bowl. Finally, she puts the bowl on the floor for Peabody. It turns out Peabody likes sugar very much.

They both watch me. I feel a little awkward as I chew another biscuit. I wipe the crumbs off my face.

"She looks just like Bernadette, don't you think?" Mrs. Potter says.

Mrs. Swift shakes her head at Mrs. Potter and clears her throat.

I sit up straight. Bernadette was my mother's name.

"We knew your mama very well," Mrs. Potter says when she sees me staring.

"How?" I ask, leaning forward, spilling my tea. "How did you know my mama?"

"Later," interrupts Mrs. Swift, looking sternly at Mrs. Potter. "It's time to show you your bedroom."

Peabody sits up and perks his ears. He is very excited about the idea of a bed, and I have never slept in a real bed, ever.

48

"We expect a bath every night before bed," Mrs. Swift is saying as we all follow her upstairs.

"We do not need to be so particular about everything all the time," says Mrs. Potter, "particularly when it comes to raising a child." Her limp is quite pronounced on the stairs. She has to stop to rest several times. I wonder if I should offer her my arm.

"Now, you hush. I know what I'm talking about. I know all about raising children. A child needs a bath before bed." She reaches the top stair and rounds a corner and continues up.

"When's the last time you raised a child?" Mrs. Potter has stopped again. I turn just in time to see her rolling her eyes at Mrs. Swift. I giggle. Mrs. Swift looks back to see what we are finding so funny.

"And the dog sleeps outside. He can sleep with the pig."

I pull Peabody closer, but already his ears are flopped down. I squeeze him tight.

"Mrs. Swift," says Mrs. Potter, "the dog is used to the girl. He'll bark and bother the neighbors and you know we don't want that."

Mrs. Swift pauses for a moment on the top step. "Yes, I guess you're right," she says slowly, thinking things through. "Just make sure he does his business out of doors."

Peabody is humphing. I am humphing. Of course he does his business outdoors.

Mrs. Swift turns left and walks to a room where the last bit of sun is shining in, and already Peabody is wagging his stumpy tail like it is Christmas.

A big bed sits at one end of the room with four high posts and a canopy. The quilt is fresh as new cream and there are four fat pillows wrapped in lace.

"Oh golly," I say out loud, untying and kicking off my work boots, jumping onto the bed, and bouncing around, feeling like things are starting to finally go a little right in my life. "For sweet Pete's sake, Peabody, get up here."

Mrs. Potter has to lift Peabody up and put him next to me, because the bed is so high, and Mrs. Swift is tsk-tsking in the corner. I myself am jumping. The bed creaks loudly with each bounce, bounce, bounce. It is very old. Peabody flops over each time I leap, so I make myself stop even though I could jump like this forever.

"This is a different time," Mrs. Potter is telling Mrs. Swift. "Dogs sleep on beds nowadays." She scratches Peabody behind the ears. He thumps his stumpy tail against the bed now that I am not jumping.

If I had a stumpy tail, I would wag it, too. I breathe in the wonder all around me: the little red berries and tiny sprigs of ivy skipping up the walls, the lace billowing from the four tall windows that are so big they begin at the ceiling and end at the floor, the tall dresser with no mirror on top (thank goodness), a table with a little pitcher and bowl for washing up, even towels to mop my face. The last of the sun jumps into the room and rushes all over the wood floor, which is polished. Everything smells like lemon wax.

Mrs. Swift looks at everything. "I did well, didn't I?"

"And just who was it who carried all those buckets of

hot water? And who rubbed all that lemon oil?" Mrs. Potter is grinning.

"Now, you get in your bedgown, dear." Mrs. Potter tells Mrs. Swift they should leave the room so I can get undressed.

When they close the door, I look at Peabody. I do not have a bedgown. I don't know what a bedgown looks like, since Pauline and I slept in our shirts, although I can imagine.

I pull off my overalls and take Pauline's little notebook out of my top pocket. I stuff it at the bottom of the top drawer of the dresser, under some clothes so lacy I would look like a cupcake if I wore them. Then I jump up onto the bed and climb under the sheets. They smell like new soap and rose water and are very crisp and tucked in so tight I cannot even wiggle and I would not want to move, even if I could. That is what it feels like to sleep in a real bed; you want to stay put for a while.

The peepers chirp, Peabody snores, and I am drifting off when Mrs. Swift and Mrs. Potter come back in. They stand near the bed and watch me and I pretend I am sleeping, which isn't hard because I am so tired, and then Mrs. Potter is saying, "I told you she was the one," and then I smile and say to myself, yes I am, good golly, yes I am, and then I must be sleeping, because the ladies are disappearing right before my eyes.

49

"All healthy children need a sunbath," Mrs. Swift tells me the next morning while Mrs. Potter tries to get the stove to work so we can all have tea and maybe something to eat besides stale tea biscuits.

She shoos me out to the porch.

"What exactly is a sunbath?" I ask Peabody. Already the sun is climbing and the morning is one of the most beautiful I have seen. The smell of roses is everywhere. I lean back in the swing. Peabody jumps up onto my lap, and I push off. Back and forth, back and forth. I am feeling very lazy. Ellis is water under the bridge to me now. Peabody is watching a couple of honeybees around the potted geraniums. He is feeling lazy, too.

"Young lady!"

A harsh voice is so out of place here that Peabody and I both jump at the same time and Peabody's head hits my chin. Quick as a wink, I pull my hair tight over my diamond.

A woman stands out by the gate, a small black-and-white chicken in her arms. "Yes, you! I'm talking to you."

The woman is tall, with a thin neck and hair twisted high and tight. She has more gray hair than Ellis but not nearly as much as Mrs. Swift or Mrs. Potter, and not half as many wrinkles.

The chicken clucks and struggles in her arms. "Don't you think you're getting away again, you naughty little hen," says the woman, squeezing the hen tighter. This makes the chicken squawk louder. I look at Peabody. He is looking at the chicken.

One thing I learned from Ellis is you don't take up with just anybody who comes asking questions. I head for the door.

"Can't you hear me talking to you? Are you deaf or something? I said what are you doing up there?"

The warning light inside me is going on and off, on and off. I check my hair. I want Pauline.

The lady fiddles with the latch on the gate while she is holding the chicken. This crushes the chicken and it squawks and gets a wing loose. The lady stuffs the wing back under her arm.

The chicken thrashes, screaming, "Brawk-ack."

This is more than Peabody can take. He barrels to the very edge of the porch and yips and yaps. He gets himself in such a lather about the chicken he jumps into the air, slips, flips over, struggles, and jumps up again, never for a second stopping his yapping.

The woman takes a step back. "Well," she says to her chicken. "He's not very friendly, is he?"

"Brawk-ack!" the chicken shrieks, struggling to get its wing loose.

"Shush," I tell Peabody, rushing over and picking him up. He won't stop barking, even when he is in my arms, and he just about tips me over, he is so excited about the chicken. It is very hard to hold him and my hair at the same time. While I try to get my hair to cover my diamond, Peabody breaks free and jumps out of my arms and barks furiously.

"What a racket," the lady says, trying to hold on to her bird.

"Peabody, knock it off." I have to let go of my hair for a minute to pick him up. When I look up, the woman is staring at my face. I brace myself for what is coming, for the look I get when somebody has seen something they did not know they would get to see.

"Well," she says, eyeing me and taking a step closer. She opens her mouth and shuts it. Peabody is still barking. I back toward the door.

"I was out looking for my missing chicken here when I saw you on the porch. I live at the farm down the road. I am Mrs. Theodore Marsh. I keep an eye on the place for the old gentleman who owns this house. He lives in Florida now in a rest home. This porch is not for just anybody who feels like coming up and sitting here."

Peabody squirms and I squeeze him tighter. "I am waiting for my aunts," I say finally, not sure how to describe Mrs. Swift and Mrs. Potter. I look behind me, wondering where they are.

"Well, you can just do your waiting someplace else."

"I mean I am waiting for my aunts who live here." I look back toward the house.

"Nonsense, nobody lives here. You have the wrong house."

Peabody has gotten very quiet. He is watching the chicken to see what it will do next. I breathe out deeply, just like Pauline taught me for when things get troubled, then in again, then out. I am getting a little dizzy from all the breathing. I am also getting a little worried about the things the lady is saying.

A bee buzzes around the chicken and it clucks and

squawks and *brawk-acks* and the lady has to stop paying attention to me so she can get her chicken calmed down again.

Finally, she says, "I didn't know any aunts had moved in and I didn't know there was a child visiting, or a funny-looking dog."

I want to cover Peabody's ears so he won't hear the awful things the lady is saying, but I am still holding my hair tight. She steps closer and I know she is trying to see the diamond on my cheek.

I want Pauline. I want her to come and look into my eyes and tell me I am beautiful and how I don't need to pay any attention to a lady who is looking at me like I am the heel end of a loaf of bread.

"My aunts must be napping but I am sure they will be pleased to make your acquaintance when they are rested, ma'am."

The chicken pokes its head up from under the lady's arm. This is more than Peabody can stand. He wiggles out of my grasp and jumps onto the porch and rushes toward the hen. It squawks and gets a wing loose and in an instant is free and flutters to the ground. Peabody pounces on the chicken and the two of them roll around in the dirt, looking like a mess of fur and feathers. The woman screams and I fly down and pull Peabody off, but not before he gets a mouthful of white feathers.

"Brawk-ack!" the chicken squawks.

"Bad dog," I roar, "bad, bad dog."

"Oh, my Daphne, my Daphne," whimpers the lady, scooping her chicken back into her arms and patting it all over to see if a wing is broken.

"I have never met a more disagreeable dog. Make sure it never comes near my chickens again." Then she turns for the road. "And tell your aunts I will be back to meet them. And I will be writing a letter to the man who owns this property."

Then she flips open the gate and hurries through. Peabody barks as she marches away.

"That woman sure puts a bee in my bonnet," chuckles Mrs. Potter, who all of a sudden is standing by the swing, straightening her orange flappy hat.

"I could have used your help," I say, looking out to where Mrs. Marsh is hurrying down the road.

But Mrs. Potter ignores me. "Come on, Beatrice. We need to go to the market. I understand you like cake." Then she is limping past me and Peabody is right behind.

50

Ralph's Market is a small grocery on Main Street between the post office and Sam's Drugs. Across the street is Roberta's Dress Shoppe and beside that is a Woolworth's. Paper signs hang from all the grocery windows: VICKS VAPORUB 59 CENTS, CAMPBELL'S TOMATO SOUP 25 CENTS/3 CANS, COFFEE 85 CENTS/2 LBS, IVORY SOAP 35 CENTS/2 BARS, AND EGGS 64 CENTS A DOZEN.

The street bustles with folks. I cover my face with my hair. There's a new hole in the bottom of my work boots and the stones on the side of the road cut at my feet.

Mrs. Potter hands me a black leather envelope held together with a thick rubber band. It is worn through in some places and is very heavy with bills. "Make sure you count the money exactly. Don't let them take it from you before you count everything twice. Or three times would be even better." She raises an eyebrow to make sure I am listening.

I look up at her quickly. "Aren't you coming in?"

Mrs. Potter shakes her head. "I'll stay out here with Peabody. Lie down," she tells him, and he stands there wagging his stumpy tail. She pulls a tea biscuit from her pocket and holds it up. He flops down. "Get more biscuits," she tells me.

Three teenage boys in white T-shirts walk out of the store and light their cigarettes. I pull my hair tight. I've never been in a store without Pauline.

The boys in the white T-shirts lean against the side of

the building. One blows little smoke rings in the air. All three are watching me.

"But why can't you come in?" I glance back at Mrs. Potter and Peabody. Mrs. Potter waves me on. "They don't let dogs in markets, Bee."

I hold my hair tight as a bedsheet. I count my steps—fifteen, sixteen, seventeen. *Don't look at them, don't look at them, don't look at them.* When I have counted twenty-two steps, I am past the boys and I grab the door and hurry inside.

There are plump oranges on the shelf and peaches so ripe I know they will melt in my mouth as soon as they meet my tongue. I load some of each into my cart, along with three fat lemons for my face. There are emerald-colored green beans and romaine lettuce and tomatoes and cucumbers and green peppers and Swiss chard. I take a bunch of each. I pass the turnips, zucchini, and collard greens because when you are in charge of the grocery shopping, you get to buy what you like.

Sometimes Bobby would pull the truck over at a diner because French toast made Pauline's eyes glisten, and we ordered big stacks with strawberries on top, so I pick up all the ingredients: bread, milk, eggs, butter, cinnamon, and strawberries. Since I have no ration stamps and folks at the Ration Board would ask too many questions about why I don't have a mama or a papa, I take honey, but not sugar. I get new tea for Mrs. Swift and Mrs. Potter, a bag of dog food for Peabody, and new tea biscuits.

Pauline taught me to make tomato sandwiches, and I like those very much. You need ripe tomatoes and thick heavy bread and also some mayonnaise and some mustard.

And you need salt. I go back three aisles for salt because if Mrs. Potter and Mrs. Swift have any, it is sure to be hard as brick.

And that's the aisle where all the makings for a cake are staring me in the face. So, I do what any girl who loves cake would do: I pick up flour and a little bottle of vanilla, and while I am there I pick up a *Rumford Sugarless Recipes* pamphlet and flip through it: special cake, honey cake, cupcakes with sugarless frosting, apple corn muffins, banana cake, honey spice cake.

I put the pamphlet into my cart and go back for corn syrup because all the cakes use that instead of sugar. I pick up a chicken and a few other supper things and some rice, since I like rice very much. Then I wheel my cart to the cash register.

I used to have Pauline to help me do this, but now I have to put the groceries on the counter myself. This is not easy when you are trying to keep your hair pulled tight. Pick up the flour, put it on the counter, reach for the eggs. Pick up the vanilla, put it on the counter, reach for the milk.

Two ladies are behind me now, with full carts. I feel them getting frustrated with how slow I am going. I know they are rolling their eyes. The boys in the T-shirts walk back into the store. That's when I reach for the eggs and drop them.

"Oh, heavens," says the lady behind me, and I start cleaning up a dozen broken eggs with my hands, my hair no longer covering my diamond, my eyes full. I do not look at the boys.

When I get the broken eggs back in the carton and up on the counter, the cashier looks at my face like it is a painting on a wall to be looked at. I keep blinking my eyes to clear my tears as I reach in the envelope for a pile of money and hand it to her, without counting.

I try to be brave but as soon as I get outside, Mrs. Potter pulls me close. Her shawl smells very old with my nose crushed against it.

"Don't give heed to those who stare, Bee," she says, lifting my chin and looking in my eyes. "Be proud of who you are."

The tears really start tumbling then, and Peabody jumps so he can sniff at the shopping bags, and Mrs. Potter turns us toward home. I wipe my eyes with my shirt and carry the groceries. Peabody skips at my feet and Mrs. Potter shuffles behind, muttering to herself.

I do wonder about all the folks we pass on the sidewalk who are in such a hurry they cannot give extra room to an old lady who limps so.

51

Cordelia is squealing and grunting and making quite a racket when we get home, so Peabody and I head right out to see what's wrong.

I pick Peabody up and walk through the gate. Cordelia's food bucket is still full of tea biscuits. We go inside her shed, where she is flopped on the straw.

"What's the matter?" I whisper, kneeling beside her and rubbing her neck and scratching her back like she likes awful well.

She drops her head on her front legs. I look at Peabody. He has taken to sniffing her all over.

"Stop that," I tell him.

The shed smells like sweet straw. Pauline was wrong. Pigs don't smell bad at all if you give them a clean place to live. Cordelia knows enough to do her business outside away from her bed and her food bucket. Pigs are smart that way.

"Why aren't you eating? Do you miss LaVerne, Big Ben, and Vivian?" I whisper. "And Bobby?"

Cordelia closes her eyes from all my scratching. "Me too. I miss Bobby very much. And Pauline."

I scratch Cordelia along the back. "I don't know why Pauline couldn't see how beautiful you are." Peabody flops down beside Cordelia and licks the side of her face and then along her split ear. I like the way her light-colored lashes blink up at me. Pigs are really beautiful if you give them half a chance. Pauline was wrong about a lot of things.

I sit back on my heels. There's nothing like a little pig to help you forget how bad you are feeling about things.

I notice while Peabody is lying there that he is looking a little thin through the belly from eating nothing but biscuits.

"Come on," I say, standing up, "let's go get something for you and Cordelia to eat. I think you're both hungry."

When we get inside, Mrs. Potter is waving a plate at Mrs. Swift's skirt. Tiny flames are flickering at the hem and each time Mrs. Potter swings the plate, the sparks jump.

I scream and pick up a heavy kitchen towel and throw it on top of the flames and then scoop up the water pitcher from the table and fling water all over her skirt.

"Oh my, oh my, oh my," Mrs. Swift says as Mrs. Potter helps her over to a chair, her skirt still smoking.

"I'm sorry, dear," Mrs. Potter tells her. "It seems I've forgotten some things."

I stand there unbelieving. I bend down and lift Mrs. Swift's smoking skirt. Under all her petticoats, she wears woolen stockings so long and thick that I can't see a bit of skin.

"Don't worry, Bee. I'm not burned. All this wool protected me. I'll just go change my skirt." She stands and totters a bit and needs Mrs. Potter to help her up the stairs.

I am left in the kitchen with just Peabody, wondering about the two of them and about how good they really are at taking care of a girl, her pig, and her dog.

52

After that I take over all the cooking. Otherwise I will starve.

Each day I read one of the old cookbooks I find in the back of the big wooden cupboard by the table and then make something.

I mash potatoes to go with the plump chicken and the next day I try chicken hash. Mrs. Swift and Mrs. Potter aren't much interested in cooking or eating. While I am in the kitchen, Mrs. Swift usually hurries into the library to work.

We hear her sputtering and cursing quite a bit. Mrs. Potter tells me that Mrs. Swift is very angry about some of the things that were written about her, so she is trying to straighten things out by writing her autobiography.

"Oh?" I am interested immediately.

"She's got to, Bee. You can't trust those biographers to get it right. Good heavens, they have been writing all these years that when she spoke out against slavery and for women's rights one hundred years ago, the crowd threw apples at her. They threw their Bibles!"

I think maybe she is kidding. Mrs. Swift is old, but she can't be that old. I look to see if Mrs. Potter is fibbing, but she has already gone back to teaching Peabody to balance a biscuit on his nose. He is not very good at this trick; he keeps eating the biscuit.

"Beatrice, come in here!"

I wipe my hands on the kitchen towel and go in and see what Mrs. Swift wants.

There are so many books piled high on her desk that I have to walk around to see her. She runs a magnifying glass over the sentences in a thick black book. "I did know what this means, but I don't anymore. Look it up for me, Bee."

"Look up what?"

"*Equivocation.* In that dictionary over there." She points to a book that is so big it sits on a stand in the corner of the room.

Mrs. Potter drops onto the sofa. Peabody jumps on her lap.

"'She has a particular talent for equivocation.' Darned if I remember what that means. Do you?" She looks up at Mrs. Potter, who shakes her head.

"My memory isn't what it used to be," says Mrs. Potter, scratching Peabody behind the ears.

"Well, what's taking so long, Beatrice?"

The truth is, I have never used a dictionary. I squint, pretending I am having trouble seeing all the words.

"Just go to the *E*s and then go to *Eq*. I would do it myself but the letters are so small in that book. Why they do that is beyond me."

I flip the pages until all the words begin with *E* and then I look for *Eq*.

"Here, use this." Mrs. Swift hands me the magnifying glass. Now I have no excuse.

"E-q-u-i-v-o-c-a-t-i-o-n," she says.

It takes me quite a bit of time, but I finally find the word.

"I have it!" I say, and Peabody jumps up, because he can hear the excitement in my voice.

"Well, what does it mean?" asks Mrs. Swift, pushing her spectacles up on her nose.

"The act of being intentionally vague, ambiguous, or evasive, especially with the intent to deceive."

"Oh my," says Mrs. Potter. "That is not very kind."

"Blasted fool!" Mrs. Swift shoves the book onto the floor. "See why I need to rewrite all this? I don't have an evasive bone in my body. And I don't waffle, either. When something needs to be said, I say it. When something needs to be done, I do it. Isn't that right, Mrs. Potter?"

Mrs. Potter chuckles. "Yes, Abigail. Ever since you were a girl you have spoken your mind."

"Well, I wasn't going to hide and do nothing. Slavery was wrong, I said so. Women's rights needed to be fought for, and I did. If you hide, you become no one in particular. Who wants to be nobody at all?"

She looks over at me. "Isn't that right, Beatrice?"

53

Mrs. Potter teaches Peabody to beg (which he puts up with) and play hide-and-seek with a biscuit. One thing about Peabody, he knows when somebody is hiding something.

When he gets tired of biscuits, Mrs. Potter goes over and looks at the wall by the stove. Then she limps down to the basement and comes back up with a big ax.

"I know it was right here," she says, looking at the wall. Then she swings and whacks at the wall, sending wall dust all up and over my pot of mashed potatoes.

"What are you doing? You're getting it all over everything." I hurry and cover the pot.

Mrs. Potter takes another swing. She might limp, but her arms are strong. Plaster crumbles and wall dust billows into the room. I cover all the pots and put everything in the icebox as old plaster crumbles to the floor. There is dust everywhere. I have to wipe it off the cookbook.

"What does it matter if there was a fireplace there? We have a STOVE NOW."

Mrs. Potter whacks again, sending an enormous cloud of white powder across my nose. Peabody runs out of the room. We are still coughing when Mrs. Swift comes in from the library asking what all the racket is about. "Could you wait and do that later?"

"No, I cannot. I know the fireplace is back here."

"This is ridiculous," I say, looking at the hole in the wall.

Mrs. Potter huffs and puffs. She swings again and then goes over to sit down.

"Water, please," she croaks.

I get her a glass from the pitcher and put it in front of her. She gulps it quickly and asks for more.

"Go look!" Mrs. Potter points to the small hole she made in the wall.

I go over and look. It is very dark inside the wall, but I can make out the outline of blackened brick.

She grins. "It's been a long time since I've seen that fireplace." She gulps more water. There is a sparkle in her eye.

When we finally get the plaster cleaned up and sit down to supper, they play at their food, rolling it around and around their plates with their forks.

"Don't you like it?" My cheeks are filled with mashed potatoes.

"It's delicious, Bee," says Mrs. Potter.

"Quite good," says Mrs. Swift, rolling her carrots into her potatoes.

"Well, why aren't you eating?"

They look at each other and then away. I look at Peabody. He has finished everything on his plate except for the carrots and is waiting for more. I spoon more chicken onto his plate and set it on the floor.

"I'm full," says Mrs. Potter, pushing her plate away.

"Yes," says Mrs. Swift, standing up. "We don't eat much at our age, you know."

I stare at them. They are not going to last long if they do not eat more. Already they look very thin to me.

I try harder the next night.

I light a candle and lay the white tablecloth on the table

and the napkins. Everything looks heavenly. I serve meat loaf and rice and green beans, and once again Peabody and I eat the whole thing ourselves.

"Very nice, dear," says Mrs. Potter.

I take a very old cookbook to bed and read all about potted beef, codfish pie, creamed peas on toast, Welsh rabbit.

"What do you think?" I ask Peabody, who is snuggled against me. "Should I try codfish pie?" Peabody hides his nose under my arm.

"Me neither."

I put the cookbook down. I lie back in bed. Peabody snuggles closer. I fall asleep listening to the peepers and thinking about how Pauline would love to sleep in a bed like this.

5 4

Cordelia is looking no better three days later.

I pour the potato peels and the leftover carrots that no-body ate and mostly all the onions into her feed bucket. She sniffs delicately like she is smelling a daisy, and then she looks back at me.

"What?" I whisper, climbing over the fence and kneel-ing beside her and rubbing my hands all over her back and down her sides and scratching behind her ears. A spot of manure is stuck to her leg and I wipe that off with a clump of straw. There is mud on her chest, and I wipe that off, too. It is not like Cordelia to get dirty.

Peabody barrels out of the house and jumps up at the fence, yipping that he wants to be let in. He gives me an idea.

I open the gate and tell Cordelia I think she needs a little exercise. "Bobby says it fixes everything."

But Cordelia isn't so sure. She looks back at her shed and the warm pile of straw inside. It takes quite a bit of coaxing before she is trotting down the road.

I let Peabody lead the way and soon we are on a road we have never been on before. Peabody bounces along, but Cordelia is very slow. I am very worried about her.

We run at a turtle pace while Peabody gets very far ahead.

"Brawk-ack," I hear a chicken shrieking. "Brawk-ack."

I race ahead and just as I come up on a farm, with a white house and a big red barn with a rooster weather vane on top, I see Peabody chasing a chicken around and around a clothesline with blankets hanging down.

Chickens don't fly too well, but Peabody gets this one so bothered it *brawk-acks* and squawks and flaps its wings hard enough to raise itself to the barn roof. Before I can get Peabody picked up and in my arms and away from there, Cordelia is rooting around the barn, and soon a black-and-white hen that looks very familiar comes flapping out.

And then wouldn't you know it, Mrs. Marsh is running into the yard and hooting and hollering and screaming about her Daphne and chasing us all around the chicken yard with a broom.

Peabody and Cordelia rush for the road and I am just about to follow them when Mrs. Marsh grabs the strap of my overalls.

I pull my hair over my cheek and look up at her, my chest heaving, all out of breath.

"What are you doing scaring my chickens like that?"

"We didn't mean to. I'm sorry. I didn't know this was your house. It's just that Peabody is so interested in chickens."

Mrs. Marsh looks out at the mess.

"You'll have to pay for this. I'll be needing a new blanket, and a new hen with all her feathers!"

Peabody and Cordelia wait for me on the road. Cordelia is more trusting than Peabody and she comes back to get me. But Mrs. Marsh is ready with her broom in the air. "An ugly little smelly pig in my chicken yard? Absolutely not," she shrieks. "Absolutely not."

She whacks Cordelia on the backside. "Shoo. Shoo."

I want to cover Cordelia's ears from the terrible things Mrs. Marsh is saying. I can just tell it makes her feel awful bad.

55

The next morning I master the art of French toast.

Thanks to me we have all the ingredients at the same time: sturdy white bread (not puffy), eggs, milk, butter, cinnamon, honey, and frozen strawberries. I thawed the strawberries in a bowl overnight and they are glistening on the counter when I get up. Peabody is already on the chair watching me get everything ready.

I get out a pie plate and crack two eggs. I pour in milk and whip it all up with some cinnamon. I melt butter in the fry pan and as it sizzles I dip the bread in the egg mix and drop it into the pan.

Peabody is already raising his nose and wondering what that wonderful smell is. Then I flip the toast and when it is brown on both sides I take it out of the pan and put two slices on my plate and two on Peabody's. Then I spoon strawberries on the top and drizzle honey over everything.

Mrs. Potter comes in the kitchen and takes one look at the stack of French toast and walks closer. I look at Peabody. I put the plate I made for me on the table, right in front of Mrs. Potter. I put the one I made for Peabody on the floor. I dip two more slices of bread and drop them in the fry pan.

"Hungry?" I ask.

Mrs. Potter looks up at me, then back down at the stack of French toast. She sits down and picks up her fork and knife. Very carefully she cuts a bite, holds it up, and looks at it for a minute.

"It's been sooooo long." She glances at me, then takes a bite.

"Ohhhhhhhh." She tilts her head back a little to savor the moment and chews slowly. "It is just wonderful."

Mrs. Swift hurries into the room, wanting to know what that wonderful smell is.

"Elizabeth!" she says when she sees Mrs. Potter.

"Oh, have some," says Mrs. Potter, taking Mrs. Swift by the arm and pulling her down into a chair.

I bring a stack over for Mrs. Swift. She looks at the French toast on her plate for several seconds and then very slowly cuts a piece and picks up a forkful and looks at the way it glistens from the strawberries. Then she plops it into her mouth and from the look in her eyes you can tell all the flavors are bursting together.

"Oh my stars, it *has* been a long, long time," she says, cutting another piece and popping it into her mouth, and now there is a smile starting on her face.

French toast will do that to a person.

6

Before I can get all the dishes washed, someone knocks on the front door.

Mrs. Potter sips her tea, looking at the hole she banged in the wall. Mrs. Swift rushes in from the library, a book in her hand. "It's that horrid Mrs. Marsh."

I give Peabody a stern look. "That was a very bad thing to do," I tell him, reminding him about the chickens. Peabody jumps up from his cozy spot at Mrs. Potter's feet and races for the front door.

"We don't need trouble like this." Mrs. Swift drops into one of the chairs. "Bee, go open the door. Tell her we are not home. Find out what she wants. You must get her to go away. We can't have our plans bothered like this."

"I'm not opening the door," I say, wiping my hands on a towel and peeking down the hall.

Mrs. Marsh is trying to look through one of the windows.

"Yoo-hoo," she calls. "Yoo-hoo."

"I said, I'm not doing it." I look behind me to see why Mrs. Potter and Mrs. Swift are not answering me, but they have already left the room.

Peabody barks at the door.

"I know you're in there," Mrs. Marsh calls through the open window. "I have news. Now open the door."

I look behind me one more time to see where Mrs. Swift

and Mrs. Potter have gone and I cover my face with my hair and walk down the hall. Peabody sits growling softly while I open the door.

"What on earth took you so long, child?" Mrs. Marsh is holding a letter in her hand.

Peabody barks as soon as he sees her. He raises up the fur on the back of his neck and howls.

Mrs. Marsh takes a step back. "Well, he's no friendlier than the last time I saw him, is he?"

"Shush," I tell Peabody, picking him up. But he slips out of my arms and jumps in front of me and barks furiously.

"Well, I have never met a more disagreeable dog."

"Peabody, will you knock it off?" I scoop him up and I forget all about the diamond on my cheek and my hair falls away.

Mrs. Marsh is staring at my face. I stuff Peabody under my arm. I fling my hair across my face and hold it tight with one hand. I hold Peabody with the other.

"I need to speak with your aunts. Right this minute."

"My aunts were just here," I say slowly. "Mrs. Potter? Mrs. Swift?"

"You call your aunts by their formal names?"

Peabody wiggles himself out of my clutches, looks at Mrs. Marsh, and barks.

"Shut up, Peabody," I say, trying to keep him and my hair under control.

"Well, I am an up-front kind of woman. I've come to talk with your aunts directly." With that she steps inside the door.

This is more than Peabody can stand. He barks so

furiously he flips himself out of my grasp, jumps to the floor, slips, falls over, stands up, and barks louder.

Mrs. Marsh takes another step forward. Peabody barks louder. She takes another step and is looking into the parlor and at the little lace cloths on all the chairs and then into the library, where Mrs. Swift left her books on the desk. Peabody howls. I am no longer telling him to stop, because I do not want her in the house. But she takes another step and then another, and each time she does I back up, and she looks up the stairs. Peabody backs up and barks again and again and again.

"I will introduce myself to your aunts."

She kicks at Peabody, but he scurries out of her way and narrows his eyes and howls. There is a bustling in the kitchen and a pot crashes to the floor.

Mrs. Marsh looks at me for a second, and then she straightens her back and marches down the hall.

"Yoo-hoo," she calls. "Is anybody home?"

Peabody whines. I scoop him up and follow Mrs. Marsh.

The kitchen is empty. The back door is open. Mrs. Marsh turns, an eyebrow raised. She searches my face for lying. "I thought you said they were home."

"They were," I say miserably.

"Are you making a fool of me, child?"

"No, ma'am."

"Very well," says Mrs. Marsh, walking back to the parlor and dropping onto the plump sofa. "I'll wait."

57

I look at Peabody. Peabody looks at me.

"Come sit and wait with me, child." Mrs. Marsh pats at the sofa. Her voice is strained.

I do not sit on the sofa with her. I sit across from her. Peabody jumps up on the chair with me and watches Mrs. Marsh. He growls. "Stop that," I tell him.

Mrs. Marsh sits back on the sofa, looking down her long nose at Peabody and me.

Peabody barks.

"Shush," I say again.

"Where is that pig?"

"Outside," I whisper.

The early September sun is beating through the window and soon I am very hot. Little drops of sweat form along my hairline and down my back. Mrs. Marsh pulls a handkerchief from inside her dress and takes off her sun hat and pats the back of her neck.

I get up and open the windows as wide as they will go and I make quite a fuss over pretending I am looking up and down the street for Mrs. Swift and Mrs. Potter.

"Golly, I do not know where they are," I tell her as I am rearranging a curtain so it does not wrinkle.

"Is that so?" Mrs. Marsh begins to tap her foot and I watch it rise and fall, rise and fall, rise and fall, as if she is playing a trumpet and keeping time, but what she is really doing is waiting to prove I am a lying little fool.

Peabody watches Mrs. Marsh's foot go up and down, up and down.

"I would like some tea. Would you kindly heat some water? And while you are fixing it, please tell your aunts that I would very much like a word with them. I have received an important letter from the lawyer who represents this house."

A few minutes later I carry two cups of tea into the parlor. I set them down on the table beside the sofa, being careful to keep my cheek turned away from Mrs. Marsh. She picks up the cup without saying thank you and stirs the tea with the little spoon I put inside the cup.

"Is there any milk?"

"I'm sorry. We are out of milk."

"At least some sugar?"

I shake my head. "It was hard as a rock. We gave it to Peabody."

"You gave that dog your sugar? When it is rationed?" She looks at me as if I am a little touched in the head.

She takes a sip and puts her cup down. "I can't drink tea without milk and sugar."

I am careful not to smile. Maybe she'll leave.

"Well, there doesn't appear to be anybody here," she says, standing up. "Are you living here by yourself, child?"

"No," I say quickly. I lift Peabody into my arms. "They were here all morning. I don't know where they are now. Mrs. Swift has been working on her autobiography." I point at the library.

Mrs. Marsh looks in and her eyes pass over the desk and all the open books and the china inkwell and pen. "Well, please tell your aunts that I would like to meet with them, go over things, that sort of thing. I'll see my way out."

She opens the door and before leaving turns back to me. "And the man who owns this house has just died. Rest his soul. I am sure if he could speak he would tell me he had no idea there was a girl and a dog *and a pig* living here all alone." She takes another look at Peabody. "And kindly keep that dog away from my chickens."

Then she walks out the door and I stumble into the library and fall onto the sofa. Peabody jumps onto my lap and circles until he finds just the right spot. My stomach growls.

"Phew," says Mrs. Potter, walking into the room with a cup of tea in her hands.

"Where did you go?" I snap.

She ties her orange flappy hat. "Come on, Beatrice. Let's go have a look at that pig."

I know she is just trying to butter me up. But I follow her anyway.

58

"Do you mean to tell me any girl can go to school?" Mrs. Potter is sipping weak tea with milk the next morning. She likes three spoons of honey in each cup now.

I look up at her. "Of course," I say, taking a big bite of pie. "If you like school, which I don't." I roll my eyes.

"So you've been?" Mrs. Swift asks, holding her teacup in midair.

"Well, no. Pauline taught me to read and do math," I say quickly.

"Humph," says Mrs. Swift sharply. "How would you know what it's like if you've never been?"

Mrs. Potter cuts in: "And after high school a girl can go to any college she chooses?"

"Of course she can." Mrs. Swift leans forward. "You'll remember I was the first woman to graduate from college in this state."

I look at her. I have never thought much about school. Pauline taught me to read in the back of our hauling truck so I wouldn't have to sit in a classroom with pupils who wanted a look at my diamond. I take a bite of the Rumford honey cake. The recipe called for a full cup of honey and it is very sweet.

"Well then. That answers that," Mrs. Swift says, looking at Mrs. Potter. "Beatrice shall go to school."

"Oh no," I say, pulling my hair over my diamond. "I will

be just fine here with all the books in the library." I pull my cookbook closer and point to the mocha honey cake. "I read just fine."

Mrs. Swift takes another sip of tea. Peabody has jumped onto Mrs. Potter's lap and she is feeding him tea biscuits.

"On the day I was born," Mrs. Swift says, "my mama took one look at me and said, 'Oh dear, I am sorry it is a girl. A girl's life is so hard.'"

Mrs. Swift takes another sip of tea. "Things shall be different for you, Beatrice, which is why you shall go to school."

"I'm not going to school." I roll my eyes at Peabody, but he doesn't see me because he is licking the last of the biscuits.

"You will go to school if you want to keep living here," says Mrs. Swift, waiting for me to refill her tea. "And you will wear a frock."

A frock? I do not bother with her tea. I clomp outside, telling Peabody he better follow me or else. He is having trouble lately deciding who he likes more: me or Mrs. Potter with the biscuits.

59

The last of the French toast still sits in the bottom of Cordelia's food bucket, where it is surrounded by apple peels, eggshells, onion skins, and a large dollop of yesterday's oatmeal.

I open the gate for Peabody and he hurries into the shed. I run close behind.

Inside, Cordelia lies on her belly, her snout resting on her front legs. She watches a bumblebee. She doesn't look at us and she doesn't flick her curled tail.

"What is the matter with you, Cordelia?" I kneel down beside her and rub her neck and all along her face and between her ears. She picks her head up for a minute and then plops it down and grunts.

Peabody licks her split ear. There is mud on her belly and I wipe that off and also more manure sticking to her leg. I sit back on my heels and watch her.

Her straw is clean. Pigs never use their sleeping spot for a toilet, not if they have enough room. Pigs also like to eat. So there is something the matter when a pig doesn't eat. I try to remember if there was something that Bobby fed the piglets other than dried-out hot dogs and uneaten honey buns and gone-by apples.

Then I remember the corn. Bobby always had corn to get them to run to the finish line and he always had some in his pocket, which he handed out in little nibbles. That's how he trained them so well. Corn.

"Do you want corn?" I whisper, scratching her along her back and up around her ears, but she barely notices.

I check and make sure Cordelia has enough water by her food bucket and then jump over the fence. Mrs. Swift is working on her autobiography and Mrs. Potter is napping on the sofa.

"My pig is doing awful poorly. Can we go buy her some corn?"

"No," says Mrs. Swift. She is writing very fast and doesn't bother looking up. "That pig is fine on table scraps, same as we always fed our pigs. Now, shoo. I have a lot of work."

Mrs. Potter opens an eye, then the other, and frowns at Mrs. Swift. "Is your little pig worse than when I saw her?" she says, looking at me.

"Yes, she won't get up. She just lies on her straw. She didn't eat her French toast."

"Humph," says Mrs. Swift. "A pig that doesn't like French toast is spoiled."

"Does she drink her water?" asks Mrs. Potter.

"I don't think so." My eyes fill.

"Well, we are not buying that pig special food," says Mrs. Swift, finally looking up. "I never wanted a pig in the first place." She frowns at Mrs. Potter. "I told you a pig was a very bad idea."

"Oh, come now. The child loves the pig." Mrs. Potter reaches out to me, wanting me to sit with her on the sofa. I flop down and let her run her fingers through my hair and pull me close. I like the way her shawl smells like a dresser drawer that hasn't been opened in a long while.

Mrs. Swift bends over her notebook and scribbles. She dips her pen into her ink bottle and keeps writing.

I breathe deeply to hold back tears. "If you take me to get corn for my pig," I whisper, "I will go to school."

Mrs. Potter claps her hands. "That settles it."

Mrs. Swift lays down her pen and looks up at me. "I guess, Beatrice, we could at least inquire about the price of corn."

60

Red's Feed and Hardware is a big barn that sells grain for cows, horses, sheep, goats, chickens, and pigs.

Mrs. Potter, Mrs. Swift, and I watch the folks going in and coming out. Peabody is all interested in a swallow that swoops over our heads, and Mrs. Potter has to tie him to a low branch. I pulled a rusted wagon the whole way and now it sits between us.

"You're not going in with me, are you?" We are watching a burly man come out with a bag of grain over his shoulder. He heaves it into his pickup.

"You know we need the fresh air." Mrs. Swift stops Mrs. Potter from saying more.

Mrs. Swift hands me the fat leather envelope. "Count it twice," she says, and I slip it into the pocket of my overalls. Mrs. Potter straightens her flappy hat. I pull my hair tight and take a deep breath and walk toward Red's open door. I wouldn't be doing this if I wasn't so worried about Cordelia.

Feed stores smell nothing like Woolworth's. The scent of many sweet bales of hay fills my nose, along with the donuts a lady is frying in the back corner. There are horse brushes and cowbells and halters and chicken feeders hanging on little pegs on the wall. Big burlap bags are heaped against one another on the floor.

"Can I help you?" A man in a heavy apron looks up from behind the counter. I pull my hair tighter.

"I need corn for my pig." I say it while I am looking at the floor.

"This one here is for pigs," he says, coming from behind the counter and pulling out one of the burlap bags. "But you're going to need some help carrying it. A bag of pig corn is mighty heavy. You're an awful little thing. Did you bring anyone to help?"

"Oh, my aunts will help me. They're outside."

He looks out through the open door and raises an eyebrow.

"Right there, under that tree," I whisper, feeling an uneasiness in my belly. I pull out the leather purse and shake as I count the money.

He takes the dollar bills, counts them, and gives me my change. My hair springs back when I take the coins and try to get them into the envelope, and the feed store man has himself a good look.

The little muscles at the edges of his eyes tighten. I wonder if he will be one of the ones who say something about what is plain as the nose on my face or if he will pretend there is nothing there.

He clears his throat. He looks out the door. "You're really going to need some help, and I don't see any aunts."

"Right beside my dog. And my wagon."

He looks again. A slow trembling rises inside me.

"I see the dog, young lady, and I see the wagon, and that is all." He carries the pig corn to the door and drops it on the floor. "Have it your way," he says, turning and walking back to the counter.

The shopkeeper is right. Pig corn is very heavy. I can

barely lift it into my arms and I bump into a shelf as I push through the door, sending a couple dozen cans of Spam crashing to the floor.

"Oh golly," I say, feeling the trembling move into my arms.

Mrs. Potter is nibbling on a piece of honey cake when I drop the bag of corn into the wagon. "We have a surprise for you at home." She claps her hands, she is so excited. Mrs. Swift is trying to get Peabody untangled from the tree. I am too out of breath to listen and too worried about the trembling pushing through my body to pay attention. *Pauline couldn't see Mrs. Potter, either.*

"We were going to wait until tomorrow morning, but we changed our mind. We found some frocks in the attic for you to wear to school."

I lift the handle of the wagon and start pulling my heavy load. I don't say a word to Mrs. Potter, even though I feel her watching me, wondering why I am not excited about the frocks. All I can think about is the trembling in my chest and Pauline, who is talking in my head: *Aren't you a little old now for made-up friends, Bee?*

61

Generally it is a good idea to look at each day as a new beginning, a shiny copper penny just waiting to be spent. My first day of school is not one of those days.

Mrs. Swift walks on one side of me and Mrs. Potter limps on the other. The dampness from the road climbs through the holes in the bottom of my work boots and into my socks. I wear my overalls, mended by Mrs. Potter. "A frock would have been so much nicer," Mrs. Swift says.

The school stands in front of me, a brown wooden building with a bell ringing on top. Mrs. Potter stops on the side of the road and reaches for me. I feel her soft cheek against my own and smell the rose water on her skin. "You're going to be fine," she whispers.

I shake my head. That's the thing. I'm not going to be fine. New tears slide down my diamond. "I can't," I whisper.

Mrs. Potter pulls me close again. "You need an education, Bee."

"I don't."

"You do. To make your own way in the world, you do."

"I am fine staying home and reading and cooking."

Mrs. Potter gives me another hug and then Mrs. Swift reaches for her arm.

"You can't hide, Beatrice," Mrs. Swift says. Peabody leaps for me, but already Mrs. Swift has the rope tight. "Stop that," she tells him, and he sits down right where he is and whimpers and Mrs. Potter has to reach into her skirt and pull out another tea biscuit.

Then Peabody is all interested in the biscuit and he forgets about me.

A boy on a bike rushes toward us. His army-green lunch box waves as he tries to hold it and the handlebars at the same time. He whooshes so close I see the sweat on his forehead and hear his pedals squeak. Mrs. Swift steps out of the way just in time.

"He didn't see you?" I whisper.

"No, I guess he didn't," Mrs. Swift says quickly, and pulls Peabody close and tells him to stop barking.

The boy jumps off and leans his bike against the school and flies up the steps. Already the bell is quiet.

62

My overalls do not reach the top of my work boots. I have been growing from all the honey cake.

I stop on the top step and look back at Mrs. Swift and Mrs. Potter. An uneasy feeling fills my heart. I know now that I live with two old ladies who only I can see.

Peabody jumps and tugs at his leash, trying to run after me, and he gets himself wrapped up in Mrs. Swift's skirts. When she sees me still on the top step, she tries to wave me in the front door. I sigh, pull my hair tight, and step inside.

The school office is paneled in heavy wood and the victory blackout shades are half closed. A picture of President Roosevelt hangs on the wall beside one of George Washington and another of Abraham Lincoln. A lady in half-moon glasses looks up from her typewriter. I pull my hair tighter.

"Can I help you?"

"I . . ." I stop. I have practiced what I'm going to say, but now I'm not sure. I want to rush out and wrap myself in Mrs. Potter's pink shawl.

A girl in a plaid dress walks into the office and pushes up beside me. I stub the toe of my work boot on the floor.

"I haven't got all day, child." The lady glances at the other girl. I fidget. I suck in my breath, not sure what I want to say.

"Well, spit it out."

I push the words out quick as I can, like bullets, to get it over with. "I need to sign up."

"That so? Well, where's your mama?"

I look at my boots. I feel my diamond burning. My head smarts from holding my hair so tight.

"I haven't got a mama," I whisper.

"A father, then?"

I shake my head.

"Where did you go to school?"

"I didn't," I whisper. "Pauline taught me."

She stares at me. "No school ever?"

I shake my head.

"Well then. This is going to take a while, isn't it? You better have a seat so I can help Francine first."

She nods to the other girl. I go over and sit on a wood chair in the corner and wait while the lady and the girl talk a whole conversation. "What a pretty dress, Francine. Is it new?" she asks.

"Yes, it is." The girl's voice is tinkling bells. I have to listen to a whole long story of how her papa bought it for her and how her mama warmed it by the woodstove so it was toasty when she came downstairs from her cold bedroom. Then when she was dressed, she sat by the stove and ate hot buttered blueberry pancakes.

That gets me to thinking about my mama and papa and how I do not have either one. Finally, the lady gives Francine a box of paper for her class, and before leaving, the girl watches the way I am holding my hair.

The lady turns back to me. "You need an adult to enroll

in school, you know." She holds one hand up and inspects her nails, all painted cherry red.

I hand her a letter written in Mrs. Swift's thin spidery script:

Please admit our niece, Beatrice Rose Hockenberry. She is of superior intelligence, a capable spirit, and a pure heart.

The letter is signed *Abigail Swift* and then, in even more wavy handwriting, *Elizabeth Potter*. It put a song in my heart when Mrs. Swift wrote the letter at the kitchen table. I hugged Mrs. Swift and then Mrs. Potter, who was already stuffing my lunch pail with hard-boiled eggs and biscuits. Their hugs felt just like Pauline's. Only older.

"Well, why didn't they come themselves?" She inspects the other hand.

I pull my hair tighter and shrug.

"Well, I'll have to see about this." She disappears into the back room, and I hear her talking. Soon a man follows her out.

I stand up. I turn my face so only my good side shows. I want Pauline.

"No adult with you?" The man looks a little like Mrs. Marsh, with a high thin neck and a tight face. I wonder if they are related.

I tap my work boot against the wooden floor. I hold on to my hair and tremble. Each new person is a hazard, a flashing light, a warning deep in my belly.

"I already told her we need some sort of record to know what grade to put her in." The woman takes off her glasses and wipes them with the hem of her sweater.

I look her over good. I think perhaps she cannot hear right. I have already told her Pauline taught me everything, but I start again, very carefully, so my words will stick this time like maple syrup poured awful slow.

"I did not go to school. My Pauline taught me."

"Well, all children must go to school," the man says. "Are you telling me your mother and father never took you to school?

I stub the toe of my work boot on the floor tiles again.

"Well, that's not an answer. Yes or no?"

I pull my hair so tight my head hurts. I watch the floor and wonder how somebody who talks to children all day long could be so terrible at it.

"We need a record of your progress," he says. "How will we know what class to put you in if we don't have your records?"

I watch the floor and whisper how my mama and papa are dead and my Pauline left with Arthur, and even Bobby left. I think it is a long sad story that makes you lonely just to think about it.

"How old are you?"

I am starting to wonder why this has to be so hard. Just give me some books and a desk to sit at.

"A bit feeble, I'd say," the lady whispers to the man. I pull my hair tighter.

"Very well," he tells her. "Test her reading and we'll see. In the meantime, put her in with Mrs. Spriggs until we figure things out."

Feeble, feeble, feeble. I'm pretty sure this is not a good thing to be. The lady comes back beside me with a book and motions for me to sit down. She runs her finger against the words, slow like corn syrup. This makes my blood boil. The letters are big enough for Peabody.

She looks at me like I am light in the loaf.

"Well," she says. "Can you or can't you?"

I stare at her, refusing to say a word. "Humph," I say finally, looking at her like I have won.

"Humph," she says, looking at me like she knows better.

63

The lady marches me down one hall and then another, her soft soles squeaking. My work boots are so full of holes they barely make a sound. I try not to look at myself in the shined floor and pull my hair tight. I hold my breath and try to be nobody at all.

The lady leads me past one classroom after another, a row of dominoes, all with heavy wooden doors shut tight. We pass the janitor's closet with a deep steel sink and a heavy metal bucket with a mop sticking out. She stops at the very end of the hall, right near the back door.

"This is your room, Beatrice," she says, steering me in by the shoulder. I pull my hair tighter over my cheek, my helmet in place.

The room is darkened by a blanket that hangs over a window to block out the sun. When my eyes figure out the dark, I see a teacher knitting in a rocking chair and five children coloring.

"Hey," says a skinny boy, who jumps up and airplanes around his desk, yelling, "Zoom, zoom, zoom."

The teacher drops her yarn. "Jonathan!" Even when the teacher gets up the boy doesn't stop zooming and she can't get ahold of his arm until he airplanes around the room two more times. He is thin as a broom handle and very fast.

Finally, she grabs his shoulders and shakes him, once,

twice, three times. He slips and she grabs his collar and hurries him to his seat and shoves him down. "Now, stay."

Everyone has forgotten their coloring. My heart is aching. The teacher smooths her dress and walks over to us.

"This is Beatrice." The lady from the office presses me forward. "Please make a place for her, Mrs. Spriggs."

The teacher frowns. "You know I am only supposed to be here until the school finds somebody else. I can't have this many pupils."

"Just until we determine where she needs to be." The lady turns to me. "We do not like troublemakers in this school, Beatrice, and we do not put up with them, either. Not for a minute." Then she marches to the door, opens it, walks out, and slams it behind her.

Mind your britches, I say in my head to the children, who are staring. I pull my hair tighter against my face and make myself breathe, in and out, in and out, the way Pauline showed me. Nobody moves. I don't move. Inch by inch, I make myself invisible: first my diamond, then my face, then my chest, my arms, my belly. I wonder if Pauline would recognize me.

There are three boys and two girls in this class. I see how I will make six. The girls are at one table, the boys at another. A little girl with pigtails and thick glasses jumps up and rushes over and grabs me around the waist and hugs me so tight I let go of my hair. I reach out to steady myself and pull my curls tight.

In an instant, everyone is up out of their seats. Two boys come over by me and try to get a good look at my diamond and then Jonathan is airplaning around the room again.

A tall girl with many, many freckles hobbles toward me.

Her right leg is in a brace and she moves pretty quick by dragging her leg behind and then skipping a little to pull it up to the other. It looks really hard, walking like that. One of her shoes is a saddle shoe, the other has a black sole as thick as a book. She smiles shyly at me and tries to pull the girl in the glasses away.

"Sit down, Susan!" Mrs. Spriggs hurries to the girl in the glasses, who is now saying, "I lub you, I lub you."

"Sit down, everyone, *NOW*." The teacher pulls at the girl, but she won't let go. The girl's glasses go flying.

"I lub you, I lub you, I lub you," the girl is saying, holding on to my leg.

"That is very naughty to do, Susan," says Mrs. Spriggs, who takes the girl's arm and shakes her and pulls her back to her seat. "We just don't go telling everyone we see that we love them."

When Mrs. Spriggs finally gets all the children back in their seats, she points me to the empty space at the girls' table and I go over and sit with them on their wooden bench. She pulls a fistful of broken crayon pieces from inside a green metal can and drops them onto the table. She gives me a piece of gray paper that somebody has already colored on. "Use the back," she tells me, and then she goes back to her rocking chair and picks up her knitting.

Susan-with-the-glasses sits in the middle and the girl with the brace on her leg sits on the right. "My name is Ruth Ellen," she whispers, turning to me when Mrs. Spriggs is counting her knitting rows.

I pull my hair tight. I don't like to color. I look around the room. A Victrola stands silent. A chair is pushed into a corner, with its back facing us. The teacher's desk is big as our old hot dog cart. It stands in the front of the room, with two blackboards behind. There is a big wooden cupboard off to the side with the doors closed and nothing on top. There is a penmanship chart on the wall, a map of the United States, shelves for lunch pails, and hooks near the door with several coats hanging and army-green rubber boots lined up underneath. The floor is wide wood boards with dirt between the cracks. The walls are the same as along the hallway outside: brown halfway up, and battleship gray on top.

I do not think I was missing much by Pauline snuggling with me and teaching me to read on our soft bedrolls in the back of our hauling truck.

"Why aren't you coloring?" Mrs. Spriggs asks, looking up from her knitting.

Susan scribbles with a red crayon in one hand and a blue one in the other. I pick up a butterscotch color and draw a picture of Peabody. I have to hold my hair with my left hand, and I make him all sad-looking that we are not together.

"That's really good," whispers Ruth Ellen.

It might be the first time someone my age ever said anything nice to me.

64

"Lunchtime," says Ruth Ellen, just as my belly starts growling and the teacher rings the heavy brown bell on her desk.

"We eat right here at our tables." Ruth Ellen pulls herself up off the bench and skip-hops over to the coat hooks and brings a lunch pail back from the shelf. "We can talk if we are quiet." Susan is grinning like a jack-o'-lantern as Ruth Ellen unloads half a dozen cloth packages.

"She never comes with any food so my mama always packs enough for her. There's enough for you, too."

"No," I say, shaking my head. "I brought lunch." I bring my lunch pail to our table and wait to see what Ruth Ellen has brought. La-di-da, I am a little jealous.

Ruth Ellen has the real deal: peanut butter sandwiches, carrots sliced thin as dimes, two fat red apples that somebody shined up real good, and a couple of pieces of peach cake so heavy with peaches she can hardly lift them. Glory, I think as I watch the things come out of her lunch box.

My own lunch box is neat and orderly. The eggs and biscuits that Mrs. Potter insisted I needed, plus some boiled potatoes and a little pickle jar of milk and a fat slice of my newest recipe: mocha honey cake. It turns out Susan wants a bite.

"Thomas and Robert don't like to eat with girls," Ruth Ellen whispers. "And they make Jonathan eat at the end of the table. He peed over by the coats last week, right on top of Robert's boots." Ruth Ellen rolls her eyes.

Mrs. Spriggs pulls a sandwich out of her desk and eats it by herself. "She's the substitute," Ruth Ellen says. "The regular teacher got married and won't be back. She didn't like us much anyway. Most teachers don't."

When Mrs. Spriggs rings the bell again, it is time for recess. Ruth Ellen skip-hops outside and leans against the rough wood of the building. Susan holds her hand. The sun is hot on my cheek.

All the children from the other classes are already outside. The girls jump rope and play hopscotch on one side of the playground; the boys hit a baseball on the other.

"Why aren't we out there?" I ask, stepping away from the building so I don't get splinters in my shoulder.

"They don't let us mix with the other children," Ruth Ellen says, watching them. "We have to stay here on the dirt so Mrs. Spriggs can watch us."

My skin sizzles. Robert and Thomas hunch over a puddle and build a stick bridge for their trucks. "Don't get your trousers wet," Mrs. Spriggs calls.

Jonathan airplanes around the dirt, moving his arms as he changes direction and racing around and around our dirt area. He runs with his face lifted like he is looking at the clouds and there is a smile on his face. Come to think of it, he runs just like Cordelia.

You can just tell he is not paying attention to where he is going and he flies over the puddle, knocking the bridge over. Robert is up on his feet very fast, chasing Jonathan. He pushes him in the dirt, screaming, "That was very bad, *JONATHAN*."

Already, Ruth Ellen is hobbling over. She bends down and pulls Jonathan up by his arm. His face is red and then tears are streaming down and Ruth Ellen is smoothing them away with her hands.

All this time Mrs. Spriggs sits in a chair under a big pine tree with another teacher. She's knitting and talking and hardly paying attention to us at all. Ruth Ellen is the one who keeps an eye on Jonathan. He plops onto the pavement and watches a line of ants. He pokes a stick down and scoops up a few and pops them into his mouth. I think maybe I am in the wrong class.

Ruth Ellen skip-hops over and knocks the stick out of his mouth. "Don't eat those, Jonathan. Bugs are not to eat."

She reaches into his mouth and pulls out several ants. Now I am sure I am in the wrong class. "We have to watch him all the time," she tells me. "He will eat anything."

Jonathan looks normal. A little skinny, but lots of kids are skinny. "He does everything very slow," Ruth Ellen says.

We watch the hopscotch girls. The girl Francine is with them. I start thinking how I could blow my top, I am so mad that those girls get to play all shaded under the maple trees. I would never make anyone stand in the sun like this. Susan stops saying she lubs me and reaches up to hold Ruth Ellen's hand. She sucks her other thumb. Then the bell rings.

"We have to wait here for the others to go in." Ruth Ellen takes another stick out of Jonathan's hand. "Get ready to line up," she tells Thomas and Robert. Even they are quiet when the hopscotch girls walk by. I pull my hair tight over my cheek. You do not judge a book by its cover, I want to say.

I walk back to class behind Ruth Ellen and try to do the

little skip-hop she does. Susan takes my hand and Thomas is snapping Robert with a rubber band. Jonathan is looking like he would like to eat the rubber band.

One good thing about this class is nobody makes a big deal about my diamond. Everybody has bigger fish to fry.

Ruth Ellen asks where I live because she would like to have me over to play and her mama would want to talk to my mama for sure.

"I don't have a mama," I whisper, and I think once again how sad it is I do not have Pauline, either. "I live with my aunts." I write my address on a piece of paper and give it to her.

When we all walk out of the school, Jonathan and Susan and Robert and Thomas have to go wait in the bus line. Susan tries to keep holding Ruth Ellen's hand, but Ruth Ellen bends over and tells her no. "My mama is picking me up, same as I tell you every day." Ruth Ellen gives her a big hug, and then Susan sobs, "I lub you, I lub you," and Ruth Ellen gives her another hug.

"Do you want a ride home?" she asks me. "I'm sure my mama wouldn't mind."

I shake my head. I don't mention that Mrs. Potter is waiting under the tree.

We are interrupted by a fuss in the bus line. Francine with the new dress that her mama warms by the woodstove is telling a little girl to hold her schoolbooks.

"But I don't want to hold your books." The girl is already carrying a stack of her own books, plus a lunch pail. She is thin as Jonathan.

"Do it anyway." Francine puts her books on the top of

the little girl's stack. The little girl totters and drops several books. Two girls around Francine snicker, but a third one bends over and helps the little girl with the books.

"The little one's Mary," whispers Ruth Ellen. "She has ten brothers and sisters and a whole bunch of grandmas and grandpas living in one little house. Can you believe it? The one who just helped pick up the books is Betsy. Sometimes she's nice, but mostly she does what Francine says, just like the others."

Francine catches sight of Ruth Ellen and me, crosses her arms, and stares at us. "Wouldn't you lie down on a train track if you were them?" she says to the other girls, loud enough for us all to hear. Somehow she makes her voice sound like tinkling bells.

I pull my hair tighter on my cheek and pretend I am a wisp of smoke passing by. Ruth Ellen takes a step back and then skip-hops toward her mama, who is standing outside an old green automobile. Soon Ruth Ellen is getting wrapped in a hug and I watch them drive away.

I wipe my eye and then Mrs. Potter is limping over to me. Her flappy hat is all crooked. Peabody jumps, trying to get into my arms.

"Well, how was it?"

Francine is watching me. She turns to her friends and they all laugh.

"Guess," I say, turning away and clomping off for home.

66

I run straight upstairs to Mrs. Swift's bedroom. It is wall-papered with blue cornflowers and there is a white iron bed with a lace spread and puffed pillows and a stuffed chair in the corner. There is a yellowed copy of a very old newspaper, *The Liberator*, on her bedside table. I am not here for those things, though. I am here for the hand mirror on her dresser.

You hold your breath when you have not looked at yourself in a long while. You close your eyes and tell yourself it can't be that bad. You count in your head, *one, two, three*, and then you are afraid to open your eyes.

67

I do not remember my diamond being so dark. It looks like somebody poured raspberry juice on my forehead and it trickled down over my eye and fell especially hard on my cheek. *Spatter, spatter, spatter.*

The moaning deep in my belly rises and I can't dam it up or push it back. I rush to my bed and let my sobs shake me like a puppet. I do not want to cry like this in front of Peabody, because it makes him whine so, but whatever grit I had inside me is gone. I am soft as petals.

I wrap myself around and around in my blankets, rolling myself up so tight I can't think of getting undone, even if I wanted to, and the tears fall. Peabody is getting good at jumping up on the bed himself now, and he nestles up beside me. Mrs. Potter shuffles in and tries to hug me, but I don't let her. I don't want someone who nobody can see to hug me. Peabody, though, is greedy. He likes hugs very much.

Mrs. Potter rocks in the rocking chair. She sighs over and over and the chair creaks against the wood floor. I pretend I am falling asleep and I hope she is very sorry she sent me to school.

After a while she limps to my dresser and shuffles through the top drawer. She pulls out Pauline's little notebook and fans through it. I close my eyes again when she brings it over to the rocking chair and sits down. Before long, she is gig-gling. I guess some folks really can play the ha-ha game by themselves.

The next morning Pauline's little notebook is lying on my pillow. I push it under my mattress as far as it will go.

68

Cordelia sniffs around the back of her food bucket trying to get at an old scrap of potato peel and half a pickled egg. She has brightened up since I got her the corn. Already she is gaining weight.

I open the gate and Peabody runs through. He chases Cordelia around and around the pen. My pig squeals so loud Mrs. Potter comes out the back door to check on what is that noise. I wave her away. I do not want to talk to either her or Mrs. Swift, possibly forever.

Cordelia grunts and squeals. Peabody chases her around the pen four times and then she rushes into her shed, and when they fly out it is Cordelia chasing Peabody and Peabody who is yelping.

I sit on the ground with my knees pulled up to my chin, just watching my pig and my dog and feeling the sun on my back. I am thankful the food bucket is empty and that Cordelia is not a bag of bones. Every time the tiniest memory of my awful day at school floods my thoughts, I push it away.

I do not hear Mrs. Marsh until she is up next to me. "I see you still have that nasty little pig. Well, it won't be staying long, and neither will you or your dog. I have news." She flaps a long, thin envelope in front of me.

"Yessiree," she is saying. "This property is now in probate and a judge will decide who it belongs to."

Peabody and Cordelia have stopped chasing one another. Peabody growls and Cordelia pushes her snout out of the fence and grabs hold of Mrs. Marsh's shoelace. This throws Mrs. Marsh off balance.

"Oh no!" I shout, just as Cordelia pulls on the lace and Mrs. Marsh starts falling over. Peabody barks and Mrs. Marsh lands on her backside, a little dazed and unbelieving. Then she is up, picking up her letter and pushing her glasses back in place.

I have to hold my mouth to keep it from smiling.

"Well, I have never met a more unruly pig," Mrs. Marsh says as she wipes the mud and apple pieces and bits of straw from the back of her dress. "Or one more ugly. Look at those ears. They're not right. One sticking up, one down. Pigs aren't supposed to look like that. And the back of that pig? Look at that hump. That's not right. This was a runt, wasn't it?"

I want to pull Cordelia away, but she is looking up at Mrs. Marsh.

"And the tail doesn't curl right. Never win a beauty contest, would it? That is one ugly pig, if I ever saw one. You can't butcher it too fast."

I want to hold Cordelia's ears closed so she can't hear the awful things Mrs. Marsh is saying, but she's already run into the shed. "Cordelia is not getting butchered," I whisper.

"Whoever heard of a pig not getting butchered? It will need doing sooner than later. I expect soon, unless you want to take a huge pig with you wherever you're going. And believe me, you will be going. Probate shouldn't take long."

She pulls a piece of straw from her hair. "I came to see your aunts."

"They're not home," I say quickly.

"Are they ever here, young lady?" She narrows her eyes. "I think I'll go check."

I don't have time to say anything, because she turns abruptly and hurries toward the house.

I rush into the shed where Cordelia is flopped down on her favorite pile of straw and Peabody is curled up to her with his head on her belly. I scratch behind Cordelia's ears and along her backside. I also kiss her quite a bit because she needs a lot of snuggling to get back to feeling good about things.

69

On Saturday, there is a knock on the door and we all take cover. Mrs. Swift slides her ledger into the kitchen drawer. Mrs. Potter drops her hammer. I scoop Peabody in my arms. "Shush," I tell him. We are all getting very good at this.

"That blasted woman." Mrs. Potter looks at the wall in the kitchen that is nearly demolished. "I have just a little more to go."

The knocking goes on and on. "Go see who it is, Beatrice." Mrs. Swift gives the kitchen one more look, notices her spectacles, and tucks them in her apron pocket.

The knocking stops for a minute and then begins again, even louder.

No one moves. "Humph," I say, finally turning and walking out of the kitchen, edging my way along the wall, holding my dog with one hand and my hair with the other. I am careful to peek out the window without being seen.

"Well, who would've thought," I say, looking at Ruth Ellen standing on our porch. I rush and open the door.

Ruth Ellen holds out a basket covered with a blue-and-white cloth. "You aren't coming to school. I thought you might be sick." She leans on her good leg.

"Yes," I say, wondering what is in the basket, lifting the cloth, and smelling warm bananas and walnuts and cinnamon.

Her mama is waiting in the green automobile parked on

the road. She leans over and waves. A little boy in the back with hair the color of a sweet potato leans out the rear window. I pull my hair tight.

"Oh, what a sweet dog, Bee." Ruth Ellen scratches Peabody between the ears. He thumps his stumpy tail on my chest.

"I know you've been sick, but if you're feeling better, we were wondering if you could come to our house? My mama will drive us. She'll bring you home, too."

Mrs. Swift and Mrs. Potter slip into the library. "Yes," I say, trying to keep Peabody's tail from smacking me.

"Can I meet your aunts first?" Ruth Ellen tries to look past me into the house.

I block her view. "My aunts are napping. Maybe some other time." If I weren't so mad at them, I might tell them where I am going. Instead, I slam the door behind me.

Ruth Ellen opens the back door of the automobile for me and I pull my hair tight. She climbs in the front. "Mama, this is Bee. And Peabody. Bee, this is my little brother, Sammy."

Sammy makes propeller noises like he is a fighter bomber and Ruth Ellen's mama turns around and smiles and tells me all about how nice it is that I am Ruth Ellen's friend.

If they notice my diamond under my hair, they don't say anything. Ruth Ellen must have already warned them. Then of course Peabody steals all the attention from everybody by jumping all over all of us and then Ruth Ellen's mama starts the motor. "I didn't know this was the house Ruth Ellen meant until we got here. I didn't know anybody was living in the old Bradford place."

"Yes," I say slowly, "I am living here now."

"I didn't know the place sold. Are there lights? All the electricity was shut off for a long time. The town was worried about vagrants breaking in and starting fires."

"Yes, there are lights." I do not mention how we use a lot of candles and how my aunts cannot cook or how they want me to wear clothes from a hundred years ago. When you are used to living in the back of a hauling truck you do not worry so much about small things.

70

Ruth Ellen's house sits way back in the woods and is about the size of an apple crate with a little chimney poking out the top. Peabody sticks his nose out the window so he sees all there is to know about the dirt driveway and the thin shed with chickens poking in the grass and especially the turkey-sized gray-and-white cat napping on the front porch.

You can tell Ruth Ellen's mama is as particular about the house as she is about Ruth Ellen. There is a neat little white-washed fence around the house and another fence around a little postage stamp of a victory garden. The corn is heavy with cobs and there are pumpkins soaking up the late September heat. Pauline used to tell me she would like to live somewhere long enough to learn how to grow things. Maybe I will ask Ruth Ellen's mama if she will show me how.

Peabody barrels out of the automobile and runs for the cat and he gets clawed pretty good. He screams and then rushes after the chickens and I have to go grab hold of him and whisper firmly that he better behave or he won't be invited back.

We all go up on the porch and then Ruth Ellen opens the door and her mama says, "Well, make yourself at home, dear," and Sammy runs around pretending he is a fighter bomber. I wonder if he knows Jonathan.

"Why don't you show Bee around while I cut the cake?"

Ruth Ellen's mama pulls mugs from the cupboard. "Do you like cake, sweetheart?"

Do I like cake? I nod, wondering if she uses real sugar.

Ruth Ellen takes me in the little toast-sized kitchen, where there is a card table sitting between the big black stove and the sink. It is set with a lime-green checked cloth, four small plates, and four navy napkins. Ruth Ellen's mama puts the mugs on the table and fills them with milk.

"I got everything ready for you," Ruth Ellen says, looking all proudlike of this teeny room, which is less than a quarter of the size of our kitchen. "Come on, I'll show you the rest."

There is a parlor off to the side with a thin little camel-colored sofa, one of those lie-back-and-sleep-all-day chairs with a forest-green afghan thrown on top, and a rocking chair with crocheted pink cushions. The walls are covered with old wallpaper that has surely seen better days.

Ruth Ellen skip-hops over to a little table by the sofa and picks up a picture of a man in an army uniform and goggles, standing with his arms folded in front of a plane. He is smiling.

"My papa," whispers Ruth Ellen. "It is very dangerous to be a gunner." She rubs and polishes the photo, even though there is not a speck of dirt on the glass or in the whole house as far as I can see. "We haven't heard from him in a long time."

She sets the picture back on the table and we look at her smiling papa for a moment. Then Peabody and I follow her to a little bedroom on the other side of the kitchen, with a bed for her mama and another picture of her papa. This time her papa is wearing bathing trunks and is squeezing

Ruth Ellen's mama very hard and Ruth Ellen is giggling beside them and Sammy is in his mama's arms. There is also a picture of Ruth Ellen's mama sewing at a big factory. "She makes parachutes now for pilots and their crews. Maybe one will save our papa."

Ruth Ellen shows me a little white bathroom with roses on the walls and a rose-flowered rug on the floor. Upstairs under the eaves is the room Ruth Ellen and Sammy share. Ruth Ellen's bed is pushed up against the wall and it is covered with a pink quilt and Peabody and I are both thinking we could really stretch out here, and Sammy's bed is pushed against the other wall and has a navy-blue spread. He has drawn many pictures of fighter bombers and they are hanging all over his side of the room.

Ruth Ellen has drawn a picture of her family: her mama, her papa, Sammy, and her. Looking at it makes me wish I had a family just like hers.

71

After we have our snack (fruitcake made with honey, and Peabody gets an old used-up ham bone), my belly is ready to go off and take a nap of its own. But Ruth Ellen's mama says it is time to go get some exercise and she asks if I want to come and I look at Ruth Ellen, who is waiting for me to answer, and I think how everything in this house seems pretty fun, so why not? Lordy, why not?

We climb into the back of her mama's automobile and go bumping along many back roads. I have never seen so many farms and cows and horses grazing in meadows and alongside stone walls the way we see when we are in the places Ruth Ellen's mama knows about.

Ruth Ellen and Sammy hang out the windows looking for something by the side of the road, and Ruth Ellen's mama drives real slow. Ruth Ellen asks if I want to help and I say okay, but what the heck are we looking for?

"There's some." Ruth Ellen points out the window and her mama stops the car. I look into the woods to see what it is we are stopping for.

"Right there, can't you see it all?"

Sammy opens his door and airplanes outside, making very loud propeller sounds. Peabody jumps out of my arms and flies out after him, yapping.

"Shush," says Ruth Ellen's mama, "you'll wake them."

I look at Ruth Ellen. She is giggling as she climbs out

of the car. Her mama pulls a wagon out of the trunk. Before I can say Jack Sprat, there go the three of them over to a bunch of old logs left by maybe the power company when it was cutting limbs away from the electric lines, and then all three of them are kneeling down and whispering to the logs.

"There are fairies living around the wood, so we have to be very careful when we pick it up and carry it back to the car," Ruth Ellen tells me when she sees me with my mouth open.

"And we do have to ask their permission," says her mama. "We don't want to take any wood that they need."

I would think it might be a little upsetting to have your friends from school see you picking up logs left by the power company and then whispering to fairies, but not Ruth Ellen. She and her mama are telling the fairies all about how they are going to make Ruth Ellen's favorite wild apple pie for supper tonight because her mama got her sugar ration stamps at the Ration Board on her way home from work yesterday.

"You need to whisper to them. They don't like loud noises."

I shrug. Then we load all the wood into the wagon and stack it in the trunk. We drive to Red's Feed and Hardware and it doesn't take me longer than a jackrabbit to figure out what we are doing.

"I'll give you fifty cents for it all," says the shopkeeper, looking over our pile when Ruth Ellen's mama opens the trunk.

"A dollar for half of it," she says, her voice crisp. "I need half for cooking."

"You drive a hard bargain, Mrs. Deerfield." He winks at

her but she pretends not to notice and smooths the wrinkles in her dress instead.

"Deal?" she asks.

The shopkeeper nods.

"Done," says Ruth Ellen's mama, smiling like she has gotten a very good deal for all that work. We all unload half the wood and stack it up and we follow the shopkeeper into the store, where he opens the cash register and pulls out the money. I see the moment he recognizes me from the day I bought the pig corn. He tries to get a look at my diamond, but my hair is tight.

Ruth Ellen's mama sees everything. She reaches up and touches my shoulder and pulls me close. I let my eyes wander over to the butterscotch candies sitting on the counter. She notices that, too. Then she goes over and picks out a butterscotch for each of us. Even Peabody.

72

It is a very big production to bake a wild apple pie. It takes the rest of the day.

First, you have to stop in an old field on the way home and pick a hundred thousand wild apples, being careful of all the yellow jackets buzzing around. That takes all afternoon, partly because I have to keep ahold of Peabody, who wants to go swimming in an old farm pond at the bottom of the hill, and this gets me to thinking about Pauline and about the hole in my heart and I look around at the others to see if they can see it, too. I catch Ruth Ellen's mama watching me a few times, and I think maybe she can.

Our next job is to make sure Sammy doesn't eat all the apples before we cut the bad spots out.

Then we pull out the stems and peel and slice them all and pour them into a bowl with flour, cinnamon, nutmeg, and the rationed sugar. Then we make the crust and roll it out and pour the apples in and bake it. When it is finally out of the wood oven, sparkling from the sugar sprinkled on the crust, Ruth Ellen's mama sets the table and calls us all to dinner. We each get a big mug of cold milk and a big slice of warm pie.

We put our napkins on our laps and Ruth Ellen's mama says grace, which considering the beautiful pie in front of us is a very nice touch.

"Take care of Papa," she whispers.

"And tell him we love him," says Ruth Ellen.

"Amen," says Sammy. He doesn't wait any longer to stuff a big forkful of pie in his mouth. "Wowie," he says.

"Holy cow," I say. "Mrs. Potter would love this."

After a few bites, Ruth Ellen's mama says, "I didn't think Old Man Bradford would ever sell that house. It stood empty for so long. I am glad somebody is living in it. Was it a lot of work to get it ready?"

"Oh no," I say, reaching for another bite. "My aunts had it all ready for me when I came."

"I will drive you home," says Ruth Ellen's mama when we are done and the dishes are washed and put away. "I wouldn't want your aunts to worry, with you walking home on a dark road."

I get the front seat on the way home, and Ruth Ellen's mama tells us a long story about stars and how they are all very beautiful but some are different than the others, and how that makes them very, very special. "The red star is the one folks remember," she says, pulling up to my house. "Look at it."

I look heavenward. A red star overhead is blinking, maybe even winking. Ruth Ellen's mama leans over and hugs me good night. It is very nice.

"You can come stay by us anytime you want," she says, and even in the starlight I can see her eyes have caring for me all over them.

"Can I pick you up Monday morning for school?"

I shake my head. "I am not going back," I whisper, and I pull Peabody into my arms and climb out of the car. I turn toward the house. There is a candle burning in the window.

I think I maybe see Mrs. Potter sitting on the porch waiting, her shawl pulled tight.

"I'll pick you up at seven on my way to the factory," she says, ignoring what I've said. "Make sure you're ready, sweetheart. It takes Ruth Ellen quite a while to get to her class. Maybe you could help her carry her books?"

"Oh, Mama, I don't need help." Ruth Ellen folds her arms over herself, but her mama acts like she is already thinking about her factory job and about all the parachutes she will be sewing for the war effort. "We'll see you at seven, then."

And before I get a chance to answer, Ruth Ellen's mama is driving off and I hug Peabody close to my heart and lift the heavy latch on the gate and walk past all the thorny roses. It is a house with a lot of protection.

73

It turns out things are harder for Ruth Ellen than I was thinking. She has to carry her books at the same time she is trying to open the door to the school and rush ahead in the funny skip-drag-her-thick-shoe-to-the-front-and-skip-again way she walks. Plus, everyone is always looking at her. Ruth Ellen can use some help.

I hold the door for her and take half of her books. It is hard to do this and hold my hair at the same time.

We only get a few steps before I see Francine with her friends. She is the tallest. I take a deep breath.

At traveling shows, it is always the same. The biggest girl speaks first. The others stand just the tiniest bit behind. Not too far, because the tall girl needs logs to lean on. She would not be doing this if she were alone.

I hug the books to my chest with one hand and pull my hair tighter across my face with the other and try and look at the floor. Ruth Ellen skip-hops along and grabs my arm.

Francine steps out and blocks our way. I try and steer us around her. I pull my hair tighter. I want Pauline. Or Bobby.

The other girls circle around us, but Betsy backs up a little to make more room for Ruth Ellen. All the other children in the hall notice what is happening. You can tell because they look up for a minute, see what is going on, and then look at the floor again and hurry past. They must be used to Francine. I could run back outside, but I don't think Ruth Ellen would make it.

"I never saw anybody who looked like you before," Francine whispers. I take a few steps back. Ruth Ellen's eyes are big as supper plates.

"Oh, don't run away. We won't hurt you. Will we?" She looks back at the other girls. One has pink ribbons running all through her hair. The other wears thick glasses like Bobby.

"Come on, Francine. We're going to be late to class." Betsy turns and walks down the hall. The others edge up and push me closer to the wall, getting me all wedged in. I can smell somebody's sweet pea perfume. I want to go home. I want Mrs. Potter and Mrs. Swift and Peabody and my high bed. I want to hide under the covers and let my little dog hide with me.

I am shaking. I hold tight to the books while Francine moves even closer.

"You get burned or something?" Her voice is low so no teachers can hear.

"Why don't you just shut up?" Ruth Ellen's voice is quivering. She moves closer to me, but Francine pushes her away.

I swish my mouth, working up a pile of saliva and moving it down my tongue, just like Bobby taught me. I pucker my lips and when Francine begins to laugh I blow as hard as I can, aiming for her eye. A clear sticky pile of goo lands on her cheek and drips down her chin.

Bobby was right, I think as I grab Ruth Ellen's hand and hurry away. Knowing how to spit can come in pretty handy.

74

We are all in class one morning with our hands on our hearts saying the Pledge of Allegiance when Ruth Ellen slumps against her desk and moans, "Oh, ohhhhh, ohhhhhhh." She lays her face against the wooden top of our table and starts to cry.

I reach over and touch her shoulder. "What is it?"

Mrs. Spriggs drops her knitting and hurries over and keeps asking what is the matter and then Susan wraps herself around Ruth Ellen's leg and Jonathan comes over and tries to wedge in and even Thomas and Robert are looking like tears are about to fall.

"The doctor tightened th-th-the brace last night. It hurts sooooo much." Ruth Ellen's tears blur her face. She shakes. I take her hand and hold it. Big bruises cover her leg.

Susan starts crying just looking at all the tears and she keeps reaching for Ruth Ellen and Jonathan rushes to get a glass of water from the water pitcher even though nobody asked him to.

"She needs to lie down." I look around the room for a good spot. Thomas and Robert are already pulling the blanket off the window and spreading it on the floor by the Victrola.

"I should telephone your mother to pick you up," Mrs. Spriggs says.

Ruth Ellen shakes her head. "She's working at the

factory." She sniffles and looks at me. "Do you think your aunts could come get me and take me to your house?"

I am quick to shake my head. My aunts are a secret I can't share, and they can't help me now. "They don't have a car," I whisper.

Mrs. Spriggs hunts through her purse and pulls out two aspirins for Ruth Ellen. "Well now, what shall we do to keep our mind off things?"

"Play tag," says Robert.

"Jump on trains," says Thomas. He looks at Robert and breaks out laughing.

"Play music," says Jonathan. He rockets over to the Victrola.

"There's no records," Thomas says. And that is true. There are no books, either, other than a couple of Dick and Jane books and a dictionary in the wooden cupboard. Sometimes Mrs. Spriggs puts a towel over the Victrola so we can dry our watercolor pictures on top.

"Well, I've got a lot of lessons to plan," Mrs. Spriggs says.

I wonder what those lessons could be, since all the time I've been in this class, the only things we have done are color and paint with watercolors and make clay finger pots. She goes over and picks up her knitting needles and sits in her rocking chair. She told us she is making a baby blanket and as soon as her daughter has her baby, she will move to Florida. Good riddance, I think.

"I could read," I tell her. "But not those Dick and Janes. Aren't there any others?"

"You could go into the other class," says Ruth Ellen, propping herself up a little on her arm and looking like maybe the aspirin is starting to work. "They have books in there. Please, Bee. I would love a good story."

This of course means I will have to parade in front of Francine.

"Oh no," I say. "I can make one up. Listen to this." I settle back on my edge of the blanket.

"No," says Ruth Ellen. "I want a real story you read to me."

75

It is hard to put yourself before the lions. It takes several deep breaths to find the courage to walk into the den.

The class is chanting. "Ten times ten is one hundred. Ten times eleven is one hundred and ten. Ten times twelve is one hundred and twenty." I pull my hair tight.

Francine runs her eyes all over my cheek as soon as I knock softly and walk in the door. She dirties my diamond just by looking. I stretch my hair like there is a rubber band across my face.

The teacher comes over. "What is it? I am in the middle of a mathematics lesson."

"A reading book," I say, my eyes watching the floor, not daring to look up. "We would like a book."

"The retards would like to read," says a boy in the back of the room, laughing.

"Sit down, William." The teacher points to a bookshelf. "Go pick something out. But hurry. I am teaching a class."

To get to the bookcase I have to walk past five rows of desks. I can't think from all the whispering and pointing and giggling. I don't take time to look. I pull the first one.

76

It takes a while to quiet my heart. When it is still, I begin:

"*Heidi*. Chapter One."

Susan gets up from where she is lying beside Ruth Ellen on the blanket and comes and sits in my lap so she can watch what I am doing. Jonathan goes over by the coat hooks.

"Get back here," I tell him. "Now, sit down and listen."

Our teacher barely looks up from her knitting. Her baby blanket is now as big as her lap.

Her knitting needles *click-click* as I read: "The little old town of Mayenfeld is charmingly situated. From it a footpath leads through green, well-wooded stretches to the foot of the heights which look down imposingly upon the valley. Where the footpath begins to go steeply and abruptly up the Alps, the heath, with its short grass and pungent herbage, at once sends out its soft perfume to meet the wayfarer."

"Ahhhh," says Ruth Ellen, already calming a bit. "I didn't know you could read so well, Bee."

"Keep going," says Thomas.

And I do:

"One bright sunny morning in June, a tall, vigorous maiden of the mountain region climbed up the narrow path, leading a little girl by the hand. The youngster's cheeks were in such a glow that it showed even through her sun-browned skin. Small wonder though! for in spite of the heat, the little one, who was scarcely five years old, was bundled up as if she had to brave a bitter frost. Her shape was difficult to distinguish, for she wore two dresses, if not three, and around her shoulders a large red cotton shawl. With her feet encased in heavy hob-nailed boots, this hot and shapeless little person toiled up the mountain."

"She must be so hot," whispers Ruth Ellen.

It is surprising to see everyone sitting still. Just a few minutes ago, Susan was telling me she lubbed me a dozen times, and Thomas and Robert were running around the room pretending they were fighter bombers, and Jonathan was wandering over to see if there were any banana peels left in the trash bucket.

Now even Jonathan is sitting close to me so he can see the picture of the little bundled girl climbing the hill. We are all flopped around each other and everyone is quiet and listening, even Susan. She gets tired of sitting in my lap pretty quick and goes back to Ruth Ellen and Ruth Ellen runs her fingers through her hair, and that is enough for Susan. Soon she is sleeping.

I don't get a chance to keep going, though, because a man with bottle-round spectacles walks into our room.

77

"Beatrice Rose Hockenberry?" The man is old as Ellis and his hair is slicked to the right with pomade. His trousers fold in funny places from all the wrinkles and look as if they were made for somebody taller, the way they drag on the ground. He waits for someone to answer, but I hide behind my hair.

No one moves, not even Jonathan. We are not used to visitors. The man turns to Mrs. Spriggs. She is tucking her knitting into the desk drawer. "Beatrice?" she says sharply.

I pull my hair tighter. Susan holds on to my leg. "I lub you, I lub you." Whatever could the man want? A slow trembling moves into my belly. I hand the book to Ruth Ellen.

Mrs. Spriggs hurries her big old self over and pulls Susan off. "I'll be right back," I whisper. "Draw me a little pig, okay?"

I follow the man down the long hallway. We walk into the office and past the lady in the half-moon glasses. She is filing her cherry fingernails and doesn't look up.

He leads me into a small room off to the side, with a desk and chair pushed against the wall. He turns the chair around and motions for me to sit. He leans against the desk. It is very hot from the sun racing through the big shut window.

"I am Mr. Taft. I am from the school district. I am conducting research. Do you know why I've asked you here, Miss Hockenberry?"

I shake my head.

"Your principal says he does not know much about you and I would like to get to know you a little better."

I hold my hair tight.

The pomade has dripped onto his forehead and his skin gleams. "Now, we know nothing about your mother and father, or how you came to be at this school, for that matter. It seems you have no records."

I nod.

"Can you tell me about that?"

Oh, golly. I pull my hair tighter. I watch the floor. I take a deep breath and whisper how my mama and papa were killed in an accident when I was four and how Ellis kept me on and how Pauline took care of me. "She taught me stuff."

He writes it all down.

I kick at a piece of lint on the floor.

"Where did you live?"

"In the back of our hauling truck. We moved from town to town with our traveling show."

The man leans forward. "You didn't actually live any-place?"

"We lived all over. We worked for Ellis's traveling show."

"What did you do there?"

"I worked the hot dog cart with Pauline. I did not like it, that is why I came here, to this town, for a fresh start. I live with my aunts now."

He writes that down. Then, "What did, ah, Pauline, ah, teach you?"

"How to read, how to do math, all about the stars and the planets and trees and birds and the weather and about manners and, well, just about everything a girl could need to know. A lot more than I'm learning here, actually."

He writes that down. I stand up. "Can I go now?"

"Sit down, young lady." He looks down at his papers, then at me. "We haven't gotten to your anger yet. We need to talk about that."

"I never said I was angry." I wonder about this man's hearing. Lordy.

He writes quite a bit down, then looks back at me. His glasses make his eyes big as half dollars. "My report here says you showed indications of anger and difficulty when reacting to your handicap."

"My what?"

"The birthmark on your face. I would like to talk about that."

I scrape my heel against the floor. "I do not talk about that," I whisper.

He writes that down. "Well, I *want* you to talk about that, Miss Hockenberry. Do you know how you got the birthmark?"

I sigh. I think I had better get this over with so I can get out of here. I sigh again.

"I was sleeping in the back of our hauling truck one night after Pauline shut down the hot dog cart and Ellis closed the merry-go-round and the Ferris wheel and the Tilt-A-Whirl. And after every one of the stars had blinked out for the night so no one could see, that is when an angel came and kissed me on the cheek."

He leans back, takes his glasses off, and very slowly wipes them. Then he puts them back on.

"You do not get a mark on your face by being kissed by angels, Miss Hockenberry. You are born with it. It is a birthmark."

I sit back on the hard wooden chair and look out the window. I watch the sun shining through the pine tree where Mrs. Spriggs knits.

"I know all this," I tell him, speaking very carefully because he writes everything down. "Folks have always been telling me this, how my face is something gone wrong. Pauline made sure I knew all about how the mark is so deep you cannot wash it off. Except maybe with lemons you can fade it some."

I sit up. "When you think about it, though, isn't it better to believe in a kiss so soft you cannot hear it or see who is giving it to you? You are special when you think like this."

He writes that down, too. "You are talking about make-believe, Beatrice. Don't you know the difference?" He looks up and waits for me.

You start to wonder about folks who are always trying to make you come around to their way of thinking, like they are the only ones who know the true way about things.

78

I am in the bathroom doing my business when Francine and her friends come in. I yank my feet high on the seat and wrap my arms around myself and try to block out what they are saying:

"I'm going to bury her in spit the next time I see her."

"At least she'll look better than she does now."

(Lots of laughing.)

"I bet she cries all the time. I would if I looked like that."

"Maybe she never looks in the mirror. I know I couldn't."

(More laughing.)

"She could use pancake makeup like the movie actresses do, and hide it."

"She'll always be an ugly duckling, no matter what. No swan could ever hide under that face."

Could too, could too, could too. I lean my face against the wall of the john, holding on to my sobs so Francine and her friends won't hear.

79

I am weeping when Ruth Ellen finds me. Of course, she is a good friend so she makes me open the door and tell her what is wrong.

Sticks and stones do break bones and names do surely hurt me.

"Oh, Bee." She turns my face to her and wipes my tears off my diamond. She hugs me awful hard and it turns out her hugs are almost as good as Pauline's.

That afternoon, Ruth Ellen's mama picks us up from school so she can show me how to make chicken soup. She has been promising me because I asked her one day what was the most nourishing thing I could make.

"Why, chicken soup, of course."

I don't tell her I why I need to know: Mrs. Swift and Mrs. Potter are getting thin as paper now that I am going to school and being friends with Ruth Ellen and I don't have time to make so much cake. Some days I can almost see through them.

Ruth Ellen and I climb into the front seat and we are all squished tight as clams, which is just how I like it. I start feeling a little better about everything.

When we get out past Sam's Drugs, we see Francine walking home. She is wearing the dress her papa gave her. I pull my hair tight across my diamond.

"Poor child," says Ruth Ellen's mama. "Poor, poor child."

Of course we want to know why Ruth Ellen's mama would say such a thing about someone so horrid.

"Well," she says after biting her lip for a minute, "I am only telling you so you will have some compassion for someone who is hurting. Do you understand?" Ruth Ellen nods. I am not so sure.

"I want you to know that we are not the only ones with pain in our life. Okay?"

Ruth Ellen nods again. I am still not sure.

"Well, her father left. He ran off with a showgirl. Her mother was so depressed that her doctor sent her away for some rest and now Francine lives out past the cemetery with her grandmother. It is very sad to have so much trouble in your life."

I wonder about somebody like Ruth Ellen's mama feeling kindness for somebody as awful as Francine when she and Ruth Ellen and Sammy have it harder than anybody I know. There is still no word from their papa.

80

"Well, first you need a chicken," Ruth Ellen's mama tells me. "Like this." She pulls a bowl from the icebox that holds a picked-over chicken. I have to bend real close and squint my eyes to see even a few bits of chicken clinging to all those bones.

"There's hardly any chicken left," I say, standing up, taking the apron Ruth Ellen's mama is handing me.

"Yes, you do need someone to show you how to get four meals from a chicken, don't you, sweetheart? My mama taught me and her mama taught her and I suppose it went all the way back. It's a very important skill to learn."

I tie the apron strings round and round my belly, trying not to show everybody that I feel brokenhearted over not having a mama or a Pauline to show me things.

Ruth Ellen's mama pulls an onion and some carrots from a box under the sink and celery from the icebox. She hands me a knife. "This is to flavor the broth, so big chunks are fine. There's no need to peel the onion. It will make the broth golden. Just chop it into four pieces."

She scrapes four carrots with the edge of her knife, chops them up, and plops the orange chunks in the pot. I cut the celery. She pours in enough water to cover the bones and I shake in salt and pepper.

Ruth Ellen's mama checks the stove by holding her hand over the burner and decides it is not hot enough. She reaches into the apple crate beside the stove and pulls out some of the wood we found the other day and shoves it into the stove. Then she puts the pot on the biggest burner.

Ruth Ellen pesters me to come outside with her because she wants to build fairy houses by the victory garden, but I tell her to take Sammy out and play with him. I need to learn more about cooking.

"Can't your aunts show you how?" Ruth Ellen can be quite a bother when her leg is hurting and she wants to get her mind off things.

I do not want to get into a conversation about my aunts. I look from Ruth Ellen to her mama to Sammy. They have all stopped what they are doing and are looking at me. They are wondering about my situation, now that Ruth Ellen brought it up. I can feel it in the air. "My aunts can't cook," I say softly.

Ruth Ellen's mama reaches over and scoops up the carrot peels and tosses them in the compost bucket for the chickens. "Well, you are always welcome here whenever you want. You know that, Bee, right?"

My throat closes and all I can do is nod.

Later on, after we sit down and say a long prayer for Ruth Ellen's papa, and after her mama has to wipe away quite a few tears (and some from Ruth Ellen's and Sammy's cheeks, too), we get to eat the best chicken soup I have ever tasted, rich and golden and sure to nourish even my aunts back to health.

81

Ruth Ellen and her mama and Sammy drive me home, and this time when we pull up to my house, they all pile out before I can say no.

I am trying to think how I can get rid of them, but then Peabody barrels off the porch and Ruth Ellen's family makes a big fuss over him. They don't see him much now that I leave him home with Cordelia. Peabody might be house-trained, but he is not chicken-trained, and Ruth Ellen's hens have too many tail feathers missing.

"We'd love to see inside." Ruth Ellen's mama is already standing on the porch looking in the window. There's a light on in the kitchen and one in the library. "I haven't been in this house since I was a girl." She giggles, sounding young enough to slide down the stair railing. "Not since Berna-dette's birthday party."

I am near the porch swing, so I don't have to stumble too far when I fall into it. "You knew my mama?" I whisper.

"Your mama?" Ruth Ellen's mama raises her eyebrow. "What on earth do you mean?"

"My mama's name was Bernadette. Bernadette Hocken-berry."

"Yes, Bernadette married Tommy Lee Hockenberry. You are their daughter?"

I nod. "And she lived here?"

"Well, of course she did, sweetheart. We were all the

same age. My friends and I came to Bernadette's sixteenth birthday party. Her father—your grandfather, I guess—rented a monkey and a trainer for the day. Only rich folks could rent a monkey like that, and a carnival truck pulled up right here in front of these roses and a young man came in with the monkey. Of course, that was the only party your grandfather ever allowed.

My head spins. My heart whirls. I say it again. "My mother lived here?"

"Well, yes, dear. Of course she did. Sweetheart, are you all right? You look a little pale."

In this house that I picked out myself, the birthday cake house with the frosting dripping off and all the protection? My mama lived here?

I try to hold myself together before all my pieces slip apart. I breathe slowly and listen to my mind try to explain things to me.

Ruth Ellen's mama feels my forehead to see if I have a fever. "Didn't your aunts tell you all this? I know you were young when your mother and father died, but didn't anyone tell you these things?"

I shake my head.

"Pleeease." Ruth Ellen interrupts. "You promised me I could come over. I want to see the inside."

"You have to let us in," says Sammy, who is already turning the knob and opening the door.

I hop up and rush to stop him, but I am weak from all my parts falling on the ground. Before I can count to three they step inside, and I don't see any way out of it without being rude.

"Oh, it looks just the same. Look at that staircase.

Bernadette's room was up there, the most beautiful bedroom I have ever seen." Ruth Ellen's mama goes over and puts her hand on the rail. Sammy is already running up the stairs.

"Wouldn't you like to wait in here?" I say quickly, telling Sammy to get down here and shooing everyone to the parlor and showing them where to sit. I point out how the little lace runners are for keeping your head off the upholstery.

"Would you like some tea? And some honey cake? I made it myself."

"I love cake," says Sammy, jumping off the sofa, and Peabody jumps down with him.

"You wait here," I say sternly. "I will bring everything out."

Then I go out and get the tea ready and cut fat pieces of honey cake, wishing I didn't have to keep my aunts secret. "Would you like some cake?" I whisper, but Mrs. Swift and Mrs. Potter are so quiet you would think I live alone.

"You do your shopping yourself?" Ruth Ellen's mama asks when I carry everything in on the same tray I used for Mrs. Marsh. "You do all the cooking? And the cleaning? And get your own ration stamps?"

"I don't use sugar," I whisper.

Ruth Ellen's mama looks slowly over at Ruth Ellen. I start to feel a little self-conscious. I pull my hair down and look in my teacup.

Generally, it is not good to feel sorry for yourself. You can get in a pickle that lasts for days. I make myself stand up. "Well, would you like to see the rest of the house?"

"Oh yes," says Ruth Ellen.

First because it is so impressive, and because I am not

sure how Ruth Ellen's leg will do on the steep stairs, I show them the library.

"Some terrible things have been written about my aunt so she is correcting that. She's writing her autobiography."

Ruth Ellen's mama walks over to the desk and looks through the papers and at the pen and the inkpot.

She picks up one of the books on the desk. "Why, these are all biographies of Abigail Swift."

"Yes, my aunt."

"Your aunt is Abigail Swift? The aunt you live with now?" She waits for me to answer but I am getting a little worried about how things are going. Peabody is flopped on Mrs. Potter's sofa watching us. He is wondering how things will turn out, too.

Ruth Ellen skip-hops over to look at the papers on the desk. Her mama flips through the book. "Why, Bee, Abigail Swift would be one hundred and twenty-five years old! Surely this cannot be your aunt. This is Abigail Swift, the famous abolitionist and suffragist."

"Yes," I say, fumbling with my words. I can tell Ruth Ellen's mama thinks I am making everything up.

She puts the book gently on the desk. She reaches for my shoulder and rubs it while I am fighting back tears. "Why don't you come home with us, Bee? You could stay with us for a while."

I back up and scoop up Peabody. I want my bed upstairs. I want to hide under my blankets and make Peabody hide with me. I want all the thoughts rolling in my head to go away. I shake my head.

"My aunts would wonder where I am. Besides, Peabody wouldn't want me gone. And I have to take care of Cordelia."

8 2

You can tell Ruth Ellen's mama is running the whole thing through her mind and she's not sure what she should do.

Then Sammy is pulling on her sleeve, telling her it is almost time for *The Adventures of Superman* to come on the radio and he doesn't want to miss any of it.

Ruth Ellen's mama mulls things over. She looks at how the library is so neat and everything is polished and how there are little lace cloths on all the sofas in the parlor. I watch her line up on one side of her mind why she should let me be and on the other why she should take me home.

"I'm fine," I say quickly. "My aunts must have just stepped out for a walk."

"Mom, I don't want to miss my show," says Sammy, grabbing her arm and pulling.

Then she hugs me. "You can stay with us anytime you want, Bee," she whispers.

I nod. "I will think about it." It takes quite a bit more convincing that I am really all right, and finally they go.

Mrs. Potter hobbles into the library with a big slice of honey cake and sits on the couch.

"Where were you?" I snap.

"Right here, just like always."

"Well, no one could see you. No one can ever see you. Except me." I look at my dog. "And Peabody."

"Yes, I guess not." Mrs. Potter gives Peabody a bite of cake.

"Well, I could use some help sometimes."

She scratches Peabody between the ears. "Some things you have to do for yourself, Beatrice."

"But I do EVERYTHING for myself."

"It's better this way. It will make you strong. Now come sit beside me." She pats the sofa. I look at the two of them snuggled up, and go over to the other side of the room and sit in Mrs. Swift's chair.

I sigh many times to show her how mad I am. She pretends she cannot hear.

"Ruth Ellen's mama said Mrs. Swift was an abolitionist and suffragist a long time ago."

"I know, I heard." Mrs. Potter gives Peabody the rest of the cake.

"I thought the cake was for you."

"A bite is all I need these days." She rubs Peabody's back. Her fingers are thin as the pen on the desk.

"How come you didn't tell me my mama lived here?"

Mrs. Potter doesn't look up from scratching Peabody. She is scratching his belly now. "We were going to tell you when it was time."

"Well, don't you think it is time?" I am very hot. "How old are you?" I ask.

She stops scratching. She takes her time answering me. "I'm old enough to be your grandmother, Bee."

"How come you don't let anyone see you but me?"

Mrs. Potter laughs. "Who'd want to look at me? I'm not much to look at." She straightens her shawl.

Her skin is soft and creased and very old and she has gotten much thinner since I started going to school and making friends with Ruth Ellen. I look at her closely: her hair pulled up in a tight bun, her pink shawl cinched with a large safety pin, her cane leaning against the couch.

Mrs. Potter chuckles. She sips her tea and puts the cup on the side table. Then she holds her arm out. "Here, touch me, Bee. I know what you are wondering. Do I feel real?"

I go over and sit beside her. I put my fingers on her arm. Her skin is warm and soft and wrinkled and old. I lift it to my face and feel it against my cheek. Her arm smells like rose water.

"Who are you, then?" I whisper.

Mrs. Potter leans over and hugs me. I smell the warm wool of her shawl and feel the tenderness in her arms as they wrap around me.

"Maybe if you thought of us as your companions you'd be getting it right," she whispers in my ear.

It is a voice light as air.

That night Pauline's notebook is sitting on my pillow. This time I don't stuff it under my mattress. I open to the first page:

Little Bee is sleeping. I will keep a journal of her days because no one kept one for me.

And on the second page:

We stop at a diner in Plymouth and Bee eats French toast for the first time. She has been smiling all day.

On day three:

I bought Bee a book at Woolworth's. I set up a milk crate and she is sitting on it, asking me, "What's that, what's that?" I am waiting on folks and grilling up hot dogs and answering what's that, what's that, and I am a little sorry I bought her that book.

I throw the journal across the room.

How could she leave me?

Peabody pushes my door open and comes in and jumps up on my bed when he hears me crying. He circles until he finds just the right spot near my belly. He whines when I cry, so I make myself stop so we can both fall asleep.

The next morning, the notebook is back on my bed.

I throw it across the room.

I hurry downstairs and find Mrs. Potter and Mrs. Swift in the kitchen talking quietly.

"I want you to tell me about my mama," I say, sitting

down beside them. "And I want you to tell me who you are and why only I can see you."

Mrs. Potter opens her mouth but Mrs. Swift waves her hand and shakes her head slowly. Mrs. Potter closes her mouth.

"Not now, Beatrice. Later, when we are rested."

Already their edges are beginning to blur, like the wind is blowing awful hard. I pack my school lunch and do not bother to cut them cake. They wouldn't eat it anyway.

At school, we are greeted with an empty teacher's desk. There are no knitting needles and no baby blanket.

We are like this for the whole day, with the lady in the half-moon glasses coming in to check on us and teachers up and down the hall taking turns. None of the teachers stay very long and no one tells us anything.

Left to ourselves, we read *Heidi*. Jonathan gets the blanket from the corner where the janitor leaves it all folded up now. He spreads it out and then we all pile on top, giving Ruth Ellen lots of room for her brace. We are past the part where the little bundled-up girl meets her crabby grandfather who no one likes very much.

Susan does not understand all the words, but my voice settles her down and she loves to lie snuggled up to Ruth Ellen. Even Robert and Thomas like the book. I can tell because when I say I am so parched I am sounding like a frog, Robert is the first one to the pitcher getting me a drink of water.

But on Monday everything is different when we walk into class.

White ruffled curtains hang in the windows. The glass has been polished. Best of all, soft music is playing on the Victrola.

I look over at Ruth Ellen. Her mouth drops open. Jonathan rushes right over to the Victrola.

A tall woman stands up from the rocking chair. Her back is as straight as the map pointer she holds at her side. Her hair is piled on top of her head and her glasses are perched on her nose. Instantly everyone is quiet. Susan hides behind Ruth Ellen and the rest of us are starched shirts, folding all the noisy pieces of ourselves into place.

"I am your new teacher, Miss Healy. Please take your seats." The woman pronounces every word like she has read the dictionary many times. She does not raise her voice and she does not smile.

We rush to our seats.

"Slowly, slowly. I do not allow running." She moves over to her desk. It is covered with books. Our *Heidi* sits on top.

"I do not allow whispering or chewing on your hair or any shenanigans whatsoever. There will be no talking when you are doing seat work. Children will sit at their tables until it is time for recess. We will have three recesses a day because children need a lot of fresh air. We will eat our lunch outdoors when the weather is promising."

I look over at Ruth Ellen, raising my eyebrows. "Three recesses?" I whisper.

"Young lady?" It seems Miss Healy has ears on the back of her shoes. Otherwise, how does she know I am whispering when she is looking over at Jonathan?

I shiver.

"I do not like secrets. Do you have something to share?"

I shake my head quickly.

"No, ma'am," I whisper.

85

It takes us about two minutes to realize Miss Healy does not knit and does not do anything like Mrs. Spriggs. First of all Miss Healy has very definite ideas of what we should be doing with our time and she walks around and around the class making sure we are doing it. I bet she walks a mile before lunch.

She stops by Susan many, many times. Susan is having trouble staying in her seat, which is no surprise to me or Ruth Ellen or anybody else, but it takes Miss Healy a few minutes to catch on.

"Perhaps you'd like the rocking chair?" she asks finally, and Susan flies over and spends the rest of the morning rocking and looking through the fat Sears catalog Miss Healy brought to class. "What do you see, Susan?"

Susan keeps climbing off the rocking chair and plods off to be near Ruth Ellen, but Miss Healy reminds her that Ruth Ellen is busy with her own work and perhaps Susan can find a picture of a boot. After that she looks for a rain slicker and then a hat.

"Very good, Susan. That is very, very good." Miss Healy gives her a chunk of soft banana and a big hug. Susan stuffs it into her mouth and looks happily into Miss Healy's eyes. "I lub you." Miss Healy smiles softly, clears her throat, and walks over to see what Jonathan is doing.

He is looking out the window at the leaves on the maples

that are now golden. He nods his head to the Glenn Miller music that is playing softly.

He has not run around the room once. He hasn't looked in the trash bucket, either.

Miss Healy rubs Jonathan's back. "Do you like that music, Jonathan?" He nods. "Why don't you draw me a picture of what that music feels like? Can you do that for me?"

She puts a fresh piece of starched paper in front of him, and a brand-new box of crayons. Jonathan dumps the crayons out and looks at them for a while. Ruth Ellen and I are holding our breath, the crayons are so new and perfect.

86

When Ruth Ellen and I come outdoors for recess, Francine and her friends are standing where we always stand, up against the building. I think they want a good look at our new teacher.

"Hey!" says Jonathan. "Why are you in our place?"

We all watch Francine to see what she will say. She is wearing the same dress from her papa. All I can think about is how I spit on her the last time I saw her. And now I know about how her papa ran off with that showgirl.

Francine takes a step closer and points her finger at my chest. "You spit on me again and I'll make you eat the dirt you play on, you little retard." She pushes me. "Maybe I'll do it anyway." She laughs and then her friends pull her away before Miss Healy sees anything and they run off for games no one asks us to join.

Miss Healy pulls her skirt up past her knees and runs back and forth from the building to the broken basketball hoop. She is out of breath when she gets back and her face is very red, but she turns around and runs again and again. It is rather funny to see a teacher run. She bounces a lot, and she gallops. It is surely something we have never seen before.

Ruth Ellen and I try not to laugh at the way Miss Healy looks sort of like an old horse. Susan holds on to Ruth Ellen because she didn't have enough hugging while she was sitting in the rocking chair. Thomas and Robert crawl around the stone foundation of the schoolhouse. Jonathan kicks a puddle, splashing mud up on his pants.

Miss Healy stops in front of us and lets her skirt fall back to her shins and she pants for a while to catch her breath. "Why are you just standing here?"

Susan wraps herself around Ruth Ellen's arm. There is a bunch of screaming over by the hopscotch because Francine must have won the game. Miss Healy is waiting for an answer.

"We aren't supposed to mix," I say finally, my cheeks hot because I have to say it out loud.

Miss Healy stands there looking at me, all out of breath from her running, and I feel a little hot under her glare.

"Phooey," she says finally. "This playground is for everyone. Now, go play."

Holy moly. We watch her lift her skirt to her knees and run off for the basketball hoop again.

87

Robert wants to know if I can keep reading.

Miss Healy looks out at the class, with everyone looking all happy with the prospect.

"Well, certainly. After all that fresh air, a book would be wonderful."

Before she has a chance to say anything else, Robert is up getting *Heidi* off her desk and Thomas is unfolding the blanket and spreading it on the floor. Susan is grabbing Ruth Ellen's hand, pulling her over, and then we all pile around each other and Robert is handing me the book.

"Where were we?" I ask, testing them to see if they were listening.

"Heidi is all alone with the mean grandfather," Thomas says.

Jonathan is nodding. Susan snuggles up to Ruth Ellen.

"Okay," I say, taking a big breath:

" 'Where am I going to sleep, grandfather?'

" 'Wherever you want to,' he replied. That suited Heidi exactly. She peeped into all the corners of the room and looked at every little nook to find a cosy place to sleep. Beside the old man's bed she saw a ladder. Climbing up, she arrived at a hayloft, which was filled with fresh and fragrant hay. Through a tiny round window she could look far down into the valley. 'I want to sleep up here,' Heidi called down.

'Oh, it is lovely here. Please come up, grandfather, and see it for yourself.'"

While I am reading, Miss Healy drags the rocking chair over and sits beside us. She begins winding Mrs. Spriggs's bits of yarn into a ball. I don't let myself get too interrupted because I am reading about Heidi's new bedroom. I know how important it is to have a bedroom that helps you feel good about things.

"'I am making the bed now,' the little girl called out again, while she ran busily to and fro. 'Oh, do come up and bring a sheet, grandfather, for every bed must have a sheet.'

"'Is that so?' said the old man. After a while he opened the cupboard and rummaged around in it. At last he pulled out a long coarse cloth from under the shirts. It somewhat resembled a sheet, and with this he climbed up to the loft. Here a neat little bed was already prepared. On top the hay was heaped up high so that the head of the occupant would lie exactly opposite the window."

Miss Healy reaches over and gently pulls my hair back from my face and ties it with a piece of yellow yarn.

"You can't see where you're going with your hair hanging in your face all the time, Beatrice."

Without my curtain, I am a window with the light pouring through.

88

When it is time for recess, Miss Healy warns us, "You all better be doing more than standing in the dirt when I get out there."

We are not sure what to do with ourselves. Jonathan goes over to the pine tree where Mrs. Spriggs used to sit and pokes a stick to wedge off the bark. Robert and Thomas build another bridge. I watch Francine and her friends. I pull the yarn from my hair and my curls fall back against my diamond.

"I just don't see how come they get jump ropes and chalk for hopscotch," I tell Ruth Ellen.

"Everyone's afraid we'll get hurt." She is trying to braid Susan's hair, but Susan won't stand still.

"Phooey," I say, letting the word roll around on my tongue, feeling the coolness of the sound in my mouth. Hearing me sound just like Miss Healy makes Ruth Ellen laugh. And when Ruth Ellen laughs, Susan does, too.

Francine and her friends give up on hopscotch and race to the end of the field. I know what they are up to. They are copying Miss Healy.

"Come on," I say, sprinting for the far woods. I am a jackrabbit and I stretch my legs too far, and get myself off balance and nearly trip.

I slow down and check behind me and see Ruth Ellen and Susan standing by the wall and Jonathan is still poking at the bark. I hear Bobby telling me in my head how it may seem as if long strides will make you faster, but they really slow you down.

He may be right, but he didn't know about Francine. She is standing off to the side now and is watching. I speed up.

I ignore all the things Bobby told me about running much slower than you need to so you can work up to fast. I push faster.

I pump my arms and now my chest hurts. The blood pumps in my head and I am dizzy. I don't see the log until I trip on it and fall in a heap in the grass. I am hurt pretty bad, I tell myself as I roll around, holding my knees. I hear Francine hooting, and then Ruth Ellen is pulling me up and she and Susan are wiping the blood off my legs.

We get the bleeding stopped by the time recess is over, and we stand up against the building waiting for all the other kids to go inside. I pull my hair tight.

Francine looks me in the face. "You are nothing but a bunch of retards," she whispers so Miss Healy won't hear. "And you, Beatrice, you will always be ugly and dirty as the sole of my shoe." She scuffs her shoe in the dirt to make sure I get her point, and when she thinks I have had long enough to think about it, she shoots a pile of spit into my hair, already stretched tight over my diamond.

She laughs and then she and her friends walk into the building and Ruth Ellen reaches for me.

I feel the spit drip over my diamond and a hurricane whirls inside me. My toes tremble and then a tornado roars up through my belly and before I know it I am the eye of the storm.

89

I tell Ruth Ellen's mama no thank you about the ride she is offering home from school, because when you are a tornado the only thing to do is be alone.

Peabody waits for me on the porch swing every day now and seeing him sitting with his ears all raised up as I turn the corner warms my heart about as much as anything. He wags his stumpy tail so hard he shakes his whole self and then he jumps off the swing, dives down the steps, and leaps into my arms. I bury my face in his soft butterscotch fur and forget for a moment all about the storm inside me.

But tornadoes have a way of stirring up again, of coming back, of ripping through, and I tell Peabody how I need a plan. "But first we need a snack. And so does Cordelia."

Mrs. Swift and Mrs. Potter are not in the house. It seems that every time I want to ask them about my mama they have disappeared.

I pull a tea biscuit for Peabody from the tin on top of the icebox and slice myself a piece of apple cake and pour some milk for both of us. I tuck an apple into the pocket of my overalls for Cordelia.

My little pig has been growing these past few weeks from all the corn and she is getting rather plump. She is very interested in spending most of her time lying on her favorite pile of straw.

"You need some exercise," I tell her, huffing and puffing

to get her up and out of the gate. Luckily, there is a robin on the grass up ahead, and Cordelia changes her tune.

I run slowly and I let my dog and my pig get in front. Every time Cordelia wanders off to look at a red squirrel running along a stone wall or to see what a chickadee is chickadeeing about, I have to clap my hands and tap her on the backside with a stick like Bobby used to do at the Little Pig Race.

Peabody has no trouble. He is heading straight for Mrs. Marsh's chickens.

"No. We are going the other way." When I finally get them both turned right, I tell them to just run and be quiet because I am thinking up a plan on how I am going to get Francine back.

90

Day after day I practice my running, over and over, again and again.

Cordelia needs quite a bit of encouragement. She is very slow. She is much more interested in her pile of straw or the carrot peels hiding at the bottom of her food bucket.

I tell her all about what Bobby told me:

You have to want to get better. You have to look for your own finish line and tell yourself you will cross it, and you have to keep trying and trying and you will find the strength deep inside yourself to keep going, and when you find it, you will be proud of yourself like never before.

Cordelia hardly listens. As soon as we get in the woods, she heads straight for a cluster of mushrooms, a dragonfly on a daisy, a clump of crows. After that, I leave her home. She doesn't have the same motivation I do. She doesn't know Francine.

Peabody, though, loves to run. We get so we can run all the way to Ruth Ellen's, straight through the woods. I put one foot in front of the other and after a few days I can cover a lot of ground. Do not bounce, I remind myself. Push your arms out in front of you. Find your pace.

It feels good to stretch my legs out (but not too far) and feel the October sun shining all over my diamond and to let all the whirring inside of me grow quieter with each step. When I feel the blood pumping in my head, I slow down and push ahead with my dog bouncing along beside me. It is good to have a dog that loves to run.

Bobby was right. It turns out I love running in the woods. It is peaceful and the leaves crunch under my feet. There are many more birds to watch when you are in the woods. Plus, all this time I am thinking about an idea. It is a good one, I think. That's the thing about running. You get very good ideas.

About halfway to Ruth Ellen's, my chest starts heaving and my blood is pumping in my head and my legs start telling me to quit because they are hurting awful bad.

I am no quitter, I tell them, and I slow down to tortoise pace waiting for my second wind. Bobby said when I find it I will be stronger than I thought I was.

Peabody slows down, wondering when we can get going again, and I plod at a snail's pace and then, slowly, slowly, I find it. I feel a surge of energy and I am a jackrabbit, darting; a deer, leaping; a horse, galloping. My legs scissor and my arms pump and my lungs pound strong and free now that they do not carry heavy buckets of water around anymore.

As we run out of the woods and down the hill leading to Ruth Ellen's, the smile that spreads across my face hides my diamond. I laugh out loud because when I fly like this the sun can't help but stick to the soles of my shoes.

91

Ruth Ellen and Sammy are out in the garden picking pumpkins. They are fighting.

"It's still green. You can't pick that one," Ruth Ellen is
saying when I run up and bend over double to catch my
breath. Peabody darts off for the chickens. I try to stop him
but I am too out of breath.

"But I like the green ones," Sammy says.

"The green ones are terrible in a pie. Mama will be mad."

"Why do you both always tell me what to do?"

Ruth Ellen stands up and skip-hops over and grabs Sammy's hand and makes him stop picking the green pumpkin.
He lets out a yelp for his mother. Then they see me. Peabody
comes flying around the corner, chasing a chicken, and I
flop onto the ground, too tired to do anything. Ruth Ellen's
mama hurries out to the porch and yells at Peabody to put
the chicken down and get up on the porch this very minute
and sit down and be still, and for some reason Peabody does
what he is told. "Good boy. I shall get you some cake. Now,
stay there!"

She looks over at me. "Hello, Bee!" I wave and she goes
inside for cake.

"What's wrong, Bee?" Ruth Ellen's face is red from bawl-
ing out her brother or from being in the sun so long picking
pumpkins, I can't tell which. It takes me a long while to get
my breathing back. I stay flopped in the grass.

"What happened to you?" Ruth Ellen leaves Sammy and the pumpkins and hobbles out to me. "What's wrong?"

"Nothing," I say, a big grin stretching across my face. "I . . . know . . . how . . . to . . . get back at her, Ruth Ellen. I'm going to race . . . Francine."

Sammy comes over and lets out a wild hoot. "I can run fast. See?" He jumps over the garden fence and flies down by the clothesline, screaming, "I am Jesse Owens. You can't catch me. I am Jesse O-w-e-n-sssss."

"Why don't you just leave Francine alone?" Ruth Ellen goes back to loading a big pumpkin into her wheelbarrow. She makes her voice sharp. "You only make it worse for yourself."

Worse for myself? I am still not breathing regular. Ruth Ellen picks another pumpkin. Sammy is flying up by the chicken coop and he dashes over the wooden tub his mama uses on wash day. "See?" he says when he gets back up by me. "I am Jesse Owens."

I smile at him. "Yes, you are."

"Well, I can't run." Ruth Ellen heaves another pumpkin into the wheelbarrow.

"I know that. I have to be the one to race her. She treats me the worst. You can coach us, Ruth Ellen. All Olympic runners need a good coach."

She looks up like she is getting the wormy part of the apple. Which, I guess, she is. "I don't want to be a coach!"

I can hardly believe my great idea is getting wrecked before I even start. And I know it is a great idea. Only great ideas come when you are running. It is the way of things.

I put myself in Ruth Ellen's shoes for a bit and walk around in them for a while. Everything is uneven and feels different. I go and climb over the fence and help her pick. It is a very good year for pumpkins. There are lots of them.

"What do you think we should do?" I plop another pumpkin into the wheelbarrow.

"Careful, Bee. You'll crack them."

She picks more pumpkins and doesn't answer. "What do you think, Ruth Ellen?" I ask again.

When she looks up her eyes are tearing up. "I'm tired of not being able to do what everyone else does." She yanks a pumpkin off the vine and throws it in the wheelbarrow, where it splits.

"That's why I have to run, Ruth Ellen. We have to show Francine that you can't just hide children like us away so folks don't have to look."

Her mama calls us in for sweet potato pie after that. As we are sitting around the table, me, Ruth Ellen, her mama, and Sammy, they tell me stories about their papa: how he used to take them to the ocean and they would fly kites in the dunes, how they hunted for hours every Christmas for a tree and he always insisted on the most straggly one in need of a home, and how he taught Ruth Ellen and Sammy to catch trout without a worm. There are so many Papa stories that I start feeling a little better, too. I lean back in my chair and think how being in this house fixes things.

Then I ask for another piece of sweet potato pie.

92

"I bet we could whip you silly if we raced you." I make my tone real sharp and know-it-all when I am standing by the school building, waiting to go back to class. I want to get Francine's goat.

"You could never beat us," she says, stopping and scuffing the sole of her shoe in the dirt so I remember. She narrows her eyes. "Never."

"Let's find out, then." I lean back against the wall like I am Al Capone and I like doing this. "Are you scared?"

She laughs. "I am not scared of you, Bee." She glances at her friends. "We will race you all." Ruth Ellen, Susan, Jonathan, Thomas, and Robert crowd around me. Jonathan is poking a stick between the rough wood clapboards, Susan is wrapped around Ruth Ellen.

"Are you afraid to race me alone?" I spike my voice with dare.

Francine laughs. "No, Bee. I'm not afraid of you." Then she steps closer and whispers, "I would just die if I looked like you."

I stare her down. Her voice is no longer tinkling bells. It is a hollow jug. If she thinks she is making me soft in the belly, she is wrong. I am past all that now.

93

I check my shoelaces over and over. "Double knots," I tell myself. "You will trip if you don't tie them."

I have been going over this for the last two days, making sure I remember everything Bobby taught me.

"Don't stop, keep going. Slow down if you have to, but don't stop. No bouncing."

"You have to cheer for me like I am Jesse Owens," I tell everyone.

Robert says, "Who's Jesse Owens?" and then I have to tell them how Jesse Owens, the grandson of a slave, won four gold medals running in the 1936 Olympics in Berlin.

Miss Healy helps me mark a course that starts in the shade of the ball field and zips across the hopscotch squares and dashes over to our dirt spot, then shoots back to the shade. When we are alone at our third recess, without Francine and her friends watching, everyone helps me practice. Robert and Thomas fly their fighter bombers and Jonathan airplanes and Miss Healy bounces too much and we are all red in the face when we finish.

"I think we need a fourth recess," Miss Healy says, and we stay and run the course again.

I tell Francine when she is in the bus line that we can wait a whole extra day so she can have a practice run. "I already tried it today, and I don't want you telling me I didn't win this race fair and square."

She glares at me. She looks at my work boots and up to my overalls and finally stops at my face. "I don't need to practice to beat someone like you, Bee."

"Fine by me." I hold my nose like someone is smelling awful bad and walk away.

94

Susan is pulling all the papers and crayons and her coloring books out of her desk drawer because she cannot find her glasses. Ruth Ellen skip-hops over to help her and Jonathan uses the time to go over by the coat hooks and look in the trash bucket. A quiver has started in my belly.

"No, no, no." I go over and pull on Susan's arm. "We are late. I have a race to run."

Ruth Ellen pulls my arm. "Bee, she can't watch without her glasses."

My belly is beginning to do more than quiver. It is rolling over. My ears pop, ready to explode. "Okay, everyone help Susan find her glasses. But we have to hurry. Francine is outside already."

Miss Healy looks all sympathetic about my situation. I do appreciate that about her: how she seems to know how I am feeling about things. "Did you look by the blanket where you were reading?" Without waiting for anyone to answer, she hurries over and picks up the blanket, shakes it, and Susan's glasses tumble out.

Of course then we have to listen to Susan telling Miss Healy she lubs her and Miss Healy has to tell Jonathan to put the eggshells back in the trash. I blow my hair out of my eyes in a loud wet sputter, sounding just like Pauline. I do not want to slow myself down by getting all upset, so I count to ten.

9 5

Francine is already at the start line. She gives me the stare-down when we walk up. Susan reaches for Ruth Ellen's hand. Jonathan pushes closer to me.

"Don't worry," I whisper. "She is just trying to make me feel bad so I won't run fast. Don't pay attention to her."

I tell everyone to go to their spectator spots, just like we practiced yesterday. Jonathan and Miss Healy are at the start, Thomas and Robert are at the hopscotch squares, and Susan and Ruth Ellen are near the end.

Miss Healy steps up to the start line. "We want a good, clean race. No cheating." She looks longer at Francine than at me. "Ready?"

I nod. Jonathan is scraping a stick in the grass. I think he is looking for a worm. "Jonathan," I say.

"Get set!"

"Go!" screams Miss Healy, and I do not have any more time to be thinking about Jonathan.

Francine is very fast. Her legs are long like a colt and when she stretches them out she sails over the grass. I pump my legs hard and we are neck and neck until we get to the hopscotch squares, where Robert and Thomas are jumping up and down and waving their arms and yelling like I am Jesse Owens. This helps me quite a bit. I move ahead.

Francine is on my tail in two seconds and we are crossing over our dirt playground with me only a foot in front.

I feel her breathing down my neck. I force myself to be fast like LaVerne and not slow like Cordelia. Then I make myself stop thinking about pigs. Francine edges closer. She is close enough to spit on me.

I check to make sure I am not bouncing and that my arms are bent at the right angle, and push on. My work boots slap at the grass as we move off the dirt and head back to the finish line. All along the rest of the way, kids are lined up screaming. The boys from the ball field and the girls who jump rope and the ones who hopscotch and Francine's friends are all jumping and hollering.

It's no wonder Francine gets past me, there's so many kids cheering for her. She glances behind to see where I am. Robert and Thomas are not cheering me on, they are dive-bombing. It looks like Jonathan might be peeing on the tree. My lungs are aching and my blood is pounding in my head and my legs feel heavy like I cannot lift them up anymore.

But then I see Ruth Ellen and Susan up ahead and they are screaming, *"Bee!"* and I pump my legs faster, faster, faster and I find my second wind and I fly just the tiniest bit ahead of Francine.

Susan jumps up and down and she lets go of Ruth Ellen's hand and rushes onto the track and tries to grab me. "I lub you, I lub you," she says.

Kids everywhere along the racecourse are hooting and hollering and jumping up and down over Susan running on the track and trying to hug me. "I lub you," she calls, "I lub you," and she is reaching for me and grabbing hold of my arm.

"Susan!" I yell, trying to shake her off.

She doesn't pay any attention, she keeps holding on and

I scream for Ruth Ellen and search for Miss Healy. Already I am way behind.

And then Susan's glasses fall off and she trips on me as I try and not step on the glasses and I step on her foot and we are like a snowball, rolling and rolling until we stop.

Susan wails a high painful shriek and holds her foot. I hold my head, feeling dizzy, and seeing stars spatter all over the grass.

I pull myself up just in time to see Francine sprint ahead and cross the finish line, her arms raised. I let my head fall back on the dirt. Ruth Ellen hurries over to Susan and then Jonathan runs up and pats me on the head. I don't care if anyone sees that I am crying.

Miss Healy has lifted her skirts and is running toward us. She looks me in the eye and tells me how sorry she is that things worked out this way and then she has a look at Susan's foot. She lifts Susan in her arms and speeds off for the school. Ruth Ellen helps me up and I lean on her, and then we all follow Miss Healy.

Francine hardly notices that we are leaving. She is too busy being cheered and getting patted on the back.

Susan's foot gets wrapped in a white plaster cast and she is back after a few days. We all go back to standing on the dirt because the principal came to our class and pulled Miss Healy out in the hall for a discussion as soon as he found out about the race and about Susan's foot. He slammed the door so we couldn't hear.

We showed him. We pressed our ears to the wood:

"What in the world were you thinking?" His voice is low and gruff and irritated like I am when I am trying to explain chickens to Peabody.

"We were having a race."

"Together? You put the children together?"

"Phooey."

"What?" The principal is sounding hot under the collar. "What did you say?"

"They don't need to be separated. It's not right. They don't get half of what the other children get."

We all look at each other. We have to cover our mouths because we are about to giggle and spoil everything. It is hard to do. I am so proud of Miss Healy for standing up for us like this. I am already letting my mind run off and picture us getting the shady ball field and having the time of our lives and Francine and her friends standing on the hot dirt.

But then the principal answers. "I know, Miss Healy, that you do not have much experience teaching children like these, so I will overlook your recklessness. But it is very important that they do not mix."

"But why?" Miss Healy is asking.

"Because they get teased. Isn't that obvious?" Then the principal is saying that if she can't obey a few simple rules, she'll have to pack her satchel and leave and not come back.

Susan starts boohooing. She doesn't like yelling, and Ruth Ellen wraps her in her arms so no one can hear. The principal is making quite a noisy spectacle of himself out there in the hall. Ruth Ellen whispers to Susan how it will be okay, not to worry. Ruth Ellen is very good about things like that. She knows how to make you feel better.

After that all I can do is watch Francine gloat. It is very painful.

97

A few days later, Jonathan finds a dead sparrow by the bushes. He carries it over and Ruth Ellen screams and Susan sobs and buries her face in her hands.

Jonathan pats the sparrow softly, waiting for it to sing or maybe fly. The bird's neck is crooked and a wing is bent backward.

"Oh, Jonathan," I say, stepping forward. "It can't sing anymore. Look, it can't move."

I touch the bird. Its feathers are soft and warm from the sun beating down. It is very still. Jonathan tries to put the sparrow into his pocket.

"No," I say softly, showing him how to cradle the bird in his hands. "We need to bury it."

Miss Healy suggests a funeral and tells us we can dig the grave on our next recess. We give this job to Thomas and Robert. We find a rusted old shovel in the janitor's closet.

Jonathan leads the way, carrying the sparrow in the old cigar box that held all our broken crayons when Mrs. Spriggs was in charge. Ruth Ellen and Susan wrapped the little bird in tissues, but not before Susan cried tears over all the feathers.

We follow behind, and Thomas and Robert carry the shovel. Miss Healy comes last, carrying the Bible. Francine and her friends are already playing hopscotch when we come out.

"Over there," I say, pointing to the spot by the bushes where Jonathan found the bird. "Maybe that is close to his home."

When the hole is dug, I get down on my knees and help Jonathan set the box deep in the ground.

"Now you can say something nice about the bird," I tell him.

Jonathan stands back, his eyes brimming. He looks about to say something and then chokes. He does this twice, and then Miss Healy pulls him to her and lets him cry into her shoulder.

"Bee? Can you say something about the bird?" I think back to my mama and papa's funeral to see if I can remember anything that the preacher said, but all I remember are the angel statues.

Jonathan looks up at the sky for a moment and then whispers, "I love birds because they are music," and we all stand around thinking on that.

Susan sniffles quite a bit and wants to lub all over Ruth Ellen. I stand up and wipe the dirt off my knees and glare at Francine when she walks past. I know she is wondering what we are doing over by the bushes.

98

I stay after school to help Miss Healy put all the new books she bought for us on the shelves. There are more than two dozen, all shapes and sizes. We find just the right spot for *Heidi*. Holy moly, our classroom is a library.

Then Miss Healy pulls a paper bag from the bottom drawer of her desk. It is filled with reeds. "What do you think if we tried making baskets in this class? I think that learning to do things with our hands can be very relaxing when we are worn out from all the schoolwork."

She is smiling at me and not looking like a horse at all. I do like her way of looking at things. Miss Healy has a heart full of kindness for children. She knows all about what we have to put up with.

We separate the reeds so the long pieces are in one pile and the shorter ones in another. We put the piles in two baskets and carry them over by the window. When we finish, Miss Healy goes down to the office because the principal wants to talk with her and I close the door to our classroom and walk outside.

I am not expecting Francine and her friends to be waiting outside for me, but here they are against the building. The cigar box is flipped upside down in the dirt. The dug-up sparrow lies at Francine's feet.

"You're such a loser, Bee," Francine sings softly, tapping

at the sparrow with the toe of her work boot. "You look like crap and you run like crap." She kicks the little sparrow from one foot to another.

The bird is covered with dirt from being rolled around, and now the other wing folds at a funny angle. Francine kicks it again.

Sparks inside me ignite. "Leave it alone," I say, pushing Francine as hard as I can against the building.

It is not hard enough. "You little retard," she says, pushing me back, and I fall in the dirt beside the cigar box. I look frantically for Miss Healy, or anyone else. But I am alone. Only Francine's friends are with us, the one with the thick glasses and the one with the ribbons in her hair. They stand like soldiers, waiting for their general's call. Betsy stands off to the side with a smaller girl, who is crying softly.

Francine looks at me on the ground and laughs.

"What's the matter, Bee," she says after a bit of silence, "you fall out of the ugly tree? That must be what happened, and then you hit every branch on the way down. Isn't that right?" She laughs at her own joke.

"Shut up," I say. "Shut up. Just shut up." I jump up, suck up spit, and shoot it at Francine's face. My aim is true. Francine screams, "Grab her, grab her!" as she wipes the spit dripping down her cheek. "You idiots, hold her."

One of the girls grabs my arm, but I yank it away. Francine kicks the smaller girl, who isn't helping, and she falls to the ground. She looks up at me, her eyes tearing, and then Betsy helps her up.

I try to jump away, Francine grabs me.

"Against the school," she yells. "Hold her." I try to break free, but there are three girls against one. They hold my arm up to the side of the building and then they grab my other arm and I am the butterfly Eldora pinned to a piece of cardboard, its wings fanned so everyone can have a good look.

I want to go home. I want Mrs. Potter and Mrs. Swift and my high bed. I want to hide under the covers and let Peabody hide with me. I want Cordelia to nuzzle my neck because I am feeling awful bad about everything.

Francine comes closer. I see the mad in her face. "How can you even stand to be alive, Bee? You wreck this world for the rest of us who aren't stained all over our face."

I squirm, but I can't break free.

Then she raises her hand and holds it in the air a foot from my face and I turn my head as far away as I can and wait, already wincing, a moth in a web.

And then it comes: a wave of pain against my diamond. My head hits the schoolhouse. I stumble as the ground rises to my knees and I slip to the dirt. I hear Betsy yelling at Francine and then everything goes dark.

Many minutes later, when I finally pull myself up, I am alone. Even the sparrow is gone.

99

I take three days to plan my revenge. While I am hiding under my quilt with Peabody tucked up beside me, waiting for my diamond to stop aching so, I decide that with Francine, I will go all out.

I do not tell Mrs. Potter or Mrs. Swift because I do not want them to change my mind.

On Friday I wait for Francine to walk past as she goes inside after recess. When she gets up to me, I step in her way. I have rehearsed the whole thing over and over in my mind, plus practiced with Peabody, and that helps my shaking legs quite a bit.

I pause for a moment while all her friends crowd around so they can hear everything I have to say.

I look Francine square in the face. "How's your daddy?" I say it sharp like I am a rail spike. "Heard from him lately?"

Ruth Ellen gasps behind me, but I hammer on. "Yes, we hear your daddy ran off with a showgirl, isn't that right?" Ruth Ellen is kicking me with her good leg. I turn back and scowl.

Francine turns beet-colored and backs up. I am glad she knows what shame feels like. Betsy moves away.

Already, Francine's eyes are tearing up. My revenge is sweet like sugar frosting and I hardly feel Ruth Ellen yanking on my sleeve. "And what about that dress you always wear? Did your papa buy it because he felt so bad about running off?"

She looks at her friends, who are trying to get around her and into the school. "Is that why you wear the same dress *all the time?*"

I go on and on because I have tapped a well inside me, and it is bottomless and endless. I don't stop until Francine runs crying into the school.

Ruth Ellen twists my other sleeve and pulls me around so she can look in my face. "My mama told us that secret so we would be kind." She flings the words in my face. "How could you do that, Bee?"

"What do you mean? After all Francine did, you want me to be kind? And forget?" I back up and stare at her. "I don't think so, Ruth Ellen."

"You went behind my mama's back and told a secret she told just to us. And now that's going to get my mama into trouble. You are not the only one with pain in your life, Bee."

Then she drops my sleeve and skip-hops away like she can't get out of my life fast enough.

100

The next day is Saturday and I spend the whole day being mad at Ruth Ellen. As anybody worth her salt knows, getting good and boiled up under your skin is what helps you start feeling better about things.

On Sunday I am ready to think on if I was wrong. I sit on the porch swing wrapped in a blanket with Peabody snuggled up to me and list all the awful things Francine ever did to me and Ruth Ellen on one side of my mind and what I did to Francine on the other. On one hand I am sure my revenge was right, on the other I am a tiny bit unsure.

When you chew on your troubles like they are taffy, sometimes things get so stuck inside you do not know the right way of things. I turn to my dog. "What do you think?" But all he does is wag his stumpy tail.

I am lonesome without Ruth Ellen. I drink many cups of tea to get any bits of bad taste out of my mouth and sit on the swing for the rest of the morning. It is November, but the sun is shining, and it is warm in my blanket. When nothing else helps, Peabody and I go out and watch Cordelia.

We watch her eat these things from her food bucket: apple peels from the apple cake, eggshells from the batch of pickled eggs Mrs. Potter said we needed on hand, celery ends, potato skins, carrot peels, and leftover casserole that nobody wanted, not even Peabody.

I notice how Cordelia is blooming and blossoming right

in front of my eyes from all the love and all the corn and how she must be three times the size she was when Bobby bought her from that farmer outside Springfield. I wince about the horrible things Mrs. Marsh said about butchering, and I hope Cordelia has forgotten all about it, because I sure am trying.

"Come on, Cordelia. What you need is some exercise. I'm going to give you another chance at running."

I've been thinking on how I would like to see where Francine lives. "I want to have myself a look," I tell Peabody and Cordelia. "But you'll have to be very quiet or we'll get caught. And we surely do not want that."

It takes quite a while to get Cordelia interested in leaving her pen. She is very fond of her shed and the straw pile and her food bucket and the fence where the squirrels cross.

It is quite a long way to the cemetery, much farther than to Ruth Ellen's. The cool air fills my lungs as I pump my arms and feel my body move. My muscles warm and stretch. I stop several times to call, "Here, pig, here, pig," and pull out some corn so I can get Cordelia back on track because she is more interested in chasing chipmunks than running to Francine's.

There is a hill overlooking the cemetery, and we run to the top. A small gray house with a steep roof and a black door sits on the other side. I wonder why Francine's grandpa would build a house right here so close to a cemetery, with all the statues so near they could watch you sleep if you leave your windows open. Sometimes, what folks do makes no sense to me.

The house is quiet as brick. There is no smoke rising from the chimney, no clothesline creaking from heavy blankets, no dog barking on the front step. It is all an empty sheet of paper: no chickens, no children shooting jacks on the porch, no cat. It's quiet and stripped bare; only the shadows move.

After a while the door swings open and Francine walks out. She pulls her jacket tight over the dress her papa gave her. She sits on the top step and hugs her knees and rocks herself. After a while, her shoulders shake.

The wind picks up and the bare branches above us scratch at each other like old bones. Peabody sits close by me, watching the lonely scene. Cordelia is nosing around the bottom of an oak tree. She likes acorns especially well and I am glad that aside from a few grunts she is mostly quiet. We are too far away for Francine to hear us anyhow. And even when she looks up in our direction, and I slip behind a tree, I don't think she can see us.

I think about my house, where Mrs. Potter is always waiting on the porch and the swing creaks in the wind and Peabody jumps and yelps as soon as he sees me and he flies down the steps and into my arms. There is always the smell of something good baking in the oven (thanks to me). Cordelia will snuggle up and nuzzle my ear anytime I want and Mrs. Swift is forever asking me to look things up in the dictionary and telling me how girls need to make something of their lives.

"Let's go home," I say to my pig and my little dog.

Things may not be perfect at our house, but they are much better than this.

101

Mrs. Potter says we all need days of rest, because it makes us stronger. She and Mrs. Swift nap most of every afternoon now. Mrs. Swift leans back from her autobiography after just a few minutes of work and dozes in her chair. Sometimes she does this while I am looking up a word for her in the dictionary. They eat nothing now, not even cake, and they sip only weak tea.

That night after I crawl into bed Mrs. Potter comes in and whispers good night and sits in my rocking chair. Peabody is snuggled up against me.

"You said you knew my mama," I whisper. "You keep promising you'll tell me about her and you haven't yet, and I really need to know about her."

Mrs. Potter looks out to the hall. Then she stands up and limps to the door and closes it. "Mrs. Swift doesn't think you are ready to hear everything. But I do. So I am going to tell you. Yes, we both knew your mama, Bee. We already told you that."

"I know, but what was she like? Ruth Ellen's mama told me my mama lived right here in this house and she slid down the stair railing and that means she ate food in our kitchen and slept in our bedrooms." This last thought is sweet like caramel and I twirl it around my tongue to make it last. "Which bedroom was hers?" I whisper.

Mrs. Potter rubs Peabody's belly the way he likes so.

"This was her room, Bee."

Of course it was, I tell myself. My mama would want the room wallpapered with little red berries and tiny sprigs of ivy skipping up the walls, the lace billowing from the four tall windows that are so big they begin at the ceiling and end at the floor, and the bed with the lace canopy.

"What was she like?"

"Well, she was a lot like you." Mrs. Potter leans back and closes her eyes. "She was about your height and skinny as a beanpole with long brown curly hair, just like you. She had one leg that was all twisted from polio."

I sit up so fast, Peabody gets bounced all around the bed and he jumps onto Mrs. Potter's lap.

"No one ever told me that." I try to remember what I can of my mama but all I see is a mama with her arms around me. I do not see a twisted leg.

"Yes, polio is what killed your grandmother. Your grandfather just about went out of his mind when his little girl got so sick with it, too. When she got better, he hid her away so no one would tease her about her leg."

"And my papa?"

"Ahhh, yes, Tommy Lee Hockenberry fell in love with Bernadette. They were both sixteen and they met when his traveling show came to town. She snuck out of the house, and your grandfather didn't know. Tommy Lee could look past her twisted leg. Your grandfather didn't like him at all."

"Why?"

"Old Man Bradford had hidden Bernadette away for a long, long time. He hired a governess to teach her at home so she wouldn't be teased. He didn't think anyone could look after her the way he did."

"But my papa was good?"

Mrs. Potter grins. "Yes, Beatrice. Tommy Lee Hockenberry gave no heed to the looks of folks who knew no better." She smiles. "And your mama was very strong. Even with her twisted leg. Doctors told her having a baby would be too dangerous for her. They said she was weakened in all sorts of ways from the polio, but she wanted you very, very much. Yes, she was strong. Just like her grandmothers before her. It runs in the family." She chuckles and winks at me.

I feel my heart racing. "Did you help her, too?" I whisper.

"When she needed us. And we were there for her mother before her. Your grandmother's name was Avalyn Rose."

I take this in. "And did you appear only to them, too?"

Mrs. Potter reaches for her cane. "Yes, Bee. We have a history of doing that." It takes a few tries for her to get up out of her chair. "Now get some sleep, Bee. It's late."

She limps to the door in the moonlight and turns around. "We've found one photograph of your mama when she was a girl. Would you like it?"

I jump off the bed. Peabody wags his stumpy tail, wondering where we are going.

"Tomorrow, Bee." Mrs. Potter chuckles. "It's in the attic in an old trunk your grandfather kept. We'll get it tomorrow when it's light. Now, get back in bed."

After she leaves, I watch the thin shadows move across my wallpaper and feel my heart soar. Now I know that my papa, Tommy Lee Hockenberry, loved my mama, Bernadette, very much. I am a little stronger just thinking about that. I look around my room at the wallpaper with the ivy growing up and when I climb into bed I pretend I am my mama bouncing around on the fat mattress. Then Peabody gives me another chance to be still and he curls up next to me and I feel my dog's nose pressed against my knee. It is very comforting to have a dog who loves you.

I wonder if my mama had a dog who loved her, too.

102

Before breakfast, before I am dressed, before I have even brushed my teeth, I knock softly on Mrs. Potter's door.

"Can we get the picture?" I have my blanket wrapped around me and my socks on.

Mrs. Potter rocks in her chair. She pulls herself up and wraps herself in an old dressing gown. Her bed is made, her pillows puffed, her quilt folded neatly at the bottom, same as yesterday and the day before.

"It doesn't look like you slept in the bed at all."

She chuckles. "Not much anymore."

The attic door is at the end of the hall. We tiptoe past Mrs. Swift's room. Mrs. Potter opens the door carefully so it doesn't creak. "Walk slowly. The stairs are very steep."

It is true. A staircase shoots straight up. Mrs. Potter takes one step at a time, bringing both feet up on a step before moving to the next. I am so eager I could fly to the top and it takes quite a bit of effort to slow myself down. Peabody is having a hard time being patient about things, too.

It is very dusty and very dark. There is no light except for the sun sifting through a small window at the peak. I breathe in the old smell of the attic.

"She used to play up here. See, those are her dolls."

I look where Mrs. Potter is pointing. There is a toy dinner table set with dishes, and dolls with dark curls sit at each of the chairs. "Look!" I say, beaming as I pick through a trunk of doll clothes and another of toy china.

Warm old wood and dust and cobwebs mingle with oak dressers and paintings and rugs. There are boxes and boxes of things wrapped in old newspaper and stacks of books and magazines.

"Beatrice?" Mrs. Potter is at the far end under the window. She has the cover of a trunk raised. I nearly forgot what we came up here for.

I hurry over and peer into the trunk. On top of a pile of photos is a framed picture of a little girl. I hold my breath and reach for it and stare into the gray eyes of a smiling girl in pigtails. Except for the mark on my face, she looks an awful lot like me.

I stare for a very long time. "There's no more pictures?" I ask finally, feeling the sad emptiness of wanting more and there not being more.

Mrs. Potter leans back on her cane. "Your grandfather didn't take any more pictures because he thought it would hurt her to see herself all crippled. He had no mirrors in this house. He was an odd man. Some folks mean well, and they are still very wrong."

I look into the little girl's eyes. I think maybe I see a part of myself. I wonder if she would like Peabody and Cordelia.

We do not hear Mrs. Swift climbing the stairs and even Peabody jumps when she clears her throat.

"What are you all doing up here?" Her voice is hard. She looks from Mrs. Potter to me to Peabody. I stand still. Peabody whines.

Mrs. Potter takes a step toward me. She gives Mrs. Swift a long silent look. "It's time, Abigail."

I breathe deeply and hold the picture tight.

"I was just telling Beatrice that her grandfather was very wrong to try and keep so many things hidden." She raises an eyebrow.

Mrs. Swift is quiet for a moment. I can see her chest rise and fall. I hold my breath. I think maybe Peabody is holding his breath, too.

Then Mrs. Swift walks over to me and touches my hair. "It's the same color, isn't it? You remind me of her, Beatrice. It's really something, isn't it, Mrs. Potter?"

Mrs. Potter grins. She feeds Peabody a tea biscuit to keep him quiet while we are all talking about serious things.

"Well, if we are going to show her the picture," whispers Mrs. Swift, "we should show her the other thing, too. Come here, Beatrice."

She walks over to a bookcase pushed up against the wall. It is lined with many old and very dusty books. On the top is a metal box. Mrs. Swift fumbles with the latch. "You do it, Beatrice, my hands aren't what they were."

She pushes the box to me. It takes a few tries to get the rusted latch to open. When I do, there are at least a dozen fat leather envelopes inside.

"There should be enough to get you through if you are careful and conserve. If you are especially thrifty, you should be able to go to college on this. There is a lot of money here, dear, and you know how I feel about getting an education and making something of yourself. It is the best revenge."

I look at her quickly and study her eyes to see if she knows what I did to Francine. All I see are deep lines around her eyes and a softness inside.

Mrs. Potter holds one of the fat envelopes to the window

and fans through all the bills. "Your grandfather might have been very misguided about his daughter, but he sure knew how to save his money."

Mrs. Potter giggles and before I know it Mrs. Swift is joining in and Peabody and I are just looking at each other.

103

Of course the first thing I want to do is go tell Ruth Ellen all about my mama. There's something about having a mama that makes you want to show her off. I tuck the picture in the pocket of my overalls.

I run all the way to Ruth Ellen's house without hardly stopping. I like running in the cold. I like how you don't get so hot. Most of the time I am fast as a horse.

Ruth Ellen is sitting on her porch winding pine boughs into a circle. Sammy is trying to help. "Would you stop hanging on me?" she tells him. "I don't want to be playing with you *all the time*. I just want to make this wreath *by myself*."

She pushes him away. Sammy sobs and runs into the house.

Ruth Ellen crosses her arms and her mama comes out on the porch. You can tell she has something to say to Ruth Ellen. When she sees me, though, pushing my toe through the dirt, waiting to talk to Ruth Ellen, she shakes her head and walks back into the house. You can hear Sammy sobbing and his mama saying things like "Shush, it will be all right. Hush now."

I wait awhile for Ruth Ellen to calm down. She ties the wreath with ribbon. I look at how nice the yard is and how the big maple limbs spread over the thin shed with the chickens pecking all around. I could live in a place like this, I think, breathing in all the crisp air around me.

"What you doing here, Bee?"

I grind my toe in the dirt, planning out exactly how I am going to say it. I do not want to get it wrong.

"Ruth Ellen?"

"What do you want?" She crosses her arms in front of her. She is a mad hen.

"Maybe I shouldn't have told your mama's secret. But I know I needed to make Francine stop hurting me and that was the only way I could think, to tell things that would hurt her in front of her friends. At least I didn't hide. It felt good, actually."

"You could have told someone that Francine was hurting you. That would have stopped her. You didn't have to tell my mama's secret. You're only going to make it worse this way." Ruth Ellen flings her words like mud.

I fling them right back: "You knew, all the kids knew, and nobody did anything to help me, Ruth Ellen."

"You could have told Miss Healy how bad it was. You could have told my mama."

I think on that. Then I say, "You could have told your mama, Ruth Ellen."

I check to see if I am getting through. Ruth Ellen's eyes are softer. That is a good sign. She sighs. The porch door slams and Sammy comes out and sits down on the top step, watching us.

"I hate Francine, too, Bee. Sometimes I don't know what to do when I am getting teased. Sometimes I don't want to worry my mama any more than she is already worried about my leg and about my papa being missing and about how are we are going to make it through another week living so bare like we do."

I reach over and hug Ruth Ellen because I have been missing her so and when I do I remember the picture. I pull it out of my pocket. "It's my mama."

"Oh, Bee," Ruth Ellen whispers, and we look at the picture for a long time, at the girl with the pigtails and the happy eyes. "She looks just like you."

"Yes," I say, and we keep looking at the picture until Ruth Ellen winces and bends over and rubs at her leg.

"Is it bothering you very much?" I ask.

"All the time. I want this thing to come off."

"Does the doctor say when?"

"No. He doesn't tell me anything, and when he does talk to me he talks like I am three. He won't tell me when it can come off. I hate him, Bee."

She bends over double then and her shoulders shake and I hold her. I am quiet so she can cry on and on because I know all about grown-ups not telling you things and how you have to be careful to pick the ones you can believe in.

104

There is the wonderful warm smell of bread baking as soon as I get in the door. Ruth Ellen stays outside because she doesn't want her mama worrying about the tears. Ruth Ellen's mama has her arms in the sink, soap suds climbing halfway up her arms. She is washing the big wooden bread bowl.

"I am sorry." I say this to her back because it is easier. I say it quick before I change my mind.

She pulls her arms from the bowl and carefully wipes her hands on a blue-and-white-checked towel, all neat and folded on the counter. When she turns, I see there are tears in her eyes. She must be thinking about Ruth Ellen's papa.

She smiles softly. "Whatever could you have done wrong, Bee? Would you like some apple cake?"

I say I surely would and she cuts me a fat slice.

"Where's Ruth Ellen?" She looks out the window over the sink.

"She told me to come in. She's making up with Sammy."

Ruth Ellen's mama smiles about that and pours me a mug of milk. I eat all the cake and drink all the milk before I talk more. I need time to think on things before I say anything.

"Now, what is it you wanted to talk to me about?" Ruth Ellen's mama sits across from me and pours herself a cup of tea. She cuts me another slice of cake.

"You know that secret about Francine's papa you told us about? How he took off with that showgirl?"

I wait for Ruth Ellen's mama to nod. Already there is worry in her eyes. "Well, I told Francine about it, in front of all her friends so everybody would know."

Ruth Ellen's mama puts her cup down. "But why, Bee? That's an awful thing to say to someone. I expect you hurt that girl terribly. And that was a confidence I shared that is going to hurt Francine's mother. I suspect I shouldn't have told you."

I nod. "Francine hurts me all the time."

Ruth Ellen's mama wants to know what I mean, so I tell her the whole long sad story of everything awful Francine ever did to me. I tell her about the ugly tree and spitting (I leave out how I spit first) and how Francine said she would lie down on a train track if she looked like me. I tell Ruth Ellen's mama about Francine saying I was dirty as the sole of her shoe and how I was too ugly to be alive. I tell her about hitting me so hard right across my diamond and about the sparrow.

It takes Ruth Ellen's mama a moment to take everything in. Then she says, "That is very terrible, Bee. I didn't know." She sets her cup in front of her and moves it back and forth slowly in figure eights. "It must have been awful to be treated by that girl with such cruelty. Did it help to hurt her back?"

I shrug because I'm not sure what I am supposed to say. She twirls her cup a few more times. Then she puts her hand over my hand.

"You know, Bee, I did the same thing when I was your age. A boy from the neighborhood tried to burn my cat's tail and I chased him all the way back to his house and broke his nose."

The picture of Ruth Ellen's mama walloping a boy and breaking his nose is so unbelievable I can't help myself and I giggle.

Ruth Ellen's mama smiles. "It was the same boy who teased your mother. I got him good."

I look up quickly. "I didn't know she was teased."

Ruth Ellen's mama nods. "Yes, she was. Not often, because your grandfather kept her hidden away. I remember that birthday party, though. We were all sitting on the porch with the monkey and all the presents and the cake and punch and that boy and his friends snuck up on us, yelling, 'Cripple, cripple, what you doing with a cripple.' Your grandfather sent everyone home right after. I broke the boy's nose a few days later."

"Did it help you feel better?"

"For a while. Maybe I should have told someone instead, though. As I've gotten older I've wondered if I didn't hurt myself by hurting him. I don't know." She looks at me. "It's complicated, isn't it?"

I nod. She cuts herself a piece of cake. "You know, Bee, I'm not sure your grandfather gave your mother a chance to handle the teasing herself. He hid her away. That's not right, either."

No, I think, but it might be easier. I sigh. "What else do you remember about my mama?"

"Not a lot, I wasn't with her much, but I do remember she laughed a lot and she looked just like you."

That reminds me. I pull my mama's picture from my pocket. "It's the only one we could find."

"Yes, that's her! See? She looks just like you."

Except there's no diamond. I rub my mama's face, touch the spot where a mark could begin but doesn't.

Ruth Ellen's mama sits back and watches me. "Bee, have you noticed you don't hold your hair over your face when you are here?"

I stop chewing so I can tell her that yes, I have noticed that.

"And Ruth Ellen says you do not hold your hair down like that when you are in class anymore, either."

I nod that, yes, I have noticed that, too.

"And I imagine you don't when you are home, either?"

"That's right," I whisper, running my finger over my mama's face.

"Everyone is always going to notice your birthmark, Bee. It's like Ruth Ellen's brace. You can't help but notice. But it's what people do after they notice that's important. Do they treat you like a person with dignity? Or do they baby you and coddle you or make fun of you or worse?"

"Yes," I say, sitting back, thinking on that.

"You have to be strong, you have to stand up for yourself, you can't hide and you can't let yourself be hidden away." Ruth Ellen's mama sips at her tea.

"Your grandfather was wrong," she whispers. "Very wrong." Her voice trails off and then she gets a funny look on her face. I can tell she is thinking on things.

105

After Christmas, Ruth Ellen and I catch Mrs. Marsh nosing around the school. The morning after that she is waiting by the office when we come in the door, all bundled up for the snow.

"Humph," she mumbles when she sees me.

"Humph," I say, walking right by.

That afternoon when I am reading *Heidi*, Mr. Taft says he needs to talk to me. Good grief. Again? Susan grabs hold of me and I have to pull her off before I can stand up and follow him.

We walk all the way back to the dark little office and I sit on the same hard wooden chair. I sit on my hands so I will not try and pull my hair over my face. I want to see if I can be different.

Mr. Taft says he wants to talk about my home situation. "Now, tell me more about these aunts you live with. Are they able to care for you?"

I am still mad at them because Christmas was not very much fun with me making a big stuffed turkey and mashed potatoes and honey-glazed squash and them not eating a thing. I would have liked to invite Ruth Ellen over for leftovers, but how can I explain my aunts to anyone?

"Beatrice?" Mr. Taft leans against his desk and folds his arms over his chest. Lordy, I already went through this whole thing. I do not want to do it again. "We are fine," I tell him. "F-I-N-E."

"And you're eating well and getting plenty of exercise and sunshine?"

I nod.

He writes that down. Next he wants to know how I am feeling about my birthmark, like it is any of his business.

I shift around in my seat, trying to get my pride strong. "I am fine. F-I-N-E." I am sharp in my voice like I am finished with him.

I do not tell him how Ruth Ellen's mama helped me get some things straight in my head. I wonder if Mr. Taft notices how I am not hiding and now I am not holding my hair.

Snow falls outside the window and the dirt where we leaned against the building for recess is blanketed in white. Everything is changed. I breathe deeply, just like Pauline taught me.

Yes, I think as I stand up and walk right out of his office. I am different now.

106

The letter arrives two days later.

Dear Madams,

You are requested to meet in the office of the principal on Friday to discuss the guardianship and class placement of Beatrice Rose Hockenberry.

Anthony Hutchins, Principal

"Did you notice there is no 'Thank you kindly'?" asks Mrs. Swift. "Terrible manners. Just terrible." She is sitting at the kitchen table, sipping from her cup. She has switched to plain hot water with a bit of honey, hardly any nourishment at all. Mrs. Potter is very quiet. I put a piece of molasses cake in front of her, but she won't take a bite. Peabody wants to sit up on her lap, but she won't let him. She looks weak as her tea.

"Why don't you eat? You won't last long if you don't eat."

"I just need a little nap." There is a long pause while Mrs. Swift stirs her hot water.

"You're not going, are you?" I reach for Mrs. Potter's cake and take a bite.

"That's right. We're not going to that meeting, Bee." Mrs. Potter sips her tea.

"Why not this once? Why can't you be there for me when I need you?" I finish the cake. Mrs. Potter looks down at her tea. I jump up. "Why do you hide here all the time and never let anyone see you? Why don't you at least show yourself to Mrs. Marsh? You know she's the cause of this whole thing. She was at my school the other day!"

"We came for you, Beatrice. Not for anyone else." Mrs. Swift sips at her hot water. "And we won't be here forever, just until you can stand on your own feet."

They've been talking like this lately, and each time they do I feel a bear gnawing at the bottom of my belly. "Where are you going?" I have to reach out and touch Mrs. Potter to make sure I can still feel the warmth in her arm. Already she is fading so I can hardly see her.

"We will not leave until everything is set." Mrs. Swift looks up at me. Her eyes are thin pools of violet.

"Until what's set?"

"Soon enough, my dear, we'll explain everything." Mrs. Swift stands up and takes Mrs. Potter by the arm and they help each other walk to the library for another nap.

"Oh, would you look up the word *prevaricate* for me, Beatrice? I have a feeling it is going to make me very angry, but I do need to know."

107

"Where are your guardians?" the principal wants to know when I get called to the office.

"My aunts?"

"Yes, they were supposed to attend this meeting. They are already half an hour late."

"Oh," I say, whispering, "they are ill."

The principal sits forward. "I don't care whether they are feeling well or not. They must be present at this meeting. We need to discuss your situation. You are not supposed to be here. They are."

Lordy. I tap my foot. My face is hot. My diamond must be blood-red by now. "They are so old, they do get terribly tired," I whisper. I look at the floor.

The principal sits back and looks at me for a while. I want to cover my diamond because I know it is being looked at, but I sit on my hands instead.

In a few minutes, Mrs. Marsh knocks on the door and wants to come in and the principal tells her to have a seat, like they have this all arranged.

She sits forward and looks over at me. "I tell you there are no aunts. She is in that house herself."

And then Ruth Ellen's mama is here, wanting to come in. "May I have a word?" She is tapping at the door. "It is about this child."

The principal sits back and says how this is very odd,

that Ruth Ellen's mama has not been invited, but since there is no one else who will speak for me, yes, she can come in. I hear her tell Sammy he must sit quietly in the hall with his book.

Then she comes into the office. She is surprised as I am to see Mrs. Marsh, but she is quiet about it as she sits beside me on the sofa and takes my hand. I thank her with my eyes for coming. I told her yesterday I didn't think my aunts would come.

"Her aunts are feeling poorly and are wondering if I could speak for them? They are quite aged. I have never seen a child better cared for, if that helps."

"This is highly unusual," the principal says. "I don't know."

Mrs. Marsh stands up. "I keep telling you, there are no aunts."

"How can you say that?" says Ruth Ellen's mama. "Why, I just had tea with them this morning."

"I thought you said they were feeling poorly," says Mrs. Marsh. She has narrowed her eyes.

"I brought ginger tea to them. Beatrice told me yesterday that they have been feeling poorly and probably wouldn't be able to attend this meeting."

I know Ruth Ellen's mama is making everything up. She gives Mrs. Marsh a sharp look and turns toward the principal.

"The house is clean and polished and cared for. The ladies love their niece dearly. And they said to tell you her older cousin Pauline is coming back to live with them. She's twenty-four and is surely old enough to be Bee's guardian as the aunts are growing older."

I look up quickly. Ruth Ellen's mama winks very slowly and carefully so no one else can see.

"This is a lie," says Mrs. Marsh. Her face is red, darker than my diamond. "I have been watching over the house she is living in for several years. The gentleman who owned it has recently passed and now it is in probate while ownership is determined."

"What do you have against this child, ma'am?" Ruth Ellen's mama asks. "Don't you know she is the heir?"

And then everyone is looking at Mrs. Marsh, which is a very nice change.

The principal clears his throat and turns to Mrs. Marsh. "Do you have proof that the child is living alone?"

Mrs. Marsh is losing ground. "Well, no," she sputters. "Except no one is ever there."

"Maybe they're out a lot," snaps the principal, "taking walks or napping or doing things old ladies like to do."

He leans back and crosses his arms over his chest and watches me for a minute. Then he sits up. "Okay, we will proceed as before. Back to class, Beatrice."

Ruth Ellen's mama sits up. "Sir, when you suggested this class, it sounded like a nice safe place for Ruth Ellen because she was being teased so much about her leg. Now I see it is something much different. I do not think these children should be hidden away to make things easier for them. It embarrasses them and makes them different, and they will never learn to be part of anything. Perhaps if anyone needs a special class like this it is all the poor-mannered children you have around here."

And that's how all the attention flies off me. Ruth Ellen's mama has given me a present, tied with a bow. Thank you, I say with just my eyes, and she smiles back, and I am proud of her speaking up like this.

"I shall pursue this," Ruth Ellen's mama says. "There is a great deal of discussion about this over at the university among the professors and their students. I attended a meeting last week. They call themselves progressive."

The principal sputters. "I don't know," he says. "Children like this need to be separated in a class by themselves. They need the care and attention that can only be provided when they are separate."

"They need to be included," says Ruth Ellen's mama, standing up and getting ready to walk out. "They don't need to be looked at."

I am glowing so much over Ruth Ellen's mama's accomplishment, and then I realize what is so funny about what the principal is saying.

I let my head fill with the pictures of Robert and Thomas dive-bombing and Susan climbing all over Ruth Ellen, and Ruth Ellen letting her, and then of Susan falling and me losing the race and Jonathan coming up and patting my back.

"You're right," I say, grinning more and more and more until my smile stretches across my diamond. "We are in a class by ourselves."

And then I laugh out loud.

108

Miss Healy wants to know all about the meeting when I get back to class. She brings me over to the rocking chair, where we can talk privately.

"There has been some speculation here that you may be living in some unusual circumstances. Is there any truth to what I am hearing?"

She takes my hand and squeezes it. She looks at me kindly. I know she wants the best for me.

"My aunts love me very much," I tell her. "I am fine."

Miss Healy nods. I go over to our table and Susan wraps her arms around me and Ruth Ellen asks where I have been. I look at the arithmetic paper in front of me. The numbers swim around like they don't know where they belong. I rub my eyes. My stomach rumbles.

After a while, Miss Healy comes over and kneels beside me. "Why don't you go out and sit under that tree, Beatrice, and work on your basket for a while. When you get some of those loose ends all woven together, you can come back in and make another start." She hands me a piece of banana bread. "You might be hungry."

I think maybe she is right about things. I put on my coat and go out and sit in the sun and wonder about how sometimes things fall apart and how sometimes, if you work on it, they get put back together. And then I set the basket in my lap and begin weaving, stopping every so often for another bite of banana bread.

At supper that night I tell Mrs. Potter and Mrs. Swift about the meeting and about what Miss Healy asked about them. They have not touched the molasses cake I put on the table.

Mrs. Swift looks over at Mrs. Potter and clears her throat, a thin, fleeting sound, and Mrs. Potter turns to me. "I think, dear, it is time to get Pauline."

Maybe so, I think, my heart breaking all over again as I try to block out the last time I saw her, when Arthur was pulling her away.

109

The next afternoon while we are sitting around Ruth Ellen's table eating spice cake, her mama wants to know if I would like to learn how to make shepherd's pie.

My mouth is so stuffed I have to wait a minute to answer, but I nod right away and I think she gets the idea. "Peabody would love it," I say.

While we are browning the hamburger, Ruth Ellen takes Sammy out for some fresh air so Ruth Ellen's mama can help me cook. She has been telling me it is very relaxing to be chopping and measuring and sautéing and mixing. "It is nice to keep your mind concentrated on something and not on your troubles."

Yes, I know all about needing to do that, I tell her while I am watching her mince garlic. I wonder if she chops and minces to help her forget they haven't heard from Ruth Ellen's papa in so long. She hands me another clove and shows me how to smash it with the side of the knife so the skin falls off. Then she shows me how to chop in a fine mince. "You kind of roll the knife, see?"

Then we chop onions. I am very good at this and I show her how I do it.

"Why, that's the best onion dice I've ever seen!" Ruth Ellen's mama starts giggling because she knows how much experience I've had with chopping onions.

It is relaxing to be cooking with Ruth Ellen's mama. I forget all about the meeting in the principal's office and start daydreaming about how I would like to bake a birthday cake for myself with real sugar and real buttercream frosting. I do like buttercream very much.

"You can take half of this shepherd's pie home to your aunts for supper. Do you think they will like it?" Ruth Ellen's mama is hunting through the cabinet for a big enough pan to bake everything in.

I think so. I tell her all about how they don't eat much and I am quite worried about them.

"Tell me more about your aunts, Bee. I haven't gotten to meet them yet."

I chop celery and think about how to describe Mrs. Potter and Mrs. Swift. "Well, they are awfully aggravating sometimes because they do not let anyone get to meet them. They do not like Mrs. Marsh at all."

"No," agrees Ruth Ellen's mama. "I can see why."

She giggles and then I do, too. I reach for another stalk of celery. She peels and washes six potatoes and hands them to me. "We need these in small bite-sized pieces."

She starts peeling and chopping carrots. "Bee, your aunts are really real and you're not just making them up so you can have a place to live? Because you know you could live with us anytime you want."

I look at her and my eyes start filling up and I do not know if it is the onions or the kindness she just said.

"They are real," I tell her. "Peabody loves them, too."

"Well," she says slowly, "I guess you cannot fool a dog." And then Ruth Ellen's mama, being the way she is, so good about children and what they feel and what they have to say, says she believes me.

But she tells me that perhaps it is time to go get Pauline.

"Funny," I say. "That's just what my aunts said."

110

We have to wait for spring. Even a stay-put show like the one Ellis set up in Poughkeepsie has to close for winter.

I use the time to write to *The Billboard* and get a subscription. Bobby told me he won't try and find me until the war is over and he is done building bombers but I want to be ready. So I stuff some money in an envelope and carefully write the address on the front and mail it, hoping I have done everything right.

One day in late February, the postman drops my first copy of *The Billboard* in our mailbox. Without even telling Mrs. Potter or Mrs. Swift, I grab it and race up to my room and stretch out on my bed, with Peabody beside me. There is a picture of Lawrence Welk on the cover and a "Gone to War" ad from Wurlitzer on the back. It seems all the people who make pianos, accordions, and phonographs have stopped making music and are now working on the war effort until we get our victory. "Work faster," I whisper.

I flip open the pages and look around for an advertisement that says "Anyone knowing whereabouts of Robert Benson." I look at each inch of print. A traveling show in Norfolk is looking for a tattooed man and a carnival in Little Rock wants someone to run a penny pitch and a fun house. A show in Baton Rouge will pay a merry-go-round foreman twenty-five dollars a week.

There's a "Hotzi Notzi" pincushion for sale where you

get to stick your sewing pins in Hitler's behind, and a story about greeting cards being a big seller during wartime, especially Valentine's Day cards. There are money belts and boxes of paper shamrocks for sale and oodles of fortune-telling cards. I search through the entire issue twice, but there is no mention of Robert Benson. Peabody is wondering if I am going to look through everything again. No, I am not, I tell him, tucking the magazine under my pillow. Reading the whole thing again won't make me feel any better, but I know what will.

"Come on," I say, and we go take the compost bucket full of scraps out to Cordelia. I have never known anyone who loves getting their back scratched as much as my pig does, so while she is rooting around the apple peels and the squash seeds and the stale bits of bread stuck in the snow, I spend a good long while getting all the spots itched that need itching. She is getting so huge she doesn't want to run anymore. I don't care too much. I love her anyway.

Every so often she looks back at me to let me know I am doing everything just right.

111

One day when the lilacs are blooming outside Ruth Ellen's front door and there are baby chicks in her chicken shed peep-peeping and the barn swallows are back for another year, I know it is time to find Pauline.

Ruth Ellen's mama has planted early peas in the victory garden, and honeybees found the apple blossoms. Everything is reaching and stretching and growing, even Peabody. He is no longer a bag of bones and he has decided he likes napping with Ruth Ellen's cat more than chasing her, at least when the sun is shining.

We are all sitting around Ruth Ellen's kitchen table eating fried donuts and making our plan. I tell them how Ellis sent Pauline to his show in Poughkeepsie and she should be there now.

"But I thought you moved around all the time?" says Ruth Ellen. She is trying to find Poughkeepsie on the map.

"Our show moved. But Ellis was trying to keep the Poughkeepsie carnival in one place during show season— hire more singers and a flying trapeze and chimps and stuff like that—to attract more folks. That way he wouldn't have to worry about getting enough gasoline."

We look at how to get to New York. "Poughkeepsie is big," says Ruth Ellen, bending closer to the map.

"Yes," I say, knowing all about cities, because I think I have maybe seen the world.

On Saturday they pick me up in Ruth Ellen's automobile. We hope that with their gas ration stamps and my leather envelope, we will be able to get to Poughkeepsie. Ruth Ellen's mama has packed a picnic basket with peanut butter sandwiches and lemon squares. I think that is a nice touch. Pauline loves lemon squares.

Mrs. Potter and Mrs. Swift are half hidden behind the curtain. Mrs. Potter promised to give Cordelia plenty of corn and now she is holding Peabody up for me to see. I wave to them and hope everything will be just the same when I get back. I choke back tears and stare out the window until we turn a corner and the house disappears.

Part III

112

I do not tell anybody that Ellis keeps snakes under his hat. I don't tell them about the smell of Beech-Nut on his breath, or the way he creeps up on you so quiet your heart freezes solid. If I told them, we would never get Pauline.

My legs are already wobbling and all I'm doing is sitting in the backseat of this green automobile between Ruth Ellen, who is reading ahead in *Heidi*, and Sammy, who has his *Captain America* comic book on his lap. I make myself breathe in and out, in and out, just like Pauline taught me. I am better at breathing now that I am better at running. I look out the window at all the houses and all the little victory gardens getting cleaned up and ready for another planting season.

We have to pass the road that leads to the cemetery and Francine's house and I wonder if I will have to battle her again. I know Ellis is not the only wolf in the forest.

I breathe in and out, in and out, and just thinking about Ellis makes the warning light inside me go on and off, on and off.

113

The thing about traveling shows is you hear "The Farmer in the Dell" long before you see the rides. I have a headache before I get three feet out of the car.

"Woweeee," says Sammy.

"This is it?" says Ruth Ellen, skip-hopping through the gate. "You lived at one of these?"

The warning light is going on and off inside me and it feels like I have a pound of butter stuck in my chest.

I nod and have to clear my throat over and over before I can get anything out. "See that long line of hauling trucks down there? Pauline and I lived in the back of one of those."

"Woweeee," says Sammy again. "Can we go on that?" He is pointing to the Ridee-O.

"No," says Ruth Ellen's mama, watching the wheel spin and the folks scream, and we see a different Theodore the Cripple getting looked at and some other Silas Meany keeps his eye on the ground in case any wallets go flying. I wonder about LaVerne, Big Ben, and Vivian and what happened to them.

I pull my hair tight over my face. Ruth Ellen's mama notices. She does not know Ellis.

The first surprise is that Eldora is working the hot dog cart. She is chopping onions under a sign that says, RATIONING = 1 HOT DOG A PERSON. EAT ALL THE POPCORN YOU WANT.

"Well, me oh my, is that you, little Bee? We were wondering what ever happened to you." She throws down the knife and rushes out from under the tarp and gives me a big sloppy kiss and hugs me very close to her big self. I breathe an ocean of perfume. She brushes at my hair with her fingers because she was always jealous of my curls. I have to pull my hair tight over my diamond.

"Has Ellis seen you yet? He was madder than an old dog that you ran off like that. He looked for you, too."

My knees shake and my legs wobble. I do not know if I have it in me to face Ellis again. I keep watching over my shoulder because I know wolves sneak up when you are not looking.

Eldora notices Ruth Ellen and her mama and Sammy. "You bringing her back?" she asks her mama.

"No." I say it sharp because I do not want Eldora to get the wrong idea about me taking over the hot dog cart again.

"Too bad," says Eldora, going back so she can turn the hot dogs. "I'm getting mighty tired of this, but Ellis didn't think fortune-telling was making us enough money. My predictions kept going wrong. It's hard to predict the future during a war, you know."

I do not have time for this. "I need to find Pauline. Do you know where she is?"

Eldora laughs softly. "Well, I'll be. You haven't seen her yet? She's resting in that last truck back there. Holy cow, won't you be surprised when you see her."

Resting? In the middle of the day? That doesn't sound like Pauline. "Why isn't she running the hot dog cart?"

"Go see for yourself." A line is forming, and I have to

keep pulling on my hair and turning away because one mama and her two boys keep trying to have themselves a look.

Eldora goes back and turns her hot dogs. I look over at the hauling truck. And then before you can say Jack Sprat, I am running toward the truck and rushing up the ladder and climbing in the back of the truck and there is Pauline, just getting up from a nap, her hair all uncombed and flying all over the place, and then I am jumping in her arms. Only there's not as much room as before on account of her belly being the size of a watermelon.

"Bee?" She whispers it in my ear like maybe she has forgot what I look like. "Bee?" And then she is crying and holding me, saying, "Oh, Bee, I didn't know how I would ever find you. Ellis said you left, and I thought I lost you forever."

And then the tears are rolling down my cheeks and I am home because she is wrapping her arms around me and we are together. The fit is not quite right, though, because of her belly, and I stand back and look at the size of it. Pauline looks at the floor of the truck. "I'm going to have a baby, Bee," she whispers.

There is a bruise on Pauline's cheek, dark as a rose at dusk. I reach up to touch it, but she winces, and turns her head away.

"He left me, Bee." She reaches for me and sobs against my shoulder and I brace myself so I can steady her. There is another bruise on her arm and she is very thin in all the places where there is no baby growing. I hold her tighter, feel her shaking. I rub her back and say many soft things in her ear. I know all about being left.

"You were right, Bee," says Pauline, hugging me so tight

again that I can hardly breathe. "Arthur said he was going to marry me. But he never did."

I want to say, I told you, you silly, but I don't. I look back at Ruth Ellen and her mama and Sammy. They have moved closer to peek inside. They are careful not to interrupt.

"The baby's coming in June. Ellis isn't going to keep me on, not with a baby. It's not been a good year for him at all."

"Oh," I say, glad things aren't going so well for Ellis.

"Did you come back to stay, Bee?" Pauline is looking all worn out. She drops onto the mattress, even with Ruth Ellen and everyone watching.

"No, Pauline," I say, going over and sitting beside her, wondering how long it will take us to pack up her things. "I came to bring you home."

114

We hurry out past a new kind of look-see booth, one I have never heard of before: Japanese Shrunken Head.

"Woweeee," says Sammy. "Is it real?"

I shrug. A girl in pigtails and glasses and worn-through overalls stands inside a miniature circus tent with red, white, and blue American flags blowing on top. She holds up a shriveled head with its mouth sewed shut and a bone-and-feather necklace around its neck.

"Come on over and feel the shrunken head of a Japanese soldier captured by real live cannibal headhunters on the Philippine Islands. Come touch for a nickel. You'll never forget Pearl Harbor."

I feel pain in my heart just from looking. I grab Pauline's hand. Ruth Ellen's mama pulls Sammy away. "Bee, would you get us out of here, please?"

I walk us all toward the ticket booth, taking another glance around to see if there might be a Little Pig Race at this show and if maybe another Cordelia is here, and that is when I see Ellis over by the Tilt-A-Whirl, sniffing the air.

Pauline sees him, too, and tugs on my arm. "Bee, let's go."

Before we can get anywhere, though, Ellis sees me, and he rushes over, poking his finger out, straight at my face.

"Well, looky, looky, looky. Look who's wandered in." He

pulls his cowboy hat back, and I check to see if I can see the snakes under there. I can't, although I think maybe his eyes are yellow.

A very large man sits stuffed inside the ticket booth. It is not Fat Man Sam, but it looks just like him. I pull my hair tight over my diamond. I pull my other arm across my chest. It is chilly in Poughkeepsie in early May.

Ellis's eyes roll over Ruth Ellen's brace. Her mama wraps her arm around Ruth Ellen and pulls Sammy close. Pauline is shaking like a leaf.

Ellis turns back to me. "You think you can just come back any time you want and work here? After you left me like that? Well, you've got another thing coming. I ought to . . ."

I am carrying Pauline's suitcase, so he might be thinking I am coming back, rather than the truth of the matter. He steps closer and my legs wobble. I gulp in my breath and let Pauline lean against me. I pull my hair tighter over my diamond.

"It's gotten bigger, hasn't it?" He reaches for my hair but I turn away. He grins. I see sharp teeth. "You take a seat in the look-see booth and I'll let bygones be bygones. Folks will pay a lot to see that diamond you got."

Ruth Ellen's mama sucks in her breath. "Now, see here," she says.

Ellis turns quick to Ruth Ellen's mama and pushes his hat. "Thanks for bringing her back, ma'am. She owes me a lot."

"I'm not coming back." I say it while I am trying to hold Pauline up. She is very heavy on account of the watermelon.

"You owe me money, sweetheart. You got to stay and work for me and pay it all back. Otherwise I'm calling the cops, saying you robbed me blind."

Ruth Ellen's mama pulls on Ruth Ellen and Sammy. "I think it's time to go, Bee."

"Oh, yes," Ellis continues, "I took you on and let you stay here after your idiot mother and father got themselves killed. I could've dropped you off at an orphan house, but I didn't, no siree. I kept you on, fed you, and put a roof over your head."

I chew on what he is saying, about him keeping me on and putting a roof over my head, but it is all bad meat. I can feel Pauline shaking under her thin sweater.

"Bee, it's time to go, *now*," says Ruth Ellen's mama. She takes me by the shoulder, but I push her hand off without taking my eyes off Ellis. "I'm not hiding anymore." I say it strong, feeling a mountain begin to rise within me.

Ellis moves closer. He drools over my diamond. That's the worst part, the drooling.

"I don't owe you a nickel," I say, backing up. "You kept me on so one day you could sell my diamond to whoever would look. And I don't call a hauling truck a roof over my head."

"You owe me money, you got to stay and work for me."

"I don't owe you anything."

Ruth Ellen's mama steps forward. "That's it. Everyone to the car, *now*. You will leave us alone or I will call the police." She grabs hold of Sammy's shirt and nearly lifts him off the ground. But Sammy struggles and gets loose and points to the shrunken head. "Is it real?"

Ellis laughs. "Of course not. Is anything real around here?" He winks at me.

The mountain rises higher. Very slowly and carefully, I suck spit into my mouth. I whoosh it around, working up more, more, more, just like Bobby taught me. I gather a thick gob on the edge of my tongue and pucker my lips just as Ellis reaches for my diamond.

I step back, a girl eyeing a wolf.

He pulls his hat off so he can see me. I am surprised at his eyes. They are not yellow; they are thin and watery like he has the flu. There's not a single snake under there.

I laugh inside myself. I am a lion, eyeing a mouse. I shoot the spit at the ground beside his feet.

"Don't ever touch me again." I say it sharp, my voice low and deep, and he must hear the mountain in my voice that he never heard before because he takes a step back.

I lift my chin. My diamond shines. I let the mountain rise higher and higher until it fills every part of me.

Then, slowly and carefully, I tuck my hair behind my ears. And I let Ellis have a good look at the girl he cannot have.

115

We all hurry Pauline as fast as she can go, rushing past Eldora and the merry-go-round and the Ferris wheel, and Ruth Ellen's mama is telling Sammy how they will never visit another carnival again, not in her lifetime anyway.

My heart soars when I see a Little Pig Race and I have to stop for just a moment and go over and wouldn't you know it, a little pig that looks an awful lot like Cordelia comes running over to get her backside scratched.

When we finally reach the automobile, Ruth Ellen and her mama and Sammy sit in the front seat so I can have Pauline to myself. It is a very nice place to be, both of us wrapped up like that. Pauline naps quite a bit and I try not to think too much about Ellis or about the watermelon between us.

When we get home and Pauline and I walk in the front door, Peabody comes barking and barreling down the stairs and it takes him all of two seconds to remember Pauline.

"Bee, you still have the little dog!"

"It's Peabody," I say, and Pauline is trying to bend over and pat him, but it is not easy with the size of her belly.

"Oh, Bee," she says, tearing up just looking around at everything: the library with all the books, the tall staircase with the railing just made for sliding down, the parlor with all the lace cloths so you don't get the furniture dirty. It is a house a girl can call a home.

"But how did you do this? Who lives here?"

"We do," I say, leading her to the kitchen. "Plus my aunts, Mrs. Potter and Mrs. Swift."

They are not in the kitchen. I put on some tea. I cut fat slices of spice cake and give one to Pauline and one to me and one to Peabody. I am going to have to cut back on sweets for Peabody, now that he is getting so tubby.

"Where are they, Bee?" Pauline is eating her cake and drinking her tea and looking around the kitchen. The room smells of roses.

"They are very shy," I tell Pauline.

She raises an eyebrow. "Really?" She eats the cake and rubs her belly. She is too tired to wait for my aunts, so I take her upstairs and show her the guest room, the one with the buttercup walls. We both lose our breath when we walk in, it is so beautiful. Mrs. Swift and Mrs. Potter must have found the strength to get very busy. I guess company coming can do that to you.

"Oh, Bee. It is so pretty." Pauline goes over and sits on the four-poster bed and then lies back on the pink-and-blue quilt. She has four fat pillows just like me.

In the corner is a tiny crib all made up with white soft sheets. Somehow my aunts already knew about the baby coming. I tap on the bed and Peabody jumps up. He isn't so sure about things, but I tell him Pauline is someone he's going to get very close to, I am sure of it, so he might as well get started right now. When he is settled up on a pillow, I lie down, too, and it is almost like we are playing the ha-ha game. Except we are in Pauline's new bedroom now and not lying on the grass outside our hauling truck and there is a watermelon between us.

"Bee, I'm so sorry," Pauline whispers in my ear. "I'm sorry about leaving you. I should have never gone with Arthur. I'm sorry about everything."

I let the words pour over me and it is like I am getting washed in the kindness. It feels very nice to be apologized to.

116

"Don't you want to see Pauline?" Mrs. Swift and Mrs. Potter are sitting at the table, both a little slumped over.

Mrs. Potter gets up and tries to fill the kettle with water. It is very heavy and so I carry it to the stove. She tries to light the match, but she can't get a spark. She never has gotten the hang of the stove. "Why are you both hiding in here?" I ask as I light the burner and put the kettle on to heat.

"We're tired," Mrs. Swift snaps. "We've been busy."

"The room is very beautiful. Pauline is very happy. Thank you." I smile at them. "Don't you want to get to know her?"

The kettle whistles and I get up and make them both weak tea. I cut us all slices of spice cake. They both shake their heads at it. "Just a little?" I ask. "You want to be strong when the baby comes. Don't you want to be able to play with the baby?"

Mrs. Potter looks at Mrs. Swift. Mrs. Swift looks at Mrs. Potter. "They're not the ones we came for," says Mrs. Potter. "But we think it's a good idea they stay. They will help you."

"We want to show you something." Mrs. Swift struggles with a book on her lap. I help her put it on the table. It is very old with a worn leather cover that is as wrinkled as Mrs. Potter's skin. There is a large gold cross on the cover. Mrs. Swift pushes it to me. "I've been looking everywhere for this. I finally found it up in the attic while we were looking for that crib. Why your grandfather kept it hidden up there, I have no idea."

The pages are brown as paper bags. In thin letters, the first page says *The Holy Bible*.

"Go to the next page."

I flip it open. The page creaks. There is a handwritten list of names in faded ink, beginning with Josiah (1701–1753) and Beatrice (1710–1745) Bradford. The last name changes, and the ink turns to black, but the line is straight to Elizabeth Bradford Potter (1759–1839) and further on is Abigail Bradford Swift (1818–1893). My grandfather, Edward, is recorded, and he may have told my mama he was cutting her out of his life, but he didn't, not really. Her name is beneath his: Bernadette. And beside it is my papa's name, Tommy Lee Hockenberry. And under them both is me, Beatrice Rose Hockenberry.

"You know what this means?" Mrs. Potter asks. She traces the line to her own name and then to Mrs. Swift's.

I shake my head because I don't know what to make of everything yet.

"I am your great-great-great-great-grandmother," says Mrs. Potter. "And Mrs. Swift is your great-great-grandmother."

I stare at the page. I look at both of them. Mrs. Potter is grinning. She takes Mrs. Swift's hand and squeezes. "Abigail is my granddaughter. She always was rather forthright, to say the least. Even as a child."

I hold tight to my chair.

Mrs. Swift pulls an envelope from the back of the Bible and pushes it over to me. "Open it."

It is a deed to the Josiah Bradford house, built 1732. There are house plans attached. Although much has been changed, like the porch added and all the gingerbread dripping over everything, you can tell it is the house I am sitting in.

"What I'm trying to tell you," says Mrs. Swift, sipping her tea, "is that since there are no other living relatives, the house belongs to you, Beatrice."

117

That night when I am all tucked in my own bed with Pea-body nestled up beside me, and I am feeling all contented that I have found a home where I can stay, Mrs. Swift and Mrs. Potter come in for their good-night hugs.

If I wanted to, I bet I could wrap my arms around Mrs. Swift twice, that's how thin she is getting. Lately she has been getting so tired that I have been doing a lot more than just looking up a word now and then. Now she has me flipping through book after book, reading chapters, cross-checking dates, confirming facts.

I hold her close, feel how thin she is. She nearly topples over from the weight of my arms, but she squeezes me back. I feel the tears on her cheek when she whispers, "You really are a cygnet among ducklings, Beatrice."

I pull back and she sees the question in my eyes.

"If you don't know what *cygnet* means, look it up." Then she gives me one more hug and leaves me alone with Mrs. Potter.

"I found her. I found my Pauline," I say after a while. I have always been better at telling deepest-heart things to Mrs. Potter.

"That took a lot of courage, going back to that show, didn't it?" She reaches for my curls and braids them so they don't fall all over my face. She rubs my forehead and down the sides of my eyes and then softly touches my diamond.

"Seems to me you've found Pauline—and a whole lot more, Bee."

I snuggle deeper in the pillows and Peabody snuggles closer to me. "Yes," I whisper. "Yes, I have."

118

Pauline gets grumpy as the weeks go on and she gets more and more uncomfortable.

We do not talk anymore about where my aunts spend their time. Pauline and I come to a truce of not talking about them. One night, though, while we are playing the ha-ha game on Pauline's bed, I tell her how Mrs. Potter is really the lady in the orange flappy hat.

"Oh, Bee." Pauline groans and flips over, which is not easy to do now that she is a whale. "There's nobody here but us. Now, go to sleep." Her voice is muffled and angry.

After that I show her the Holy Bible and the deed, just to set things right. She rubs her hand across the cover's wrinkled leather and opens it and runs her fingers down the names. I whisper that she needs to stop so she doesn't erase anything.

"I just can't believe that your name is here. And this is your mama, Bernadette. And that is your papa."

She shakes her head and stares at the Bible, and then we settle into another truce of not talking about the house anymore, either, because all Pauline can concentrate on is the new baby coming. She does say, though, that one day we'll have to find a lawyer to look into everything.

119

Francine has left me alone since my revenge plan. She turns red as my diamond and looks at the ground whenever she sees me. This happens quite often now that we are playing on the same playground all the time. That rule got changed for good when Ruth Ellen's mama made such a fuss and Miss Healy stood up to the principal a few more times and now we mix—at least when we are out at recess.

We still have our same classroom at the end of the hall near the janitor's closet, but who knows what will happen with that rule? Ruth Ellen's mama invited the professors and students from the university for a meeting at her house and she served wild apple pie. She asked me if I might like to come to a meeting. Maybe if I go, Ruth Ellen would want to, too. I told her maybe I would. It is good to know about a lot of things.

One day I am late getting to school on account of Pauline waking us all up in the middle of the night because she was awful sure her baby was coming early. She fell asleep before anything big happened and Peabody and I had a terrible time getting back to sleep. When a baby's coming, you do not want to miss anything.

I run all the way to school, I am so tardy, and when I finally get there, Francine is out by the road talking to a man with heavy black glasses. At first I think it might be Bobby and my heart jumps, but then I know it can't be

Bobby because he would never have anything to do with someone like Francine.

The man is shaking his head and Francine is crying into his shoulder. When she pulls back, her face is very red. Her books are all over the ground.

She tries to jump up in his arms and hold him around the neck but he is still shaking his head and slowly he untangles her fingers. "Don't go, Papa," she sobs, and she tries to grab onto his neck, but he is pulling, pulling away. When he is free of her, he hurries off to his car.

My mouth is open. Francine notices me and runs for the school steps. *Hey*, I want to tell her, *you forgot your books*, but I don't. I watch her grab the door and then stop and lean her head against the wood and her shoulders shake.

It is hard to see someone lose their papa. Slowly I scoop up her books and walk up the steps. She is trying to wipe her tears away before I get there.

"Here," I whisper. My curls are falling wherever they want and I do not try to pull them over my diamond.

She looks at me for an instant, at my diamond shining, and takes the books, and hurries inside.

120

When Pauline's baby is born one hot night in June, we start learning all about being a family. This basically means no sleep for anybody.

We wake up every few hours for another feeding. Pauline cries when the feeding doesn't work right. I brush her hair because it is very comforting to her. I make her lots of tea and lots of toast, up the stairs and down the stairs, over and over again. "You have to drink more water," I tell her when I've brought her the tenth glass of the day. Of course I have to keep going out to the well to fill up the bucket. The water in the kitchen sink still runs like butternut squash.

Every time the baby cries, I bring her to Pauline, which seems to be the solution to everything. When the baby is well fed and Pauline is especially tired, she lets me bundle the baby in a blanket and walk across the floor, over and over, but she tells me I can't leave the room.

At night I have to be careful of bumping into Mrs. Swift or Mrs. Potter. They come around a lot so they can see the baby. Sometimes they pick her up when Pauline is asleep. The baby settles down in Mrs. Potter's arms, just like Peabody.

"How wonderful it's a girl," says Mrs. Potter, rocking slowly.

"Yes," says Mrs. Swift. "The world can be a wonderful place for a girl, can't it, Elizabeth?"

I don't want anything to upset Pauline, so I don't mention anything more about Mrs. Swift and Mrs. Potter. Generally, it is not good to worry things when you are so happy. You tend to cloud things up.

Sometimes when Pauline and the baby are asleep I sit myself carefully on the bed and watch the moon move across their foreheads. Pauline is very careful not to roll over on top of the baby. I am glad of that. She opens her eyes and looks at me and smiles. "Oh, Bee. My Sweet Pea Bee. I am so happy."

"Me too," I say, looking down at the little baby, feeling my heart swell to bursting.

"Come lie down beside us," Pauline says.

And I do.

121

Pauline is slow about coming up with a name.

This is very aggravating to Mrs. Swift. "Girls need strong names. None of those silly names like Patience or Charity."

"Imagine growing up with a name like that," says Mrs. Potter. "You could never get rip-roaring mad about anything. The babe's got to be named Elizabeth."

"Why should she get your name? Why not Abigail?"

"Elizabeth is a good name. You know she's going to need a strong name, just like Beatrice."

I never thought of my name as strong, but I do now, and I thank my mama and my papa for giving me a good beginning. Mrs. Swift and Mrs. Potter bicker well into the night. I hear them through the walls. I fling one of the shoes that Ruth Ellen's mama bought me one day with her ration stamps after she saw the holes in the bottom of my work boots. "We have so much," she whispered. "We can share."

Mrs. Potter and Mrs. Swift are quiet for a minute. Then they pick up again.

"Well, how about Sarah?"

"Not quite right."

"How about Constance? Leah? Martha?"

This is when I have to get up out of bed and bang on the wall. "Be quiet in there," I snap.

They hardly stop. "How about Gertrude?" says Mrs. Potter. "You know I've always liked that name."

This time I roll my eyes. I fall asleep thinking about the name I would choose. It is Sophie.

122

I have to run out to Ruth Ellen's and tell her all about how Pauline named our new baby Sophie and how I am the one who came up with the name.

I stop and give Cordelia a long scratch all along her backside. She is getting so big she could use some more exercise.

"We'll go chasing chipmunks when I get back," I promise.

Pauline is not happy at all we have a pig, but as soon as I can get her to look past all that and see Cordelia as she really is, I know she will come around. I am already planning on showing Sophie how beautiful pigs are right from the start. I scratch Cordelia between the ears just like she likes. "Hold your head high," I tell Cordelia. "Don't worry about Pauline." I give her one more scratch and then I am off, running for Ruth Ellen's.

I concentrate on my breathing, on the way my body moves. I don't bounce and my stride is the length that is right for me. I start out slow and don't run as fast as I could because I know I have a long way to go and I will make it if I keep putting one foot in front of the other.

Don't stop, I hear Bobby telling me. *You have to keep trying and trying and you will find the strength deep inside yourself, and when you find it, you will be proud, really, really proud. When you have a goal like that, you will get better, I promise.*

When I get to the house all is quiet, and I think maybe

nobody is home, but that is funny because Ruth Ellen's mama's automobile is parked in the yard. Of course with gasoline rationing so strict now, most folks are walking.

I go up on the porch and knock. There are some whispers and then Ruth Ellen's mama opens the door. Her eyes are red. I look behind her and Ruth Ellen and Sammy are sitting at the table. There is a candle lit. They are crying, too.

Oh no, I think, my heart dropping to the floor, and I am losing my balance and need to hold on to the door before I collapse on the porch right in front of Ruth Ellen's mama.

"Come in, Bee," she whispers.

I am too afraid to ask anything. So I stand there and look at Ruth Ellen and then Sammy, both of them with red eyes and tears dripping down.

"Your papa?" I ask finally.

"It's his birthday and we still haven't heard anything," says Ruth Ellen's mama. "It is a very long time to have no word. It is very hard for us. Come sit and say a prayer with us, Bee."

My prayer is all about how I am thankful that the news isn't worse. I pull a chair over. Then without even having to say anything, Ruth Ellen reaches for my hand and gives it a squeeze and her mama takes my other hand and they both take Sammy's. And then we are all one circle, breathing in and breathing out, and I notice it gets quiet and peaceful. "Ruth Ellen, it's your turn," whispers her mama.

Ruth Ellen squeezes her eyes awful tight as she says, "Please, Lord, we thank you for our many blessings and pray that you send your angels to watch over all our soldiers and that you send an extra one—an especially strong one—to watch over our papa because we love him so and it has been a very long time."

She stops because she gets all choked up and I see that her mama's eyes are wet and even Sammy is crying again. It must be very hard to miss your papa so. We all squeeze hands tighter after that and I ask angels to watch over Bobby, too. I don't know if he is building fighter bombers or flying them. I send a prayer out either way.

Then Ruth Ellen's mama gets up and gives everybody a hug, even me. I look at this family I love so much. I think they have it harder than anyone I know, with their papa gone so long and them trying to be brave and sometimes not feeling too brave.

"Bee, isn't your birthday coming up soon?" Ruth Ellen's mama wants to know.

I nod. "Yes, I will be thirteen."

"Well, we have been saving something for you."

Ruth Ellen's mama drags her chair over to the counter and stands on her tippy-toes so she can reach the highest cupboard. She opens the door and pulls out a bag of rationed sugar.

"We thought you'd like to make yourself a cake," she says, climbing down and handing the bag to me.

"A real cake with real sugar," giggles Ruth Ellen.

After we have several chocolate cupcakes with no-sugar frosting (since they were saving sugar for me), many mugs of milk, and many more stories about their papa, I tell them it is time to go home because Pauline and Sophie are waiting.

Ruth Ellen's mama says she will be over soon for a visit.

"I can sleep a little easier knowing you are not alone in that big house, Bee." She smiles, and now I see there are tears not just for their papa. Her eyes are filling with caring for me.

I do not bother going over everything again about Mrs. Swift and Mrs. Potter. Sometimes it is better to let things alone.

Then I hug them all, this family that I love so much. And when I go home, I walk the whole way because I do not want to spill any sugar.

123

It turns out that Pauline likes to clean house much better than me. This works out very well for all of us.

When she is cleaning drawers or sweeping a floor or arranging spices or putting practically anything in order, she sings. It is usually a song like "Silent Night" or "O Come All Ye Faithful" or "Angels We Have Heard on High." I guess Pauline hasn't had enough Christmas in her life.

She ties Sophie to her chest with a wide strip of flannel and walks around for a big part of each day with a feather duster or she folds towels and blankets and washes dishes. She spends a very long time each morning cleaning the room she shares with Sophie, waxing and dusting and polishing everything, over and over.

She won't step inside Mrs. Potter's or Mrs. Swift's room, which is fine with them. She still doesn't believe me when I bring up the lady in the orange flappy hat, and Mrs. Swift and Mrs. Potter say that is surely for the best. They are usually resting now and don't like to be disturbed.

When I have had enough of Sophie and her crying, I hurry into the library and close the double doors. Mrs. Swift and Mrs. Potter are already there.

"My head. My aching head." Mrs. Swift rubs her temples and closes her eyes, leaning back in the chair at her desk. "Why does that baby cry so much?"

Mrs. Potter giggles. "All babies cry—a lot. You sure did."

She gives Peabody another biscuit. He jumps on her lap and circles around until he finds just the right spot.

"Humph," says Mrs. Swift, opening another book. "Beatrice, look up the word *acerbic*."

I don't want to move. I like being snuggled up to Mrs. Potter.

"Beatrice?"

"Oh, all right." I blow my breath out in a loud wet sputter.

I flip through the heavy book. I am getting faster at this. After a little bit, I read: "Biting, bitter in tone or taste."

This time it is Mrs. Swift who sputters. "Can you believe they wrote I was those things?"

Mrs. Potter grins. I snuggle back on the sofa.

After a few minutes, Mrs. Swift rubs her temples again. She throws down her spectacles. "I simply cannot do this anymore. My eyes, my headache, what shall I do?"

Mrs. Potter opens one eye. "Have Beatrice do it."

Mrs. Swift purses her lips and stares at me. She looks at her crooked fingers, over at Peabody, and then back at me. "I suppose it would be for the best," she says. "We won't be here forever."

"Yes," says Mrs. Potter, pulling me close.

I do wish they wouldn't talk like this. No one wants to lose their grandmothers.

After that Mrs. Swift turns the job of writing her autobiography over to me. "Now, I have arranged the books on the desk into piles," she tells me. "The ones that say the terrible things about Abigail Swift, like what a difficult, opinionated woman she was for wanting to speak her mind in a public forum, well, I pushed those to the side. No sense even reading those."

Mrs. Potter winks at me.

"How unbecoming to womankind, how narrow-minded, how forthright, they say," Mrs. Swift sputters.

Mrs. Potter chuckles.

"Are you laughing at me?"

"Of course not." Mrs. Potter grins.

Mrs. Swift rubs her temples. "I do believe a woman should be allowed to vote and seek public office, Beatrice. I do believe slavery is a sin and that all people should have the same rights as white men."

I spend the whole afternoon looking up facts about Mrs. Swift: She took a speaking class in college but was not allowed to speak publicly alongside men. She and her friends went into the woods to practice their speeches. Eventually, she became a famous lecturer and abolitionist.

"You were pretty special, weren't you?" I say when it is time for supper.

Mrs. Swift laughs and opens her eyes. Her new napping spot is right beside Mrs. Potter, with Peabody in the middle. "I wasn't afraid to make a place for myself in this world, even when conditions weren't ideal."

She bores her eyes into me like they are spikes.

"Don't you agree, Beatrice?"

After many days my notes fill only a few pages because I have to ask every few minutes, "Is this true? Did this really happen?" and Mrs. Swift tells me if it did or not. Sometimes she throws a book on the floor.

I know it will take a very long time to finish a whole book. That is fine, though, because I have discovered something: When I am writing, I don't worry so much over things, like if Bobby will come back, if Francine will bother me anymore, if Ruth Ellen will get her papa back and her brace off, or about my diamond. I don't worry so much about Mrs. Swift and Mrs. Potter, and how thin they are and how they nap all the time.

It is very nice to have your troubles disappear when you are writing.

124

"Now, there are some things we want to remind you about," Mrs. Potter is saying. I am washing the mixing bowl and putting away the eggs. My birthday cake is in the oven. The cake is made with lots and lots of snowy white sugar. There's a world of difference between a cake made with corn syrup and one made with sugar. Ask Peabody.

Mrs. Potter sinks into a chair by the table. Her limp is getting worse. "I want to remind you of some things so you don't forget."

I giggle. "You can always remind me of everything I need to know. I am right here." I drop the washrag into the sink and come over and wrap my arms around her.

"Bless your heart, Bee," she whispers. "You really are cute as a bug's ear." Then she pulls away. "Now, I'm serious. There are some things we need to go over. Sit down."

I sit. Peabody jumps onto my lap. I can smell the cake baking. It is heavenly. I do not want to talk about serious things. I scratch Peabody between the ears.

"Now, somebody who owns a house is going to have to remember everything. Like don't forget to drain the pipes before the winter. That's why the water is so filthy now. No one drained the pipes for years after your grandfather moved to Florida. And don't forget to put on the storm windows the first of October and don't forget to take them down the first of April. You'll get enough good sun then to start warming the house."

"But why do I need to know all this?" I ask, feeling anxious.

"Shush, Bee. I'm telling you important things. The roses out front need to be pruned in the fall. Don't let Peabody get near Mrs. Marsh's chickens or you'll have a tempest in your teapot. Stay away from that woman. And the front door will stick if you don't oil the hinges."

I am not listening anymore. I have scooted my chair closer and am wrapping my arms around her.

"You will be fine." She squeezes me back. Then the teakettle is whistling and she asks me to make her a cup of tea.

"Very weak, Bee. I like it very weak now." She rubs her leg and winces.

I bring the tea over and sit down and rub her leg. "How come it is bothering you so much more now?"

"Humph," she says. "I could write my own autobiography. Maybe I will when I have time." She leans over and whispers, "I didn't get the whole musket ball when I pulled it out of my hip myself. Mrs. Swift doesn't want me to tell you. But the truth is, I was a soldier. I fought for General Washington at Bunker Hill. Pretended I was a boy. I had to do my own operating on myself so I wouldn't be found out. My leg has never been the same."

"I don't want you to tell her what?" says Mrs. Swift, coming into the kitchen for a cup of tea.

"Nothing," says Mrs. Potter, and we all let it drop, which is okay by me because I really don't want to think about how old Mrs. Potter is while I am hugging her.

"Sit down." Mrs. Potter pulls out a chair for Mrs. Swift. "I've been telling Bee about the things she needs to know."

Mrs. Swift sighs deeply. "Yes, you already know about the leather envelopes in the attic. The bills are very old, but no matter. I'm sure they still work."

I put Mrs. Swift's cup on the table. "But we can do this all together, right?" I look anxiously from Mrs. Swift to Mrs. Potter.

"And I want you to go to school, Bee, and college. Nobody has been able to make anything of themselves without a proper education. Even in my day."

"But . . ."

"Beatrice, we came to show you there's a long line of women behind you who have stood on their own two feet, and to show you that you can do it too." Mrs. Swift sips at her tea.

I drop into my chair. "But where are you going? I don't want you to leave me." Already my eyes fill. "I don't want to be alone again."

"But you're not alone, Beatrice. You have a family now." Mrs. Potter puts her hand on mine. "And you've accomplished it all yourself."

"Yes, dear," says Mrs. Swift, "and we won't go until you're ready."

I look at Mrs. Potter and wonder about the musket ball in her leg. I wonder about Mrs. Swift's mama saying it was a shame she was born a girl, and about my own mama, Bernadette, who wouldn't let her papa hide her away.

As I think about them all, I feel their bones gathering within me, knitting their strength to my insides. And I feel new tears dripping right over my diamond.

125

That afternoon, while the cake is cooling, I find a new issue of the *Billboard* in our mailbox.

I rush upstairs, where Pauline is changing Sophie on the bed and rubbing Johnson's Baby Powder all over.

I show her how I look for news of Bobby every week. "But why, Bee?" Pauline scoops Sophie up in the air and kisses her little pea-sized toes.

"Bobby promised we wouldn't lose each other."

"Well, don't invite him here. I already told you I don't want to be around a man who smells like pigs. And neither do you—do you, little Sophie?" She kisses Sophie on the cheek.

"But, Pauline, he likes you. He is awful sweet on you."

She looks at me and scrunches her nose and goes back to loving on Sophie.

"I'm sure he doesn't smell like pigs now, Pauline." I say it sharp. Sometimes she makes me awful mad. I know she has it wrong. I know what matters is what's underneath. And there's a very fine man under there. Just ask Cordelia.

I decide then and there to tell her the whole story of Bobby, just like her *Story of Bee*.

"Sit down. I have something to say, Pauline."

I tell her everything, about how Bobby was the Hurricane and how one of the other runners tripped him during a race and how Ellis found him all despairing and gave him a job. I remind her about the boys chasing me and how Bobby spent day after day teaching me to run fast. With his thick glasses he might not be able to fly bombers, but he could build them. He wanted to do more than spend his life working for Ellis. "But most of all, Pauline, he really cares about me.

"He told me not to quit, to keep trying and trying, and if I did I would find strength deep inside myself, and when I found it, I would be proud, really, really proud."

She runs her hands through my curls the whole time I am talking. She gets the brush and sweeps it through my hair about a thousand times. I think I can purr.

"I didn't know all that about Bobby," she whispers.

"I guess you weren't looking very hard."

She looks at me for a moment and then brushes more and more while Sophie sleeps right beside us. "I am sorry, Bee. I am sorry about everything."

I let her pull my hair back with a ribbon and my diamond shines. "How did you get so beautiful, Bee?" she asks.

I reach up then, and I am in her arms. I let her hold me and I feel her breath on me and her heart beating. I smell the apple shampoo in her hair. The place deep inside where my heart used to ache is filled with other things now.

"I bet lots of folks would like to be more like you, Bee," she whispers, holding me tight. "I know I would."

126

We are sitting around the table after a big roast chicken dinner with gravy and mashed potatoes and I have to hold my belly, I am so full.

I am proud as a peacock I am such a good cook and I am grateful to Ruth Ellen's mama for showing me how. She says I can go over and learn more things anytime I want. I think I will any day now.

Peabody whines that he is ready for something else to eat. I tell Pauline and Sophie to shut their eyes and I go get my birthday cake. It is high and chocolate and sprinkled with coconut all over the buttercream frosting and everything about it is just right for a girl turning thirteen. I am very good at baking cakes.

Sophie's eyes are big as moons as she snuggles in Pauline's arms and watches the candles. When I set the cake down, I show her, this is how you blow the candles out. She will turn two months soon, and it's never too early to learn.

I start cutting the cake and when I look up Mrs. Potter and Mrs. Swift are standing behind Pauline and Sophie. They are so faint I can hardly make them out.

Mrs. Potter watches me give Pauline the first piece. She put a new feather in her flappy hat and it is dipping in the hot August breeze that tumbles through the open window. She has to tie the strings tighter to keep the hat on her head. Then she reaches down and scratches Peabody behind the ears. He hardly notices, though, because he is so busy eating cake.

"Do you want some?" I whisper to them.

Mrs. Swift is already shaking her head, they do not want any cake, and she is putting her finger to her lips and pulling Mrs. Potter away. I reach out for them and feel my heart breaking, but this time Mrs. Potter shakes her head. Peabody looks up as they thin out and their edges blur, but Pauline and Sophie don't notice anything but the cake. Pauline reaches for another slice.

Mrs. Potter winks one last time. Mrs. Swift smiles softly and points to the library, where her autobiography sits waiting.

And then, in the blink of an eye, they are gone.

Just like they said they would be.

Acknowledgments

I am sincerely grateful to my husband, Steven, my children, my parents, and the Still River Writers for encouraging me through the years it took to write this novel, for listening and offering ideas, and for reading the manuscript so many times.

I am also thankful for my editor, Michelle Frey, who saw Bee's heart from the very beginning and helped to make the novel all that it could be, and also to her assistant, Kelly Delaney, and intern, Stephen Brown, for their many hours of work on the manuscript. Thank you also to all the staff at Knopf/Random House who had a hand in bringing Bee into the world, including copy editor Jenny Golub, for her skill and kind words, and Kate Gartner, for designing the beautiful covers on all three of my novels.

I am grateful to my agent, Elizabeth Harding of Curtis Brown Ltd., for her guidance and encouragement.

Thank you also to my friend and former newspaper colleague Paul Della Valle for his accomplished book, *Massachusetts Troublemakers: Rebels, Reformers and Radicals from the Bay State*. His biographies of Lucy Stone and Deborah Sampson provided the clay I needed to begin crafting the characters of Mrs. Swift and Mrs. Potter.